AUNT
SARA'S
WOODEN
GOD

Sincerely
Mercedes Gilbert

Bruno of
Hollywood
N.Y.C.

AUNT SARA'S WOODEN GOD

MERCEDES GILBERT

FOREWORD BY LANGSTON HUGHES

DOVER PUBLICATIONS, INC.
MINEOLA, NEW YORK

Bibliographical Note

This Dover edition, first published in 2017, is an unabridged republication of the work originally published by Christopher Publishing House, Boston, in 1938.

International Standard Book Number

ISBN-13: 978-0-486-81939-6
ISBN-10: 0-486-81939-6

Manufactured in the United States by LSC Communications
81939601   2017
www.doverpublications.com

FOREWORD

Miss Mercedes Gilbert, who comes from Florida to Broadway as one of America's leading Negro actresses, returns again to the deep south for the scene of her first novel, "Aunt Sara's Wooden God." This is an authentic every-day story of thousands of little families below the Mason-Dixon line, bound to the soil by poverty and blackness, but living their enclosed lives always in the hope that some-day some one of them may escape the family group and go on to higher things. Their tragedy is that there is so small a foundation on which to base such a hope. The wooden god of Miss Gilbert's novel is a mulatto country boy, worshipped by his mother, but himself unable to fulfill the faith and belief she has in him, balked as he is by poverty, the color-line, and his own inner weaknesses born of conceit and fear. That he lives and dies a hero to Aunt Sara, although he tortures and hurts so many others, constitutes the ironic tragedy of this book filled with little pictures of the rural and small-town life of the South.

Those readers who enjoyed "Jonah's Gourde Vine" or "Ollie Miss" will find in "Aunt Sara's Wooden God" a kindred volume.

Langston Hughes

AUNT SARA'S WOODEN GOD

CHAPTER I

> "Ah'm gonna lay down my burden
> Down by de river side
> Down by de river side
> Down by de river side
> "Ah'm gonna lay down my burden
> Down by de river side
> Ain't gonna study war no more."

Sara Lou's song trailed off to a whisper as William's voice, raised angrily, broke the silence of the early morning.

"You're a liar! and a meddlesome black fool! and I've got a good mind to smash your ugly face in," William shouted.

"Mister Gordon jes' tole me yuh done borried money from him an' said Ma sent you to get it, an' ah know he wouldn't lie on nobody," Jim retorted.

"Yes, you know it's the truth 'cause Mister Gordon said so, and he's a white man and can't lie," William sneered.

"No! It ain't dat, ah jes' knows yuh, an' what a liar yuh is!" Jim's remark raised William's fury to a murderous pitch. Picking up a long stick that lay near by, he raised it threateningly.

"Shut up, you black fool, before I knock your head off."

"You ain't gonna let your wooden God an'

9

corn-stalk Jesus fool you into hittin' me," Jim
taunted; his voice, though quieter than William's,
carried a convincing quality of determination that
William knew meant more than mere words.

Sara Lou ran as swiftly as her two hundred
pounds would permit towards the barn from where
the angry voices of her sons seemed to be coming.
The early July morning had dawned hot and oppressive, and Byron, a small farming village in
Central Georgia, stirred itself sleepily. Dew lay
like carpet upon the green grass that covered the
surrounding woods. Overhead numerous brightly
colored birds flitted from tree to tree chirping
loudly, unheard by Sara Lou as she called:

"Yuh Will-y-um! Yuh J-i-m! Will-y-um! Stop
dat fussin' dis moment!"

William dropped the stick he held quickly, and
turned to greet his mother, his face still flushed with
a dull angry red that showed to the roots of his
dark brown wavy hair.

"Yuh boys aught'er be shame uh yo'selfs, blood
brothers an al'lers fussin' an' fightin', jes' cause yo'
pa done died an ain't nobody but me to try an'
keep yuh straight," Sara Lou scolded, as she stood
between the two boys, looking directly at Jim.

Jim started to speak, but changed his mind and
walked slowly away. What was the use, he thought.
He could gain nothing by trying to tell his mother
of William's latest deception. No matter what
he said, his mother would take William's side. He
was slow of speech, while William had answers
ready before questions were asked, and their mother
hung on every word he uttered. He was her God.
Next to her religion, she worshipped him. To her

his words were always soft and honey-coated, while to Jim, William used a patronizing tone which made the younger boy's blood boil. But their mother could not detect the underlying sneer in his smooth words and she usually blamed Jim for the frequent quarrels between the boys.

Sara Lou watched Jim as he walked away in the direction of the Gordon plantation. A little pucker in her usually smooth fair brow showed plainly the anxiety of her thoughts. In the depths of her large black eyes lurked the troubled expression which for the four years of her widowhood had dimmed the bright cheerfulness of former years, when her husband, John, had been the staid prop on which she leaned and watched her boys grow to young manhood.

A sigh escaped her lips, as Jim's figure receded in the distance. How like his father he was, she thought—the same slow steady tread, his father's height and color, the same quick flare of temper, and equally quick forgiveness.

Her mind drifted back over the years to the day, twenty years before, when she first met John Carter. He had come to Byron, to pick cotton, and had lingered on after the cotton picking season had passed. Owen Gordon, the richest white farmer in Byron, had hired him as a steady farm hand, but that had not been the main reason for his sojourn in Byron. He had seen Sara Lou, then a tall, fair young woman of twenty; her large black eyes had looked beyond him the evening he first saw her standing in her little cabin door on the outskirts of the Gordon place, but something sweet and soulful in their depths had made him want to talk to her and know her better.

He had asked about Sara Lou, that night, as he sat out in front of the little log cabin where he boarded with Lucy Salisbury, the village midwife and root doctor. (Aunt Salisbury, as she was lovingly called by the villagers,) gave her snuff brush, a tiny oak twig, a swish as she pushed it with her tongue from one side of her bony cheek to the other, and spat out a long string of brown snuff before she answered. Then, turning her feeble, squinty eyes heavenward, her jet black face seemed to take on a purplish hue as she exclaimed:

"Lawd uh mercy man, yuh ain't gone an' took no notice uh dat strumpet is yuh?" and without giving John time to answer she continued. "Dat gal jes' naturally ain't no good, cain't ever be no good, none uh her folks fore her was no good, dey was jes' a bad lot an' dat's all dere is to it."

"Whut yuh mean, a bad lot?" John questioned, mildly enjoying the distressed look on Aunt Salisbury's bony black face, almost invisible in the dim moonlight except for the white string with which her hair, short and thin, had been wrapped so tight, that her homely face looked strained and witchlike.

"Jes' dat, son, yuh see ah done knowed dem all, from her great grandma down to her, an' all uh dem 'cept Sara Lou's ma, done had half white bastard chillun."

"How did Sara Lou's Ma escape?" John asked laughing heartily.

"Well, to start wid, her great grandma, Hester, b'longed to de Saunders family back 'fore surrender. She was a pretty yeller gal jes' like Sara Lou is, an' de fust thing you knows she had a baby for old mister Frank Saunders, old missy Saunders gits suspicious 'bout it bein' his chile an' makes him sell Hester. Owen Gordon's father, Charles Gordon, bought her and put her to keepin' house for um. Well, Charles Gordon had a half brother who was jes' de limit when it comed to women, white or black. Wid him it didn't make no difference. It was jes' any woman who he could lay down wid, so he took right out after Hester's daughter, Ida, soon as she was knee high to a duck, an' when she was fourteen she had a baby for that man and they named her Charlotte. About a year after dat Ida's Ma Hester died, an' old man Charles Gordon went to live in Macon an' Ida stayed at de Gordon house to work for his son Owen Gordon, who had jes' got married. Well, Owen and his half uncle had a big fuss, an' the Uncle skinned out an' went some where up North, dat was de last heard uh him. Ida took charge uh de Gordon house and raised Charlotte right dare on de lot."

Aunt Salisbury interrupted her recital with a loud chuckle as reminiscences of Ida passed through her mind.

"Lawd, son, dat Ida was a caution. Twan't long 'fore she was sure runnin' dat Gordon home, an' when Owen Gordon's sons was born, first Lawrence an' den some years later Franklyn, Ida jes' took dem in charge and raised dem so dey wouldn't mind nobody on earth but her. She was a strong-willed woman as ever I seed, Ida was. Well, her gal Charlotte grew up right pretty an' 'bout de time she was seventeen, Owen Gordon had given us a little piece uh land an' de logs and some uh de men

had built a church, our Calvary that we still wor-
ships in, an' de next year durin' cotton pickin' time
a young preacher named Sam Smith come here to
pick cotton an' decided he'd jes' stay on an' preach
in de church an' farm. Well, den de fun started,"
Aunt Salisbury laughed, as she produced a box of
railroad snuff from the pocket of her apron, and
putting the stick she had been chewing into the box
she moved it back and forth as she nodded her head
on her bony neck with a gluttonous sound of sup-
pressed mirth.

"Lawd, son, when Ida found out dat de new
preacher, Sam Smith, had his eyes on Charlotte,
she didn't let no grass grow under her feet. She
started plotting right den how she was gonna marry
Charlotte to dat black man so as to try an' live
down dem half white bastards hur ma and hur done
had, an' den she figured dat would be a good way
to git back at us Byron colored folks dat had all'ers
called dem de Gordon Niggers.   Heh, heh, heh,"
she chuckled.

"Ida had dat preacher sneakin' up to de Gordon
place every night to dere cabin back uh de Gordon
kitchen, where she'd feed him chicken an' all de
good things she could sneak out to him, an' den she
ranged it for him and Charlotte to run off to Macon
an' git hitched."

"What happened after they got married?" John
asked as Aunt Salisbury paused in her story to rub
her snuff brush over her few charred teeth and spit
out her long brown string of snuff.

"Well, when the folks found out what had happened, dey got powerful mad and planned dat dey
would stay away from de church, de next Sunday,

but heh, heh, heh," the low chuckle shook Aunt
Salisbury's shoulders, and when she got her breath
she continued.

"Well, son, dat fust Sunday dey stayed away,
but de next Sunday Ida had got a note from Owen
Gordon sayin' dat effen dey didn't 'tend dey church
meetin' he would take de church away from
dem, and dat settled things, an' de darkies was glad
enough to meet de new Misses Smith. Well, den
Charlotte an' de preacher got long jes' fine. Folks
was running over each other to meet dem an' make
dem welcome. A year later Charlotte had a baby
boy; a little ill-formed thing dat hopped 'round
like a frog, an' 'twasn't long 'fore de pore little
critter died, an' a year later, when Sara Lou was
born, pore Charlotte died in child birth, an' de
Reverend Smith raised her all by himself. Course,
when Sara Lou was old 'nough she started working
for Owen Gordon, and when she got to be twenty
an' hadn't had no mishap ev'rybody believed she
would marry respectable and like her Ma, but no,
what did she up an' do but have a baby by Owen
Gordon's son, Franklyn."

"Dat's 'bout all dere is to it, son"! Aunt Salisbury concluded, stretching her bony arms above her
head and yawning sleepily.

" 'Cept dat Sara Lou's trouble done killed her
pore old Pa, he died foh her baby was two months
old, it was bad enuff her havin' a bastard chile, but
when as de pastor uh de church he had to turn her
out de church, well, it was jes' more den de old man
could stand so one night he jes' sleeped away." Aunt
Salisbury ended her story with a sigh, as she rubbed

her knees vigorously and hobbled towards the cabin door.

"Well, de gal is jes' human, an' ah sur' ain't blamin' her so much," John said as he knocked the ashes from his pipe and walked slowly towards the gate and called back "Ah'm sure gonna try an' git dat gal tuh marry me, eff'en she'll have me."

And John Carter kept his word. It was several weeks later when he got his first opportunity to talk with Sara Lou, he had walked around her cabin and found her sitting in the back door, her baby William held tightly in her arms, tears falling freely upon the face of the sleeping child.

It was a cool Autumn afternoon and when Sara Lou looked up to find him smiling at her, the serious expression in his eyes had brought a quick smile to her lips as she asked.

"Whut yuh want, Mister?"

"Nothing special, sister, ah was jes' passin' an' ah thought I'd jes' stop an' git acquainted," John answered, his smile broading to a grin.

"Well den, you better be on yo' way, cause dey ain't nothin' yuh nor nobody else kin do fuh me," Sara Lou answered, wearily passing her hand over her straight black hair that hung to her waist.

"Ah ain't so sure 'bout dat, dere's lots ah kin do. In de fust place, dis garden is all runned down, ah kin fix dat," John assured her, glancing over the little ragged garden that grew near the cabin.

Sara Lou had argued and tried to send him away, but he could not be gotten rid of, and thus their friendship had started, but to all of John's entreaties that she marry him, she turned a deaf ear.

"No, John, ah'se got my baby William, an yuh

ain't gonna take him an' me an' ask no questions,
an' ah ain't gonna answer none," she would always
answer to his pleading.

"Listen heah, Sara Lou, ah swear ah won't never
ask yuh nothing 'bout William an ah'll treat him
lak my very own long as ah lives if yuh'll marry
me," John promised from time to time. But it was
a year later before Sara Lou consented to become
his wife, after the news had reached Byron of
Franklyn Gordon's death in an automobile accident
in New York. Owen Gordon had spoken quietly
that morning when she came to bring his laundry.

"I'm leaving this morning for New York, Sara
Lou. Mister Franklyn has been killed in an accident," he said simply. And Sara Lou, not daring
to answer, had nodded her head and abruptly left
the house.

She had heard from time to time about Franklyn's
escapades in New York. Owen Gordon had never
mentioned him to her but news somehow travelled
in the small village, and Franklyn's wild drinking
and gambling had drifted back to Byron.

A week later, Sara Lou became the wife of John
Carter; and until the day of his death he had kept
his word, never to ask questions about William.
He had treated the child as his own son, even
spoiling him to some extent, for which Sara Lou
rebuked him with:

"Now, John, yuh'se spoilin' dat boy, an' dat
ain't right, 'cause he got hard 'nuff disposition now
to fight down."

"Don't yuh worry 'bout William, Sara, he's uh

smart chile, an' nuthin' ain't gonna spoil de young
'un", John would excuse.

A year after they were married, Jim was born,
as black as his father, but a good-looking little chap.
But even the birth of a son of his own did not
change John towards William. Until the day of
his death he had never shown any difference in his
treatment of the boys, and William had loved and
honored him with all his heart. If he had ever had
any doubt that John Carter was his father, because
of the neighbor's children's hints and jibes, he
never showed it and for sixteen years life ran a
smooth course for the Carters. John was a beloved
Deacon in the little Calvary Baptist church, and
Sara Lou's kindness to the villagers soon won
their love and respect. Her ever-willingness to aid
them in their trouble, answer the call of sickness
and distress among them, had made her a favorite,
and they lovingly called her "Aunt Sara."

She turned a deaf ear to the taunts the neighboring children threw at William, and when he came
to her sobbing that they had called him a half white
nigguh, consoled him with:

"Sticks an' stones kin break yo' bones but names
ain't never goin' to hurt yuh, son."

Even as a small child he showed tendencies of a
willful tempestuous nature, but she enthroned him
in a place in her heart that no other human being
could ever reach, excusing her partiality with the
thought that he would need all the love and tender
care she could give him to help him overcome his
faults.

And thus life had run along, smoothly and happily for Sara until her husband's death. But, for

the last few years the frequent quarrels between William and his brother had distressed her more than she cared to admit.

Jim loved William with all his heart, but he could not overlook the streak of deception that he saw, more plainly than anyone else, under William's smooth exterior. His fear for his mother's happiness was greater than anything else in his life. He knew that she worshipped William and did not want her to be disappointed in him.

On William's part, there was a deep dislike for Jim that had always been latent in him from early childhood. The realization irked him that Jim was legitimate and had a real father. He would be tortured with jealousy whenever John Carter cast a kindly glance at little Jim. And he would take any little remark directed at himself as bitter criticism. These flaring feelings had persisted with the years, but after John's death, he had stopped trying to conceal them, but allowed them to burst out in frequent quarrels and disagreements with his half brother.

Sara Lou had watched the growing dissension with fear and foreboding. Her eyes filled with tears, as she laid her hand tenderly upon William's shoulder, and asked:

"What's the matter, son? What makes you and Jim can't get along? Don't yuh love one another?"

"Oh, it ain't me, Ma. Jim is always fussin' 'bout me stayin' in Macon—going to High School," William answered, placing his arm affectionately around her waist.

"Thar yuh go—makin' love to yer ole mammy, as usual", she chuckled, her face showing the pleasure she always felt when near her handsome elder son.

William, a head taller than his mother, was straight and slender; his features, like hers, were finely molded; his hair dark brown and curly, matching well his smooth fair skin.

With a pleased little sigh she clung to him, loving the way he petted and fussed over her.

"Ah been wantin' yuh an' Jim to come an' git yo' breakfuss. It's nigh on to five uh clock an' yuh gotta git to Macon to yo' business," she said, pushing him before her towards the house.

"Ain't much doin' in my pressing shop right now, Ma. Folks wearin' overalls lots an' they don't need no pressin' shop for 'em," William remarked.

"What was that Jim was sayin' 'bout Mr. Gordon?" Sara Lou asked. A note of concern crept into her voice.

"Oh, nothin', Ma," William answered hastily. "Only he and Mr. Gordon both think I should be here workin' on the farm instead of tryin' to get a better education."

"That's all right, son. Some day me an' Jim goin' to be mighty proud of you when you'se carryin' the Gospel."

William was silent for a moment. Then, looking toward the Gordon plantation he observed: "Mr. Gordon's sure left lots of work for Jim while he's in Europe!"

"An' Jim'll git it all done. Dat sho' is a smart boy!"

"But he'll be gone a long time, Ma. There ain't no need 'er Jim tryin' ter do it all in a day when

there's so much right here on our place that needs
bein' done," William complained.

"Now Willyum, yuh jes' leave Jim do things his
own way. Dass how come Mr. Gordon laks dat
boy lak he does. White folks laks things don'
right 'er way an' not put off ontell de las' minute."

"Well, can't we have our breakfast right 'er way,
Ma?" William asked with a laugh.

"We sho' kin!" Sara Lou smiled and a few moments later they were seated at the table, before
them a steaming breakfast of fat side, hot corn
bread, molasses and coffee.

Sara Lou bowed her head as William prayed—a
routine never neglected in their home.

"I'm goin' to ride to Macon this morning with
Reverend Johnson. He's going in to see the doctor,"
William was saying.

"Ah'm glad he is caise he ain't been feelin' so
well lately," his mother replied, full of concern
about her ailing pastor.

"He's a good un for yuh to pattern atter, Willyum, when yuh starts preachin'," she added, looking at him proudly. Her desire to make a preacher
of William was the greatest thing in her life, and
although William wasn't so keen about becoming
a preacher, he made her think he was, and after all
it would afford him a chance to lead a life of ease
and he hated work.

"He's all right, 'nough, ma, but he ain't educated
and when I starts preaching, I'm goin' to be well
prepared," he answered.

"But he's chuck full 'er religion, and dat's whut
counts wid de Lawd, William."

"And the Lawd ain't 'gainst us preparing our-
self to carry His word either, Ma."

"Ah knows dat, William. Dat's why ah let yuh
go to Macon to high school, but jes' de same, don't
yuh git all puffed up wid pride caise pride goes 'fore
a fall, de Lawd says."

William's face flushed over his mother's rebuke,
as he lowered it over his plate, but when he raised
his head again, he was smiling.

They had finished breakfast when Jim entered
the kitchen. Placing a basket of fresh vegetables
on the table, he seated himself to eat his belated
breakfast. Sara Lou smiled fondly as, passing, she
patted his shoulder, and hurried away to her many
morning tasks.

Jim, a reticent boy of medium height, stocky and
as his mother put it, 'the spittin' image of his father',
claimed only one resemblance to his mother and
brother—his eyes which were large and black. Unlike William who was a brilliant scholar, he had
learned little in school; his brain just did not seem
to grasp even the simplest rudiments.

The farm had been his teacher. He loved it, un-
derstood cattle, could doctor them when sick and
bred them better than the oldest farmers around
Byron. Since his father's death he had become the
head of the house as far as earning the living was
concerned.

Sara Lou's home like the other Negro cabins, had
at first consisted of two rooms in which they lived,
cooked their meals and slept. Her husband, John
Carter, had however, enlarged it with two rooms
built under the eaves known as a jump, adding a
front and back porch downstairs and a little shed-

like kitchen. It was by far the best of the Negro homes for miles around.

"See the garden's doing nicely, Jim," William ventured, as Jim settled himself at the table.

"Could do bettuh, if Ah had some help."

"You spend too much time working over at Mr. Gordon's. Maybe that's why you can't get more done here."

"Not half as much time as yuh spend sittin' 'round in dat school or foolin' 'round in Macon loafin' and pretendin' yuh wanna learn something so as yuh kin preach," Jim retorted hotly.

"You don't know what you're talkin' 'bout. Jes' 'cause you're ignorant ain't no reason for me to be. I'm tryin' to be better myself."

"Yuh ain't never goin' to better yo'self! It jes' ain't in yuh. Ah done heard 'bout yo' carryin' on in Macon," Jim threw over his shoulder, as he rose and walked away.

"Don't you talk to me like that, you black ape. I've got a good mind to smash your face in, anyhow," William cried, catching up with him and shaking his fist under his nose.

Sara Lou, coming in to clear away the breakfast things, saw the situation.

"Now whut y'all fussin' 'bout?" she asked pushing them apart.

Jim turned and walked away.

Sara Lou watched him, a sigh escaping her lips as she said to William:

"Dat boy sho's got uh temper!"

"Yes, he's always fussin' wid me 'bout attending school. You should speak to him about it, Ma, once and for all."

"Ah sure will, son. He ought to be sham'er his-self an' yuh studyin' to git ready to carry de gospel but dat comes uh him not havin' religion an' dere by de needed grace to carry on."

"I wish Reverend Johnson would come on by. I wanna get going," William said, anxiously looking in the direction of the minister's home.

"It is funny he ain't sho'ed up yet. Yuh bettuh run over dere an' see whut's hol'in' 'im, Willyum," his mother advised.

William hurried away, anxious to visit the parsonage anyway, as it afforded him a chance to see the minister's sixteen year old daughter, Ruth. whom he and Jim had both loved since they were small tots.

His mother watched him walk jauntily away, hatless, the sun now high in the skies beaming brightly down on his curly brown hair. A sigh trembled upon her lips, as she wondered what the future held in store for her two boys so different in body and mind.

CHAPTER II

The Reverend Peter Johnson's little log cabin
built near the Calvary Baptist Church was little
more than a mile from the Carter home. Reverend
Johnson and his daughter, Ruth, whose mother had
died in child birth, eked out their meager living
working in the cotton fields and in their own little
garden and with the few dollars the members
of his church grudgingly gave him from time to
time.

Ruth was a pretty dark brown skin girl. Her
short black curly hair framed a small oval face, the
chief attractiveness of which lay in her large black
eyes set wide apart, sparkling roguishly beneath
long silky lashes. This morning an anxious look
was in their depths, as she faced William, who
greeted her with:

"Hello, Ruth, you look brighter 'en the sun."

"Go 'lon' wid you, William. You'se all'ers
making pretty speeches," she smiled, alluring dim-
ples playing hide and seek in her cheeks.

William's heart beat rapidly, as he looked into
her eyes. An almost overwhelming desire to take
her in his arms sent his blood coursing wildly
through his body.

"Ah was jes' about to come to yo' house to tell
you dat pa is too sick for drivin' to Macon dis morning, an' our ole horse Bess to top it off, done tooken
sick las' night," she was saying.

"I'm sorry to hear that, Ruth, but I'm glad I gotta see you agin 'fore leavin'."

"You jes' seed me las' night in church, William," Ruth laughed.

"Yes, but I ain't had no chance to talk to you wid Jim moonin' 'round lookin' at you like a dying calf."

"An' how does uh dyin' calf look, William?" Ruth asked sweetly.

"Just like Jim does when he looks at you."

They both laughed heartily and Ruth, anxious to change the subject, remarked.

"When yo' school goin' to open, William?"

"In October, an' I'm gonna try and make two terms in one this year, if I can", William replied, a trace of pride in his voice.

"You sho' is smart and allers was. Ah ain't never seed a body dat kin learn fast as you kin nohow."

William's voice was low and tender when he replied: "I want my success to be yours, Ruth. Promise me you'll marry me when I finish school." He pleaded, trying to look into her eyes which she had lowered to her feet, restlessly digging little holes in the soft earth. Visions rose before her of a barefoot boy and girl driving home a cow. The boy, William's brother, Jim;—in his slow passionless voice had said, as he lifted her to the broad back of the cow.

"Ah loves you, Ruth. Les' you an' me git married."

"Ah loves you too, Jim, but us ain't old'er 'nough," she had answered, hanging her head.

"But we could git engaged," Jim had urged and

explained the process of becoming engaged accord-
ing to something he had heard Aunt Salisbury say
that if two strands of hair from the heads of two
people in love were tied together and buried at the
roots of a tree, as the tree grew, they would grow
closer. They had buried the strands of hair at the
roots of a tall hickory nut tree. That was four
years ago and even if Aunt Salisbury's charm was
not always productive of love and harmony in other
lives, in theirs it had become a sacred ritual which
even William with his good looks and education
could not shake.

Ruth raised her eyes and smiled brightly into
William's face, as she replied evasively.

"You jes' go on an' git to be uh preacher. All
us folks gointer be wid you. Pa wus jes' sayin'
tu'ther day that he wish you'd preach yo' fust sermon in our own church, an' Ah kin jes' see you now
walkin' up an' down, wavin' yo' arms an' preachin'
'bout Zekiel an' de dry bones an' uh wheel in uh
wheel, an' ole sister Spencer jes' uh singin' her
little song, 'preachee, brudder Willyum, preachee,
preachee.' "

"I declare Ruth, you're a sight for a minister's
daughter, but I think I'll start preaching in Genesis
and work up to Revelations," William laughed.

"Anyhow, good luck to you an' may Sister Spencer sing longer an' louder," Ruth smiled, turning
to go into the house.

William spent a few moments with the sick minister and left promising to send Jim over to see
about his horse. He was soon on his way to the
Railroad station. Sara Lou watched him until the
bend of the road hid him from view, his goodbye

kiss making a warm glow in her heart, a prayer for his safety on her lips, as the shrill whistle of the train slowing down at the station faintly reached her ears. Far out in the cotton field she could hear Jim singing loudly as he wielded his hoe.

"Umph! Dat boy's all'ers happy," she commented giving her churning extra speed. Up and down the dasher plunged, as she hummed her little song.

The village now fully awake, was alive with the noises of cackling hens, quacking geese and turkeys. Children ran to and fro in play, their happy cries rising above the barking of the neighborhood's many mangy dogs.

Sara Lou, a clean bandanna tied over her neatly coiled hair, prepared to go forth on a mission of praying with a neighbor's sinful husband.

Jim sat down heavily on the back steps, the bucket in which he kept medicine for ailing horses by his side. He had just returned from Reverend Johnson's.

"How's de Rev's horse?" his mother asked, noticing his dejected expression.

"Ah, b'lieve she gonna die, Ma."

"Umph! Dat's too bad. Fo' de lan's sake whut ails de ole cuss?"

"Ah don' know but ah done give her uh dose uh every medicine Ah got an' it ain't done uh mite uh good."

"Well, you don de best you could do an' dat's all dat's 'quired uh anybody. But Ah gotta go over to Sally Brown's. She done sent fo' me tuh come an' pray wid dat triflin' Luke. Ah be back tuh-rechly."

"Ah hope he gits 'ligion dat'll last 'im longer den de last he got, Ma," Jim laughed.

"Go 'lon' boy, youse all'ers pokin' fun atter somebody's 'ligion. You bettuh git some yo'seff," Sara Lou chided.

"Don't worry 'bout me kaise when Ah gits it, ah'm gonne keep it sho'nough."

"Dat's zackly whut Luke done said, but last Sad'day night dat low corn liquor he drinked done tole 'im to beat Sally nigh 'bout to death an' he promised if she wouldn't jail 'im he git some mo' an' Ah goin'ter help de pore debil keep his hocks outter de jail house."

Sara Lou moved toward the gate, as Jim rolled on the porch with laughter.

"Umph, dat boy sho is uh causon," she grumbled, walking down the road, the crunching grass beneath her feet making even rhythm in her ears. On each side of the road tall leafy trees threw fitful shadows across her path.

Occasionally, a wagon passed her, the driver calling a greeting or offering her a lift for Sara Lou was the most loved person in the little settlement. Hurrying on, her voice floated back in snatches of her favorite song.

> "Ah'm gonna lay down mah burdun,
> Down by de ribber side
> Down by de ribber side
> Ah' gonna lay down mah burdun
> Down by de ribber side
> Ah ain't gonna study war no mo'."

A thin column of smoke curled up from the one room cabin that was Sally Brown's home.

"Huh!" Sara Lou grunted, as she looked over the sordid wreck the place had become, "Lawd, ain't it jes' terrible how triflin' some folks kin be."

Sally, a tall, black woman of twenty-five, standing in the door, greeted her happily.

"An' Sara, Ah sho' was scared yuh wuzn't comin'."

"Well, Ah's heah. Whar's dat no 'count Luke? Ah thou't last 'vival when he confess 'ligion we wasn't gonna have no mo' trouble wid dat scamp."

"He's sleepin'. Come on in!" Sally whispered, leading the way into the cabin, where Luke lay fully clothed upon a wooden bunk built to the wall.

"Now look'uh heah, Luke Brown, you wake up an' do it rite now," Sara Lou demanded.

"Awrite An' Sara," Luke muttered sitting on the side of the bed rubbing his eyes with his tightly balled fists.

"Come on an' git yo' vittels, Luke!" Sally called from the hearth where a pot of peas was cooking over a small bed of glowing coals.

"He don't need no vittels, Sally," Sara Lou said impatiently, catching him by the shoulder. "Whut he need is de grace uh God, an' he don't need no full stomach to git it on. Git down on yo' knees, Luke, an' pray!"

Luke knelt sheepishly, and Sara Lou started her prayer.

"O Lawd, come intuh dis house an' call Luke
    Brown by his natrul name.
Make 'im know dat you is God,
An' 'side you dere is no odder,
Dat he gottuh die,

An' dat he got an ebber dyin' soul to save,
Paralyze his throat agin' dat poison liquor dat's
    killin' his soul an' drivin' 'im from yo' presence.
Lawd, Ah knows dat you kin unlock doors dat's
    locked,
An' Ah want'uh ask you dis mornin' *heah me
    Lawd,*
To unlock de door uh Luke Brown's heart
An' walk in an' take yo' riteful place.
Wake 'im up dis mornin' Lawd to de sense uh his
    duty.
Ah know you is a prayer answerin' God,
An' Ah want you to bend down yo' ear,
An' hear my prayer for dis heah sinful man."

Sara Lou prayed on and on while Luke fidgeted
from knee to knee, at times sitting back on his heels.
    Five minutes passed. Sara Lou's voice rose
higher and higher, as she called down every kind
of calamity on Luke's head, if he refused to change.
Sally from her corner amen'd and moaned.
    Luke peeped slyly from one to the other and
groaned aloud. Sara Lou's voice rose louder, be-
lieving the groan came from a contrite heart. Raising one knee slowly, Luke gave a loud shout and
springing to his feet, darted out of the door, Sally
turned just in time to see him disappear.
    "Look uh Luke, An' Sara," she shouted. Spring-
ing to her feet she started in hot pursuit of the flee-
ing man.
    Across the field Luke raced with Sally close be-
hind him and Sara Lou waddling after them as fast
as her feet would carry her two hundred pounds.
But he had a good start and soon vanished from

view. Sally, realizing her defeat, waited for Sara
Lou, who soon reached her side.

"You think he got 'ligion, Sally?" Sara Lou asked
breathlessly.

"Ah don' know An' Sara, but Ah sho' does thank
yuh for comin' an' trying to save de po' debbil."

"Well, anyhow, we got ole Satan on de run.
Praise de Lawd for dat!" Sara Lou rejoiced.

"How's all yo' folks, An' Sara?" Sally asked, as
Sara Lou turned to go.

"Jes' fine, Sally. Willyum done gone back to
Macon dis mornin'. He's doin' fust strate in his
pressin' business dar, an' learnin' lak uh house afire
in school."

"Ah sho' glad to heah dat, we'se all crazy 'bout
dat boy."

"Yeah, he de top uh de pot an' some day he
gonna make his ole Ma mighty proud uh 'im, Sara
Lou smiled.

"Ah heah dat de Rev. ain't so spry, An' Sara."

"No, he ain't so good. Ah'm goin' tuh stop by
dar on my way home. De sisters uh de Chu'ch aid
gonna meet at my house dis atternoon so Ah gottuh
hurry. So long, Sally!"

'So long An' Sara!" Sally called, as Sara Lou
walked hurriedly away and was soon out of sight,
hurrying back home to the many duties that awaited
her.

CHAPTER III

The day began to show signs of intense heat.
Swarms of flies made buzzing sounds overhead.
The midday sun beamed mercilessly down upon the
hard, dusty, red clay road.

The door of Reverend Johnson's cabin was
propped open with a pine wood knot. In the clay
fireplace a low fire glowed, over which Aunt Salisbury bent, stirring a pot of boiling roots which sent
out a sickly bitter aroma.

Reverend Johnson, a little dried up brown skin
man, propped up in a large armchair near by,
watched her wearily, pain distorting his wrinkled
face.

For over forty years Aunt Salisbury had doc-
tored the village ills and as she expressed it, "catched
dere babies for dem." Her anger rose in hot heat
against anyone who dared call Doctor Clark, the
white physician, who lived down in the village.

"Yuh all jes' don't b'lieve in me kaise Ah'se yo'
own color," she would complain when anyone suggested his aid was needed on a case.

Sara Lou's entrance brought a bright smile to the
minister's face. She'd always been his best friend
even in the days when the church had been arrayed
against him, and had prevented his little family
from going hungry many times.

Aunt Salisbury grunted a greeting from the
hearth and turned again to stir her pot.

"Mah Rev. you sho' do look pert for a sic' man," Sara Lou beamed encouragingly.

"Yeah, but he was 'neih dead an' Ah'se had a hard time pullin' 'im through. Ef dat dere Doc Clark had'uh come 'roun' heah wid his no 'count pills, he'd uh been gone for sho'," Aunt Salisbury complained.

"Aw he ain't so bad off, An' Salisbury," Sara Lou smiled. "But whar's Ruth?" she added, looking around the neat, sparsely furnished room that served as bedroom and kitchen for the minister.

"Ah sent her to de village for lin'ament. Mine done bein' run out," Reverend Johnson explained.

"Lawd! Ah could uh sent Jim for it, Rev. Dere ain't no use uh de chile walkin' all dem miles wid a strong boy lak Jim nearby," Sara Lou said, bustling around, looking into the cupboard to see what was on hand for dinner. Seeing that they were well provided with food, she expressed her willingness to be called upon any time she was needed, and departed for home, grumbling to herself that the sick minister needed a doctor.

She would send Jim to summons Doctor Clark, she decided, as she walked around the back of her house, where Jim was busily engaged drawing water from their deep well, to fill the large wooden tubs which were used to do the family wash every Tuesday morning.

"Lawd boy! You sho' don't forgit nothin', does you?" she chuckled.

"Nothin' dat concern you, Ma."

"As soon as you'se through, run down for Doctuh Clark to come see 'bout de Rev. He rite sick dis

mornin' an' Ah ain't gonna let 'im sit dere an' die
'thout me doin' what Ah kin for 'im."

"Awrite ma, ah'se on de las' tub now," Jim replied speeding up his work.

Jim's information when he returned some time
later, that the doctor had gone to Macon and his
wife did not know when he would return greatly disturbed his mother when they seated themselves for
dinner at noon.

"Lawd! Ah'se sho' sorry to heah dat!" she com--
mented, as she dished up a large plate of collard
greens and fat side for Jim. "Willyum sho' would
'joyed dese greens an' corn bread if he wuz heah",
she finished regretfully.

"An' he would uh found fault wid dem bein' too
greasy for 'im to digest," Jim replied before he
thought.

"How come you allus findin' fault uh yo' brudder?" Sara Lou asked regarding him with a
frown.

"Aw, Ah ain't findin' fault uh 'im, Ma, ah'se jes'
tellin' de truth", Jim smoothed, bowing his head as
a signal for his mother to bless the food.

Sara Lou prayed a lengthy prayer instead, in
which she asked God to give her boys understanding
hearts toward each other. Jim knew it was a rebuke for what he had said, and ate his meal hurriedly.

Pushing his plate back, he rose, stretched his
arms above his head, and gave his body a vigorous
shake.

"Ah jes' can't eat no mo', Ma. Ah ain't got
much appetite nohow," he explained.

"Lawdy boy! You done ate two plates full. Yo'

appetite bound to go when you gits yo' belly full."
Sara Lou laughed looking up at him affectionately.

Jim reached over and patted her shoulder and
turning abruptly, left the room. Sara Lou's eyes
filled with tears. She had never showered affection
upon him. His touch had somehow had the feeling
of a starved animal begging to be noticed.

"Dat boy is as steady as an ole mule," she
mused, brushing away a tear.

"Jes' lak his pa, po John, I know he ain't happy
in heaven wid nothin' to do but flyin' 'roun'."

An hour later the living room that was usually
kept closed, was almost filled with the members of
the Church Aid, wives of hard working farmers.
The meeting every Monday afternoon was a great
event in their monotonous lives.

Ella Jones, a tall, skinny brown-skin spinster,
who, when she walked, made you think of many
bones loosely put together, was secretary of the club.

Sally Ann Peck, a portly woman with a rather
pleasant round face, a shade darker than Ella,
seated herself in the far corner of the room. She
was a newcomer in Byron, having lived most of
her forty years in Macon. Coming to Byron during cotton picking season to work, she had decided
to stay. She and Martha Green, a thin, little black
woman lived together in a little one room cabin
over by the branch. They both were grass widows,
their husbands having left them several years
previous.

From the first day of their acquaintance the two
women had never agreed on any subject. There
had been constant fights between them for five

years, but to the amazement of the settlement they continued to live together.

Sadie Smith, Mary Ella Lawson, and a few others made up the membership of the club over which Sara Lou presided as president and treasurer. The women had been working hard for five years, trying to raise enough money to fix the parsonage but money was scarce and hard to get, and after five years of hard struggle, there was little more than fifty dollars in the treasury. Today they would decide on some way in which twenty dollars more could be added.

After a lengthy prayer by Martha Green, Ella Jones adjusted her glasses, and holding her book at arms' length before her, started reading the minutes of the last meeting.

"De meetin' ob de Church Aid met las' Monday atternoon at An' Sara Lou Carter's house, she bein' de pres'dent and trea-sure. Two dollahs an' ten cents was turned ober to de trea-sure An' Sara, leabin' ten cent mo' to be turned ober by sis'ter Martha Green."

Ella lowered her book and looked at Martha Green over the top of her horn rimmed glasses meaningly and continued:

"Fifty dollahs was den paid to brodder Slack Henderson for work he gwine to do on de parsonage, leabin' two dollahs an' thirty-five cents in de trea-sure. Dat's all sis'ters," Ella Jones said, dropping back into her chair.

"Dat's good, Sis Ella. All in favor notifie by sayin' Ah!" Sara Lou said taking over the meeting.

"Now while ah'se on my feets," she continued,

"Ah want to ast whut you'all 'cided to do to git dat twenty dollahs balance fuh Slack."

"Ah move we gib uh barn party", Sally Ann suggested.

"We ain't gonna do nothin' uh de kind! De las' un we gib de young folks danced an' dat's agin de church rules," Martha Green objected vigorously.

"Shucks, dem whut danced ain't 'long to the church nohow.   Dat's de trouble wid you folks. You jes' too narrow.   When Ah lived in Macon de church was allus givin' parties an' de young folks allus dance an' Ah ain't seed no harm it done 'em," Sally Ann came back sharply.

"How 'bout givin' uh donkey party?" Sadie Smith asked timidly.

"Aw we kaint, kaise somebody done stole de donkey an' Ben Johnson whut allus draws de donkey, done gone off an' don't nobody know when he's comin' back," Martha Green informed.

Jim's entrance at this moment interrupted the meeting.   He had just come from the parsonage, where he had found Reverend Johnson prone on the floor of his cabin; having fallen there while trying to get into bed.

Before he finished speaking, the women were on their way to see about their stricken pastor, their hearts filled with fear that they might be too late.

Eager, loving hands undressed and laid him between cool, clean sheets.   They then rushed around getting in each other's way in their anxiety to help. But Reverend Johnson lay still with open, unseeing eyes, his mouth twisted to one side, unable to utter a word.   A deep guttural sound came from his throat, as a tiny froth moistened the corners of his mouth.

Ruth, coming in a few moments later, hovered close to his bedside, as Sara Lou bathed his head with cold water and tried to force a few drops between his lips. Some of the women rubbed his hands with hot salt and did all of the many things they had heard would help in a case that plainly showed paralysis.

All afternoon neighbors came in steady streams. Women busied themselves brewing coffee and laying out the food they had brought over for the watchers at his bedside. The Church Aid members sat huddled in a corner of the room softly singing spirituals and offering prayer for their sick pastor.

Slowly the afternoon faded into twilight. The long hot summer night with many sounds from the dense woodland that surrounded the little settlement closed in around them. Owls hooted in the trees near by. Crickets filled the air with their screechy song. Near the cabin a dog howled dismally, sending a shiver over the waiting household. Night passed and the first faint streak of early dawn sent many of the farmers and their wives home to do their chores.

There was no change in the sick man's condition except that he seemed weaker. A cold sweat had accumulated upon his forehead, which the neighbors observed with a sad shake of their heads.

Sara Lou sent a message to William by a farmer driving into Macon asking him to come home at once.

Another hot miserable day came to add to their misery. To Sara Lou's distress nothing had been heard from Doctor Clark, who had not returned from his visit to Macon.

The sun again hid itself behind the Western horizon. Stark dark midnight encompassed them. Sara Lou patted up the sick man's pillow and straightened the bed covers in an effort to make him more comfortable and passed quietly into the next room for a cup of coffee. Finishing her drink, she again seated herself at the head of the bed, noticing that the covers she had straightened before leaving the room, were again thrown aside. She leaned down to pull them into place, and drew back with a scream.

"Lawd sakes, folks! De Rev. is gone! He done slipped away from us jes' as quiet," she cried, tears streaming down her face.

Ruth fell sobbing across his body. Women added their cries to the din and soon the cabin was a swaying mass of screaming people, lamenting the passing of their pastor and friend.

CHAPTER IV

Wednesday morning a light rain fell mercifully, cooling the dry, hot day. The farmers breathed a prayer of thankfulness. The summer had been intensely hot and dry. Long before noon many of them had finished their work in order that they might be on hand early for the wake to be held that night.

At the parsonage Martha Green and Sally Ann Peck, their dresses tied high around their waists, were diligently scrubbing and cleaning the two rooms. Food had been stacked high in the cupboard to be cooked and served during the night at intervals between the singing and praying. Sally Ann tucked a clean sheet over the one mirror the Johnsons owned, as she remarked to Martha.

"Lawd sake, Martha, dis gonna be de biggest wake we'se had since Ah been libin' in Byron."

"Huh! T'ain't nigh as 'portant as de Rev. Smith's wuz," Martha grunted, walking over to the open door and spitting out a long stream of snuff.

"Yeah, but Ah wuzn't heah den an' dis 'un goin' to be mighty good anyhow wid all de local preachers 'tending eben down to dat personable Reverend Bruce Hanson from Iron City."

"Ah guess dat's all you thinkin' 'bout, dat Rev. Hanson. Ah done see'd you makin' eyes at 'im de las' time he wuz heah durin' de big meetin'. You'se de forwardest 'oman whar mens is concerned, Ah eber did see, Sally Ann Peck."

"You ain't 'exactly blind yo'self, Martha. Anyhow you jes' jealous kaise he don't pay you no mind."

"No Ah ain't. Ah jes' ain't forgot dat he's got uh wife. Ef'fen she is done gone off an' lef' 'im."

"Yeah, you jes' 'members dat kaise he don't notice you."

"Ah ain't nothin' uh de kind. You'se jes' uh fresh 'oman, Sally Ann Peck. H'it ain't no wonder yo' husband done gone an' lef' you."

"Lis'en to dat!" Sally laughed loudly. "Whar's yo'un gone to and why, when he lef' you six years ago? Folks sho does say some curious things 'bout why he packed hisself off."

"Aw shet up, loud mouf!" Martha grumbled, unable to find words strong enough to silence the laughing Sally Ann.

Much to Martha's relief, Sara Lou put an end to their argument when she entered the cabin to see how they were getting on. Both women went about their tasks and were soon chattering together again pleasantly.

Out in the little Calvary Churchyard men were busy digging a new grave in which the Reverend Peter Johnson would be laid to rest Thursday afternoon. Night found everybody from miles around gathered to keep the wake. Ruth, worn out with crying, lay quiet upon a cot in the corner of the room.

William. who had arrived from Macon during the aftern on, helped his mother get the people seated. At his word the singing was started and through the long summer night their songs, low and mournful, wafted out upon the air.

The day of the funeral dawned bright and clear. Long strings of wagons wended their way to the Church. Ministers from the adjacent counties took their places on the rostrum. William had been chosen to read the scripture and sit with the ministers on the rostrum, looking down upon the crowded church with solemn eyes in which gleamed the pride he felt in his position. Jim, looking up at him seated there, could not help feeling proud of his intelligence and importance.

The sun had begun hiding itself in the west behind mountains of soft pink clouds when Reverend Johnson was finally laid to rest in the Calvary Churchyard, and Ruth became a member of the Carter household.

William, placing his hand tenderly upon her shoulder, as she stood later that evening ready to accompany Sara Lou and Jim to the parsonage to get her things, said consolingly:

"Now, don't worry yourself sick, Ruth. You can't do your father any good by worryin'. He was prepared to go. You'll just have to give him up, and try and meet him in Heaven some day."

"Ah know, Willyum. Ah want to be brave an' should oughter be to show An' Sara Ah 'preciate her givin' me uh home. But rite now Ah jes' can't help missin' Pa," Ruth replied, her eyes misty with tears.

"You must feel it's just as much yo' home as it is ours, Ruth, an' we're glad to have you heah," Sara Lou told her kindly.

William watched them walk down the wide road, Ruth between his mother and Jim, her slight form swaying in perfect rhythm as she walked. A

mixture of jealousy and fear filled his heart—
jealousy of Ruth's and Jim's proximity and fear
that Jim, whom he knew had heard about his gambling and other misdemeanors in Macon, would
some day tell his mother, gripped his heart.

There were times when religious fervor held and
swayed him under its spell. But his was a change-
able nature, cold, hard and calculating, ready to
move heaven and earth to have his way. He loved
money; pitting his wit against the other fellow's
to gain something for nothing thrilled him, and
made him a slave to gambling. Of late his luck
had been bad. He had lost in continually trying to
win back his losses, and had lost money his mother
and Jim gave him from time to time to buy things
for the farm. These thoughts haunted him as he
sat alone on the steps of the front porch where he
had seated himself when the trio left him.

Sally Ann Peck and Martha Green spoke to him
from the front gate.

"We ain't aimin' to 'tain you brudder Willyum,
if you goin' out, only we'uns 'thout dat y'all would
kinder enjoy dese hot rolls and preserves for supper. An' brudder Willyum, we wants to tell you
how grand you wuz at de Reverend's funeral,"
Sally Ann continued, beaming with one of her
brightest smiles on William.

When he answered he was once more the suave
young deacon they all loved.

"Come on in, sisters, the folks will be back soon,"
he called, leading the way into the house.

Sally Ann and Martha followed eagerly.

"Ah 'clare things sho is happenin' roun' heah.
One time dar wuzn't uh thing goin' on. But now de

Rev. done tooken sick an' died almost de same day.
Minds me uh de sayin' you'se heah today an' gone
tomorrow," Sally Ann said with a resigned air.

"Ain't it de truth?" Martha echoed.

"Yeah, Martha, jes' de odder day you wuz sayin'
you wished somethin' would happen an' you sho'
done got yo' wish. An' Salisbury done tole you
'bout wishin' up things," Sally said, turning to
Martha scornfully.

" 'Nother thing. You wished up dat storm las'
month sayin' dat it wus so dry. You wished it would
rain so de ground wuz soaked through an' it rained
steady one whole week."

William laughed heartily as the two women
glared at each other, and Martha, not wanting to be
rebuked before William, retorted angrily.

"Aw, shucks, An' Salisbury's allus beatin' up hur
gums an' cookin' roots. Kain't nobody wish up
nothin' nohow, kin dey brodder William?" Martha
asked turning to William.

" 'Course they cain't," William smiled.

"When you goin' back to Macon?" Martha
asked, anxious to change the subject.

"I haven't decided yet. I might go tomorrow
but Ruth is so upset, I feel like staying and trying
to cheer her up in some way," William answered.

"Dat's you, brudder Willyum, allus tryin' to help
odder folks," Sally Ann commented.

"Ah wish lot uh other folks wuz lak dat,"
Martha said, casting a meaning glance in Sally's
direction.

"Dar you go, Martha Green," Sally spoke up
hotly. "Castin' yo sly remarks. You kain't speck
us to be lak brodder Willyum, he lives close to de

Lawd kaise he gonna carry de Gospel. You ain't bent down from carryin' too much 'ligion nohow."

Martha started to give Sally a sharp reply, but William cut in.

"Now sister, you mustn't quarrel an' you shouldn't judge for fear you be judged by the same judgment the Bible teaches us."

Sara Lou and Ruth's voices, as they came up on the porch, cut short the discussion. William stepped forward quickly, to help them with their bundles.

"Lawd Ah'se tired!" his mother gasped, sinking into the nearest chair.

"We came ober to bring you some vittels," Sally informed.

"Ah sho thanks you sis-ters. Me an' Ruth is purtty much hungry Ah 'speck."

"Ah ain't hungry," Ruth said listlessly.

"But you must eat an' keep up yo' strength, chile. Dar ain't no need uh you gittin' all sick and skinny," Sara Lou said kindly.

"Yeah, jes' brace up an' be cheerful, Ruth. De Rev. is done gone an' you kain't live by de dead. You'se young an' got uh long time 'fore you, so enjoy yo' life while you'se able," Sally Ann added cheerfully.

"Dar you go, Sally Ann Peck," Martha snorted. "Dat ain't no way to talk to Ruth kaise she got to moan 'bout her Pa's death. You jes' cry much as you want to, Ruth. Don't you try to be careless lak dis 'oman heah whut ain't got no heart a-tall."

"Let's talk 'bout somethin' else, sisters," Aunt Sara begged. "Ruth's awrite an' ain't got no cause to moan 'round. She's in good hands an' 'course she gonna git cheerful."

Sally Ann and Martha soon bid the family goodbye and hurried home to the many duties that
awaited them.   Sara Lou refused Ruth's offer to
help get supper.

"No, chile, you jes' sit down an' rest," she said
kindly.

"I tell you what we'll do, Ruth. Come on out
and let's take a walk," William offered, taking her
hand in his.   They walked through the sweetly
scented woods that surrounded the farm.   At their
heels, Jim's old dog Towser ran barking loudly.

William tried to cheer her with vivid descriptions
of his last school term, and his plans for the future,
but Ruth was silent and unresponsive, the deepen-
ing shadows of dusk gathered around them, and
Ruth complained of a headache, so they returned to
the Carter home in silence, each busy with their own
thoughts.

When they entered the yard, Jim was seated on
the front porch and greeted them with a happy
smile.

William's heart filled with jealousy as he saw the
happy light in Ruth's eyes and the animation he
could not arouse became evident when she seated
herself beside Jim.

Excusing himself early, he went to his room determined to leave the next morning for Macon,
where he hoped work in his pressing shop, and lively
nights in the Broad Street haunts he frequented,
would obliterate the unhappiness he suffered seeing
Ruth smiling and happy with his brother Jim.

CHAPTER V

The early morning sun cast fitful shadows through
the half-opened window upon the floor of the little
back room behind William Carter's pressing shop
on Broad Street in Macon.

The room was close and filled with a musty odor,
mingled with a smell of stale beer, bad liquor and
decaying food. The floor of rough dirty boards
was strewn with bottles and bits of a torn deck of
cards. In the center of the room stood a rickety
table covered with a mixture of bottles and bits of
bread and drying sparerib bones. Swarms of flies
made their invasion known, as they buzzed from
place to place and rested for brief spells on the face
of Slippery, William's helper, who stirred occasionally to brush them away, and settle himself in a
more comfortable position on the cot pushed close
to the wall on which was thrown a dirty quilt. His
face, a brick colored yellow, covered with dirt and
freckles, was thin and wrinkled, not so much from
age as from sickness and exposure, for Slippery
was still in his early thirties—a thin, stooped, me-
dium-sized man, whose past life was little known to
the crowd around Broad Street, where he had recently drifted, from where, no one, not even
William, knew.

Turning with a groan, his feet slowly struck the
floor, as he sat up on the side of the cot and stretched
his arms above his head. For a moment he sat looking around the room, his hands pressed tightly to

his aching head, then slowly he dragged himself over to the back door of the shop which opened into an alley running the length of the block behind the dingy front negro business places. Hanging on a nail just outside the door was a rusty basin which served as bath tub and dish-pan for the place.

Slippery took it down gingerly, filled it with water and started washing his face with his hands, scooping up the water and letting it run down over his face and neck. Someone passed down the alley and helloed. He answered gruffly without turning to see who the speaker was.

Loud knocks came from the front of the place. Someone was banging to get in. Slippery slouched into the room wiping his face on the first thing that his hands came in contact with, which happened to be an old shirt, and with an oath, started hurriedly towards the front door.

"Hey, Slippery, whut you tryin' to do, sleep all day?" The query came through the door.

"Who de hell's business is it, if Ah do?" Slippery answered, as he opened the door and faced Cotton Eye, who stood grinning with a pair of pants hanging on his arm.

"Well, lil' ole business man, is dat any way to greet uh customer whut comes all de way pass dozens uh cleanin' shops to bring yuh work?" said Cotton Eye grinning broadly.

"Whut you want done to dese pants?" Slippery asked, taking the pants and throwing them on a chair piled high with crumpled suits.

"Want 'em scrubbed, man, an' pressed. Dat's whut Ah wants."

"You would want dat today when my head is achin' an' Ah feels nigh ready to die."

"But you'se in business, ain't you? An' how you gonna pay de rent ef we'all don't fetch you work?"

"Oh awrite, Cotton Eye. Sho I'se glad to have yo' work but dat don't make me not feel sick, does it?"

"Sick or well, Ah wants dem pants tonight. Daddy Jenks is openin' up his place back uh de pool parlor wid dancin' an' he's got some purtty gals whut'll be 'round an' one uh dem gals is uh humdinger. Ah done seed hur. She's from Chicago. Whew, some gal, Ah says."

"From Chicago?" Slippery asked, turning quickly to face Cotton Eye.

"Dat's whut Ah said. But whut's dat to you? You ain't neb'ber said you come from dere."

"An' Ah ain't said yit. Ah jes' wanted to make sho whut place you mentioned."

"Ha, ha, ha! You sho is a slick 'un, Slippery but Ah almost got yuh den, didn't Ah?"

"Whut you mean almost got me kaise Ah didn't quite git whut yuh said?"

"Well, we'll let it go at dat. Say when is William de Parson comin' back?"

"You bettuh not let him heah you call him dat. Dat's one sho thing."

"Huh! Ah ain't scared uh 'im even if you is. Ah'se done knowed him since we wuz babies dere in Byron an' Ah'll call him anything Ah wants to. Who is he, anyhow? Everybody in Byron knows dat he ain't born rite."

"Whut you mean, ain't born rite, Cotton Eye?"

"Why, Ole man John Carter wuzn't his Pappy. He's uh white man's chile—jes' uh plain bastard."

"Whut diff'rence does dat make? How does you
know dat you ain't one nor me nor eve'ybody. For
whut we knows. We all know who our fathers wuz
'spose to be but can we prove dat dey wuz? You
ain't sho uh nobody but yo' Ma an' even if uh pusson
is born, what didn't habe uh lawful pappy, does it
hurt 'em any? An' if dey wuz lawful, did hit help
'em any? My Pappy wuz 'spose to be lawful an'
uh preacher, an' whut am I? Nothin'. It's up to
us all whut we make uh ourselves not who our Ma
or Pa was."

"Awrite, Friday, youse rite to take up fo yo' Rob-
inson Crusoe. He sho is been uh friend to you but
Ah ain't neber been crazy 'bout no half white nigger.
Dey's tuh biggity an' thinks dey is better den us
blacks, an' Ah jes' don't lak 'em."

"Dat de trouble now. We ain't satisfied fo de
white folks to fin' fault wid us, we'se jes' got to fight
one 'nothur jes' kaise we all ain't de same color.
Whose fault is it, anyhow? Kain't nobody make
demselves, don' you know that? An' to white folks,
whether you is black or yellow or brown, you is jes'
uh darky, so shut yo' trap up 'bout color."

"Awrite, us ain't gwine fight. How'd yuh make
out in de game las' nite?"

"Rotten. Loss every penny Ah had to dat ole
pusley Sugar Kid."

"Whew! Dat boy sho is lucky."

"Oh! Ah don't b'lieve it's jes' plain luck. Ah
b'lieve he's crooked but none uh us can ketch him,
dat's all."

"It sho is funny he don't never start winnin' 'til
atter he's had de deck in his hands. Den if he picks

uh queen, it's right on de bottom. Do yuh think he
nails de cards dat quick?"

"Well, yuh knows dat's why Ah went on home.
He cleaned me right quick."

"Yeh but if Ah eber finds him nappin', he's a
gonner fo sho."

"Dat's it. How you gwine ketch him nappin'?"
Cotton Eye asked dubiously.

"Ah'll ketch him, don't yuh worry an' when Ah
does, dere'll be plenty uh trouble stirrin'," Slippery
answered menacingly glancing towards the desk in
the corner of the shop, where despite William's advice to the contrary, he kept his revolver loaded
and pushed carelessly under some papers in the
drawer.

"Well, Ah got to hurry on, Slippery. Ah'se
workin' today," Cotton Eye remembered, moving
slowly towards the door. Ah jes' had to have some
money kaise dat new gal's ober at Daddy Jenks an'
she's some queen, b'lieve me," he sighed. "Hur
name's Ethel Myers but see heah Slippery, I ain't
figurin' on no opposition in dem quarters."

"Don't worry. Ah ain't interested," Slippery
assured him.

"Well, Ah'll be pushin' on. So long. Have dem
pants all slicked up by five o'clock," Cotton Eye
called over his shoulder, as he sauntered slowly
down the street, both hands in his pockets and
whistling a popular blues.

Half-way down the block he met William walking
rapidly with his small bag swinging at his side. They
had known each other from infancy but there had
never been any friendship between them. In fact, Ed-
ward Knowles, which was Cotton Eye's real name,

had been the worst boy in Byron and had spent so much time in jail that Marshall Bailey had asked him to just leave Byron and not come back, as he was an expense to the county. He had been given the nickname Cotton Eye because of his large eyes, which seemed to sit on his forehead and were a glaring white except for their small black pupils. He was extremely tall and slender, almost skinny, his color a shiny black but his broad smile, which showed all of his even white teeth, usually won the hearts of the fair sex and made him many male friends as well.

William merely tolerated him as there was nothing else to do, but it was a superior tolerance which Cotton Eye felt and resented. His lips parted in a quick smile at sight of William.

"Gee, boy, glad to see yuh back. How's Byron?" he asked quickly.

"Oh, Byron's fine, Cotton Eye," William answered, as he tried to pass on down the street.

"How's my Aunt Sofia an' yo' ma?" Cotton Eye continued almost blocking William's path.

"Yo' Aunt Sofia's right poorly, Cotton, but Ma's fine."

"Now dat's too bad 'bout Aunt Sofia. Sho wish Ah could see hur," Cotton Eye replied earnestly.

"Well, I guess in a case like this you could run down to Byron. I don't believe old Marshall Bailey would object to you seein' the only mother you ever knew when she's sick."

"Yeah, Willyum, Ah mought try it but say, whut's to become uh Ruth now dat hur pappy is dead? Who's she gonna stay wid?"

"With Ma, of course. Who else would she be likely to stay with?" William answered.

"Well dat is de truth. Aunt Sara is a kinder mother to all de folks down dere. Pore li'l' Ruth. Is she as purtty as eber, Willyum?"

"Yeah, Cotton Eye, she's even prettier than ever and a wonderful girl."

"Which one uh you boys is gonna marry hur— you or Jim? Ah 'member dat yuh both is allers been sweet on hur," Cotton Eye smiled.

"I don't think we had better discuss that, Cotton?" William answered with acerbity, and walked quickly away.

Cotton Eye's laughter echoed in his ears, as he walked on down the block.

"Black fool!" William muttered, and disliked Cotton Eye more than ever.

Slippery looked up from his task of cleaning the front of the shop as William walked in the door and threw his bag down on the nearest chair. William's face showed he was not in a very pleasant mood, and Slippery merely helloed as he continued hurriedly to the back room for the broom to sweep the floor and sidewalk.

William followed him into the back room and stood for a moment viewing the upheaval condition of the place.

"Say, Slippery, you must have had a mighty rough bunch here last night to get things in such a mess. Whew! Open the window, the place smells bad. How on earth could you sleep in such a mess?" he asked disgustedly.

"Ah don't guess Ah could uh slept if Ah hadn't

been dead drunk when Ah went to bed," Slippery
answered shortly.

"You'd better lay off that bad liquor. It don't
do nobody no good," William warned.

"Don't Ah know it, but whut else yuh gonna do
when you'se disgusted an' broke, Bill?"

"Had bad luck last night again, eh?"

"Yep and how! In fact, been havin' it ever
since you went to Byron. A new guy blowed in
town Wednesday nite dat's cleaned eve'ybody but
Daddy Jenks an' he jes' won't play him."

"Who's he?"

"Oh, some fellow dat calls himself Sugar Kid.
Brought plenty dough wid him an' done 'tached
ebe'ybody else's to his'en since he's been heah."

"What does he play, Slippery?"

"Georgy skin an' whut luck!"

Slippery had been sweeping all through his talk
with William and started out the front door to
sweep the sidewalk that ran in front of the shop
when he remembered that he had a letter for
William. He leaned the broom against the wall
and hurried back into the place, and after searching
through the table drawer for a moment, handed
William the letter.

"Jes' came yistiddy, Bill. Ef yuh hadn't come
back today, Ah wuz gonna send it on down to
Byron to you."

"No, Slippery," William spoke up quickly, after
he had scanned the postmark. "Don't ever send
my mail down there. Jes' keep it 'til I come back."

William sank into one of the two rickety chairs
and frowning, read the letter which was from one
of his creditors. A sigh escaped his lips. Slippery

coming in from his sweeping, looked at him with
deep concern.

"Whut's wrong? Anything Ah kin help straighten out?" he asked.

"No," William answered trying to pull himself
together. "There isn't anything that anyone can
do."

"Must be very serious, Bill."

"No, Slippery, jes' a man I owe, wants his dough.
Have you got any money?"

"Not uh lousy cent. Ah got cleaned out for sho
las' nite.

"That's bad news but I guess I can find some
way out."

"We'se got lots uh work hangin' 'round an' if de
folks calls for it, dere'll be a little money on hand,"
Slippery informed.

It was Friday. Most of the people who patronized the shop, got paid on Saturday and the work
would have to be ready so they spent the remainder
of the day working steadily.

Evening brought a good many customers in for
their clothes. To most of them it was the only suit
they had, and they all would attend Daddy Jenk's
blow-out, dressed in their Sunday best. Cotton Eye
appeared promptly at five and retrieved his pants
which were all scrubbed and pressed and looked
nothing like the dirty rag he had brought in earlier
in the day.

"Lawd, Slippery, ole boy, you sho' did do uh good
job on dese pants, but shux dey don't look nothin'
lak de coat now. 'Speck Ah better fetch it over
an' let yuh knock hit off wid yore hot iron. You
wouldn't mine doin' dat, would you?" he asked.

"No. For fifteen cents Ah wouldn't mine doin'
it at all," Slippery answered.

"You sho is tight, Slippery. Heah Ah brings yuh
all my work an' yuh 'fuses to do me uh li'l' favor."

"Cotton Eye, you knows we charge forty cents
for a suit. Why do you want to try an' get it done
for the twenty-five cents you paid for your pants?"
William asked.

"Awrite, awrite, we won't argue 'bout it," Cotton
Eye answered disappointedly.

"An' anyhow, whut yuh want to weah a coat
for?" Eddie Nolan, known to the bunch as Red
Shirt, asked from the chair where he had sprawled
in his underwear waiting for Slippery to finish pressing his pants.

"Yeah," Slippery echoed, "you ain't been wearin'
no coat. Why de big desire to dress up?"

"Shirt sleeves is awrite far as dese Macon
Janes is concerned." Cotton Eye explained. "But
ain't Ah done tole yuh dat uh queen from Chicago
gonna be ober dere an' maybe she ain't use to seein'
de boys in shirt sleeves an' Ah want to make uh hit
wid hur."

The boys all laughed heartily and Cotton Eye
grabbing his pants, left in a huff.

"Wear uh red silk shirt. Dat'll make uh hit wid
hur," Red Shirt called after him.

"Ah'll leab dat for you to do, Red Shirt. Dat's
how you got yore name," Cotton Eye called back.

William's pressing business was located across the
street from Daddy Jenks' more imposing pleasure
emporium, a large building with a pool parlor in the
front and a large room in the back used for dancing.
Overhead were furnished rooms and a large room

in the rear for gambling. Here every night the
boys played dice or Georgia Skin.

Daddy Jenks seldom gambled. When he did it
was for high stakes and he was generally lucky. He
had bought the building in which he ran his business,
with his winnings many years before. Money was
plentiful then, and he had gone from place to place
all through Georgia and Florida, to saw mills and
other public works on pay day, returning with his
pockets bulging with money. His poolroom brought
him in a good profit and also his furnished rooms,
but he depended mostly on his club room from which
he gleaned a neat profit.

Anything from soda pop to corn liquor could
be bought in the place, and upstairs in the gambling
room, anything from a nickel to a thousand dollars
could be played over the tables.

Daddy Jenks' imposing figure could be seen early
and late as he walked around, keeping an eye on his
boys, as he called them. He was a large light-brown
skin man with heavy jowls and small twinkling eyes,
always dressed in a suit of expensive clothes, pre-
ferably grey with a huge horseshoe pin set with small
chips in his tie, which he claimed was his lucky
charm, and wore faithfully. Across his bosom his
watch chain stretched. At one end his watch with
its large solid gold case was tucked in a pocket and
a gold penknife in the opposite pocket.

A half smoked cigar always hung between his
lips and his black Stetson hat was usually pushed
far back on his head. He was known to everyone
in and around Macon. His real name, George
Jenkins, was seldom heard. He was Daddy Jenks
to everyone, white and colored.

His prosperity was an unquestioned fact in the
community. He even boasted a brand new Ford
sedan and a chauffeur. Kongo, the misshapen mute
who drove for him, was more or less his own pro-
perty. Daddy had rescued him from the gutter when
a lad of ten, whose half-witted brain seemed only to
emerge from its stupor where cars or machinery of
any kind were concerned, but the mere fact that
Kongo drove the car for him and did his every bidding made Daddy Jenks quite a personage among his
associates. He had visited New York the previous
summer and had come back with new ideas for his
place, had brought a second-hand piano and hired
a trap-drummer.

Three girls from a show that had been stranded
while playing the colored vaudeville house had appealed to him for aid, and he had taken them in to
help entertain his guests. Ethel Myers, one of the
girls, had been rather glad to remain in Macon for
a while. It was a new field and Ethel, for certain
reasons, did not want to go back to New York nor
home to Chicago, where she was always getting into
trouble. She was a clever dancer and a good-looking girl, light-complexioned and medium height,
with a mass of short curly hair, framing a face of
small fine features. Ethel knew her good points and
made the most of them. She could sing as well as
dance, and had a dashing personality. The word
conscience meant nothing to her. She was out to
get what was coming to her. Of the three, Ethel
was the star with undisputed rights.

Daddy Jenks, a good business man, had struck a
good bargain with the girls, who were to receive
rooms, board and a percentage from the drinks sold

for entertaining and keeping the place lively by dancing for and with the customers. He realized in trying to run his dance hall at a profit to keep the men spending, there had to be girls around—girls that could be depended upon to stay until closing time.

The place had been newly painted, and colored lights hung from the wall. In one corner stood the second-hand piano and drums. Little tables lined the sides of the wall with a space left in the center of the room for dancing. A crude counter had been built across one side of the wall. The small ice-box behind it held soft drinks. White mule could be obtained by giving a certain sign. The room, a fairly large one, running the full length of the building, could be entered through a door from an alley that ran behind the place.

At nine o'clock the music started, and the place was soon filled with sweating, swaying bodies.

CHAPTER VI

Across the street William and Slippery, tired
from their day's work, finished their supper of fried
mullet fish and hominy, and sat out in front of the
little pressing shop, watching the crowd pour into
Daddy Jenks' place.

Because of Daddy's opening, many pairs of pants
had been scrubbed and pressed, but for all their hard
work, the day's receipts had amounted to a very
small sum. To William it was nothing. He
needed money, and lots of it. His gambling had
gotten him into a tight place. He would have to
pay or be exposed to his mother. To lose her confidence would mean the end of the lazy, care-free
existence he now enjoyed. It rankled him to see
money pour into Daddy Jenks' hands for which he
didn't have to make a struggle, and he voiced his
thoughts to Slippery sitting quietly smoking a
cigarette beside him.

"Sure's a shame how some folks get money so
easy and others have to work so hard for it, ain't
it, Slippery?"

"Yep. Dat's whut Ah allers thought, Willyum,"
Slippery replied and after a moment's silence, con-
tinued. "Dat would make uh fine racket for you.
De dance hall business is easy money."

"No, Slippery, not for me. I jes' wasn't cut out
for anything like that," William answered quickly.

"But why, Willyum? You know Ah allers wondered why you wants to preach anyhow. You'se uh

good talker an' is educatid awrite, but outsider dat, you ain't nothin' like uh preachin' man aught'er be!" Slippery said, eyeing William closely, his brow slightly wrinkled in an effort to read William's mind.

"It's 'cause Ma wants me to be a preacher, I guess, and because in my heart or somewhere, there is a part of me that loves honor and right livin' and helpin' others."

"Ah knowed dat by de way you helped me. Ah was nigh 'bout dead and everybody but you was scared uh me, sayin' dat Ah had de con. Ah sho was down when you picked me up."

"Well, to be truthful, there was some selfishness in that. I figured if you ever got well, you could help me with the shop."

"Yeah, but de chances was sho slim uh me gettin' well but you tooked me in an' got uh doctor for me and everything. Paid out yo' good money and didn't even know me. Youse awrite, Willyum, ah'll say dat for you an' Ah ain't never gonna fergit you."

"I try to be, Slippery, but I certainly do make a mess of mistakes for all of that."

"Us all makes mistakes. Ain't nobody perfect."

"Yeah, but I suffer for mine because they worry me. I feel ashamed of some part of me, the part that holds me back when I want to do right and makes me do wrong."

"Lawd, boy, to heah you talk a body would think you'd killed somebody."

"Maybe I have."

"Whut!" Slippery almost jumped from his seat.

William laughed long and loudly at Slippery's agitation.

"Sit tight, Slippery," he said between the laughter that shook his shoulders. "I was only joking. 'Course I ain't killed nobody and sure hopes I never will."

"Boy, you sho had me scared!"

"No, Slippery, it's money that's worryin' me. I needs lots of money right through here. I've got to have it or all my plans are busted. That's all!"

"Well, you might git lucky an' win it. Dere's Sugar Kid 'roun' heah dat's got gobs uh dough. Maybe you'll be de one to break 'im."

"Yeah, maybe, with the luck I've been playin' in lately, there's a fat chance of me breakin' anybody."

"Well, at least it's worth tryin'."

"No, I guess I'd better let well 'nough alone. I sometimes wonder why some people have all the luck and others never seem to git anywhere," William mused, continuing. "There's my brother Jim. Everything he touches seems to prosper. He's lucky with our crops even when other folks' cotton fails or the bugs eat it up. He gets good money for every bale he turns out. Then 'sides Mr. Gordon pays him to take care of his place. Now that he's in Europe, Jim's in full charge. He's gonna sell the peaches and keep the money 'til Mr. Gordon gets back. He never asks any questions—jus' takes Jim's word for everything. I couldn't get a break like that."

"Gee! Dat sho is some break. It's uh wonder dis Mistuh Gordon wouldn't have uh white man lookin' at'ter his place."

"Not as long as Jim is around. He's known Ma

all her life, and my folks as far back as my great grandmother was born right on his place. He thinks uh lot of Ma and likes Jim because he took to farming. He don't like me much—thinks I want too much education and as Jim don't crave none, he's right down his street."

"Does Jim make much money for him? Maybe dat's why he's so crazy 'bout 'im," Slippery asked, setting his chair which had been tilted against the wall, firmly on the sidewalk, while he rolled a cigarette.

"Well, he don't make any too much, 'sides Mister Gordon's rich and don't have to depend on his place any, but he likes to make it pay something. Jim will make over a hundred dollars when he sells his peaches. 'Course he'll have to pay some of it out to get them picked, but not much."

"Lawd! I'd be scared to keep dat much money 'round me, but maybe Jim banks it."

"Well, he should, but he don't. He keeps it over at Mister Gordon's house in his safe."

"Dat sho' is a mighty risky thing to do, seems to me."

"That's jes' what I'm thinkin', Slippery. Jim thinks it's the safest place. Maybe it is. But Mister Gordon's place is right on the main road and lots of no 'count people travel that road."

"Even if dey was to break in an' take de money, nobody would blame Jim, would dey?"

"Gordon wouldn't, but old Bailey, the Marshall, and the other white folks might. They ain't got none too much good blood for Jim 'cause Gordon left him instead of a white man in charge of the place," William replied.

Slippery, his chair tipped back against the wall again, watched the stream of women and men pouring into Daddy Jenks' place. Now and then a cough shook his slight form from which he quickly recovered rather breathlessly.

"You'd better put on your coat," William advised.

Rising slowly he entered the shop to return shortly with his coat and hat on. William looked up, as he stepped out of the door.

"Goin' over to Daddy Jenks' to see whut's up an' to get another look at dat Sugar Kid's dough. Kin yuh let me have uh dollar?" he asked.

William handed him the dollar and taking his chair, started for the door.

"I b'lieve I'll mosey over there too and see the sights. Wait a minute," he called over his shoulder.

A few moments later they walked into the crowded dance hall where the fun was at its height. The center of the room had been cleared of dancers and Ethel Myers had the floor. She was in the middle of a song, a low, moaning blues which she sang, as her body swayed back and forth to the rhythm of the music. Couples sprawled at the tables, others stood in knots around the room. White mule and soda pop flowed freely.

Everybody was watching the girl, who, when her song was finished, broke into a wild dance. The crowd applauded loudly when her dance ended. Turning to bow to her appreciative audience, she saw Slippery standing just inside the door. Her eyes dilated as if she had seen a ghost.

The piano and drum started up a loud jazz number and Slippery walked quickly to her side.

"Want 'er have dis dance?" he said loudly.
Then under his breath he spoke closely to her ear.
"Don't lose yo' head, Ethel, Ah wanna talk to you."

She quickly recovered herself, as Slippery guided
her around the room in a slow drag.

"Ain't dere some place whar we kin talk?" he
whispered.

Ethel nodded and they danced over towards the
door that led into the pool parlor. There they
slipped into a dark hall.

"What you want to say, Jessie?" Ethel asked,
as she slipped free from his arms.

"Nothin' much—only dat you don't know me.
Git me? An' if you say you do an' start shootin'
off yo' head an' beatin' up yo guns Ahm gonna make
Macon too small to hold yuh, dat's all."

"Well, I ain't got no call to go 'round here
braggin' 'bout knowin' you. You ain't no prize
package to know, nohow."

"Ah jes' wants to warn yuh, kaise 'round heah
Ah'm jes' Slippery an' nobody don't know anything
but dat—not even whar Ah comed from, and it
ain't gonna be none too healthy for you if you put
'em wise," Slippery warned.

"Don't worry. I'm out to 'tend to my own business, Jessie, and that's about all I kin do."

"Not Jessie, jes' Slippery. Yuh git me?"

"Awrite, say, who's the slick-lookin' guy dat you
was standin' next to over dere by the door? I mean
de high yellow boy wid de good clothes on," Ethel
asked, nodding her head towards the dance hall.

"Dat's de man I work for—Willyum Carter."

"You wouldn't mind knockin' me down to him,
would you, Slippery?"

"He don't wanna meet no tramps lak you."

"Now be a good boy, Slippery. I'm crazy to meet 'im. Why, he's got all dese guys 'round heah skinned uh mile in looks, and besides, how do you know he don't want to meet me? I sho could go for him all right!"

"Well, ah'll introduce you to him, Ethel, but remember he ain't yo' kind, so go slow," Slippery agreed reluctantly.

"I might be lots uh help to him for all you knows kaise ah'm de little gal dat's gonna put Macon in· my pocket." Ethel laughed as she and Slippery crossed the room to where William was standing, leaning against the wall.

Ethel and Slippery were a strange pair—both outcasts and without conscience. They were from Chicago, and for many reasons neither was desirous of going back there. With Slippery it was the law that he feared and the many cases that they held against him. For many years he had been a terror on the South Side, always up for stealing. The last affray he had been mixed up in, a killing had been pulled off that could have been easily traced to his door, had he waited for the tracing. That had been several years ago, and he had finally drifted to Macon, sick and broke, and had met William, who befriended him. A friendship grew between them that had become almost worship on Slippery's part. There was nothing in the world he wouldn't have done for William.

William liked him because he could use him for his pressing business. He knew the fellows around Byron and Macon, if he had gotten any of them to help him in his shop, they would have had to be paid.

With Slippery he only had to say he needed the
money for something and Slippery would make out
on just enough money to buy his food or a few dimes
with which to gamble. At times he was lucky, and
shared his winnings with William. For thief though
he was, he appreciated the kindness William had
shown him when he was a stranger and down and
out.

Ethel had no actual crime lurking in her past—
just general worthlessness. True, she had been
picked up several times in Chicago, for street soli-
citing but had drawn only minor sentences. Her
brother, a prominent Chicago attorney, had become
disgusted with her way of living, and paid her to
leave town because of the disgrace she had brought
her family. She had gone to New York and pro-
cured work in an uptown cabaret as an entertainer.
Soon tiring of that line of work, she had drifted
from the chorus of one small show to another,
until she finally left town with a small troupe that
had gone on the rocks in Macon.

Daddy Jenks' proposition had come as a God-
send. At least it offered a place to eat and sleep,
and whatever could be picked up on the side, and a
certain amount of protection from the law.

Knowing her past, Slippery did not like the idea
of introducing her to William. To a certain extent William was his hero. He did not drink, and
was ambitious to study and better himself. That
he loved to gamble, he did not hold against him,
Why shouldn't he try his luck? He was a man and
if he didn't have a fault, it would not have been
natural. Besides, the temptation was too strong for
any real man to resist, especially when he needed

money so badly for such a good purpose as schooling. He felt that William was miles and miles
above the other negroes with whom he was thrown
in contact. With a certain reluctancy he guided
Ethel over to where William was standing.

"Ethel wants to meet you, Willyum," he said as
the three stood together jolted on all sides by
dancers. "Dis is Willyum Carter—Ethel Myers."

William graciously acknowledged the introduc-
tion and Ethel smiled her sweetest, as she said:

"I certainly am pleased to meet you, Mr. Carter.
Your friend here, Slippery and I were dancing together, and I had to beg him to introduce me to
you. Do you like to dance?"

"I'm sorry, Miss Myers, I never dance," William
answered politely with a smile.

"Well, now, can you beat that! I thought everybody in the world danced."

"I've never tried and never cared for dancing,
and I'm in the world."

Ethel looked at William for a second without
speaking. William returned her gaze unconcerned-
ly. Ethel was plainly getting on his nerves and he
did not try to hide the fact, which made her all the
more interested.

"Well, big boy," she said, "You've got me there.
I thought when I first saw you that you were a live
one—different from the other tripe, but now . . ."

"Well, what do you think now?" William asked,
stifling a yawn. A surge of anger swept through
Ethel as she was made to feel his indifference to her.

"I've got just one more question to ask, then I'll
be ready to give the verdict. Do you drink?"

"No, never tasted a drop in my life, and never cared to," William answered, moving away.

"Whew! How did your mother ever let you get out? Say boys," she cried making herself heard above the din of jazz music. "Look what we have here! It never drank a drop in its life, and don't dance. Where did you folks find it?"

Most of the dancers had turned to hear what she had to say, and when she pointed to William, a loud laugh went around the room. Cotton Eye, who had been watching her ever since she had walked over to William, guffawed louder than the rest. William turned a brick red and fire showed in his eyes, as he turned and faced the girl, who went on addressing the crowd.

"Say, where did y'all git dis 'un?" indicating William. "It hasn't got a fault in the world. Why, I believe it would think dice was number blocks made for children to play wid. Ha, ha, ha! Any more in Georgia like him?"

William, almost beside himself with anger, strode over to the laughing girl and caught her by the wrist.

"Say, you little rat!" he cried. "What you tryin' to do—make a sissy out 'er me? I've got a damn good mind to knock yore block off!"

"Don't mind her, William," Slippery said, stepping over to the girl and laying his hand on William's shoulder, "She's crazy!"

"I ain't crazy," Ethel exclaimed angrily. "He did tell me he didn't drink or dance, and walked away with that dizzy look on his face."

"Well, whut of it if he don't?" Slippery broke in. "He don't have to, if he don't wanna but Ah bet

he kin take uh pair of dice or uh deck uh cards an'
send you home barefooted."

"Who dat whut can do so much wid dice an'
cards?" A voice asked from the door. A murmur went around the room. The speaker was the
stranger known as Sugar Kid, who, although he had
been in Macon only a few days, had gathered in all
of the boys' loose change and had them scared to
mention cards or dice in his presence.

Nobody knew exactly where he had come from
nor what his right name was. Some said that in
Jacksonville he called himself Sugar Kid and that
was all anyone knew of his identity. He was a
large pompous person with smoothed brown skin
and large features. His eyes were small and in
them lurked a crafty look. His large full lips hung
loosely on his mouth. His large flat nose with its
wide nostrils seemed to be always scenting something. There was an air of bravado about him and
from the day he came to Macon, the crowd around
Daddy Jenks' place had taken a dislike to him,
which grew as he cleaned the boys one by one of
their scanty bank roll. Daddy Jenks was the only
man who did not fear him, but to others he was
poison.

William had not met Sugar Kid, but intuition told
him that the speaker was the much-talked-of-
gambler. He realized that Slippery's bragging might
get him into a mess as he did not want to play with
the few dollars he planned to use otherwise. But
William loved to gamble and could not bear to be
thought beaten in anything. He had promised himself to lay off games for awhile, but with Sugar
Kid standing there glaring at him, his blood became

fired with a desire to put him in his proper place at
any cost. Then, too, Ethel's remarks had to be
lived down. The boys had laughed at him, a thing
he could not endure.

Her remarks caused them to look at him in a way
he did not like. In view of them, she had poked
fun at him. He would have to do something to
make them forget her insinuations or things would
be said that would cause him to have to flatten out
a few of them. He would show them that he could
meet the man they all feared.

Sugar Kid walked slowly over to where William
stood in the center of the room. There was an in-
dolent smile on his face, as he slowly looked him
over and winked to the others standing looking on.

"So, youse de guy whut craves to git rid uh some
dough?" he asked sneeringly.

"Well, I can't say that I exactly craves to git rid
of any dough, but I do crave annexing some of yours,
an' kin do it if I try," William answered nonchalantly, looking the gambler over.

"Atta boy, William!" Slippery shouted.

"Well, whut yuh say to playin' a li'l' skin?" Sugar
Kid asked.

"O.K. by me," William replied.

"Well, less go. Ah'll play any uh de odders whut
wants to take me on," Sugar Kid said loudly, looking around the well-filled room.

"There's only one thing I want and it's such a
li'l' thing I know you won't object," William said
looking straight into the other's eyes.

"What's it?"

"I want someone else beside you to deal the cards,"
he answered slowly.

"How come yuh wants dat? Is dere any objection to us dealin' to one 'nothur?" Sugar Kid asked, a trace of annoyance in his voice.

"Yes, there is, and if Daddy Jenks will give us a new pack an' a dealer, we'll start!" William announced calmly.

"But I don't see any sense in havin' no stationary dealer," Sugar Kid objected.

"Well, I do, and if I don't get one, I don't play," William replied with finality.

A general murmur of approval went around the room, but none of the boys dared express an opinion that would in any way show their disapproval of the swaggering Sugar Kid. Sugar Kid, sensing their feeling and not daring to object, for fear of putting himself in a bad light with the boys, consented to William's demand.

Daddy Jenks placed a table to one side for the game, and called one of his boys to deal. The music struck up for the dancers to continue but everyone was absorbed in the game that was about to be started.

Ethel Myers sided over to William's side and placed her head on his arm. William turned and looked up into her face coldly.

"Don't play him, Carter," she said softly. "I hear he's plain poison around here."

"Don't worry 'bout me," William retorted. "I've got his number." And then announced loudly. "I'm goin' to bet on the queen, Queen Ethel, and when I wins my first five dollars, it goes to buy a present for the Queen."

Everyone laughed and Sugar Kid frowned his displeasure.

"That's right, William, yuh got de best go," they all shouted.

Slippery stood a few paces away with a worried look. In a way he felt responsible for William's plight. If he lost, it would be his fault for mentioning the game.

William looked at him and smiled, and Slippery thought that whatever faults William might have, he was not lacking in courage and admired him for that.

The game was on. A few of the other boys took a hand betting quarters and half dollars. William won and won again. The few who had joined in the game were soon frozen out and only Sugar Kid and William remained. Sugar Kid won a few hands and William won again and again. Sugar Kid had laid aside his coat and then his vest for he, unlike the rest, had come well-dressed, in fact, overdressed, for he had also hoped to impress Ethel.

Sugar Kid lost a big bet, and swore loudly. William coolly played on. Everybody, including Daddy Jenks crowded around the table where the game was being played. Sugar Kid, never a good loser, continued to swear.

"Say, listen heah, Carter, I won't stan' for nobody dealin' all de time. Ah wants de deal to walk."

William, the winner by fifty or more dollars, slowly gathered up his money saying: "When the deal walks, Sugar Kid, I walks. I done told you how I'd play an' I means it!"

The game ended at daylight. William crammed the money he had won in his pocket and prepared to leave the place. Everybody had gone except

Ethel, who walked over to his side and placing her
hand on his arm, said:

"Please forgive me, William, for whut Ah said.
Ah was jes' mad cause you didn't fall for me lak de
rest uh dese tramps round heah, but I sho done
took uh tumble for you, honey!"

"Heah's five dollars. Maybe that'll pick you
up," William answered disdainfully, shoving the bill
into her hand.

"Ah don't want yo' money," pushing the bill
away.

"All right, I'll buy you a present with it, I said
I'd give you the first five I won, and I always keep
my word."

"Ah knows you'se dead tired, William, playin'
heah all night. Why don't you come up to my room.
Ah got uh little stove in dere an' Ah'll fix you some
breakfast," Ethel pleaded, her body pressed close
to William.

William looked at her for a moment in silence.
What difference did it make with whom he ate
breakfast. Ethel had a nasty tongue and a rotten
character but she certainly was good to look at.

He sat in a small rocker as she made coffee and
cooked eggs on a small oil stove in her poorly furnished room upstairs. They laughed and talked
about the happenings of the night before, of Sugar
Kid's disaster, and when she turned her back, William tucked the five dollar bill under the dresser
scarf. She would find it there, and have to keep it.

"Tired, William?" she asked, taking his hand
and pressing it gently to her face.

"Yes and sleepy too," William answered, trying
to shake off the sleep that was creeping on him.

"Why don't you lay down heah den?" Ethel said, sitting on his knee and running her fingers through his thick curly hair.

"No. I think I better go to my own room," trying to get up.

"Whar's yo' room?"

"Er, 'bout ten blocks from here—with my cousin."

"Why walk ten blocks when you kin stay heah?" kissing him. "Come on, William, don't be so mean. Ah ain't so bad, an' Ah sho is strong for you hot papa!" Ethel coaxed, turning back the bed and patting the pillows into place.

William stood up and stretched, and made a step towards the door. Ethel playfully caught him and pushed him until he sat on the side of the bed. Sitting beside him, her arms stole up and rested around his neck. Pulling his head to her shoulder, she kissed him passionately again and again.

William accepted her caresses with no pretence of returning them, his blood tingling with passion, hot and overpowering. Ethel talked softly as she removed his shoes, and unfastened his shirt and removed it. Throwing her arms around him she pushed him back across the bed. Her body soft and warm lay close beside him for a moment. His arms reached out eagerly and drew her to him in a long, warm embrace.

CHAPTER VII

William's eyes opened lazily, and slowly traveled around the unfamiliar room. The cheap muslin curtains fanned in and out of the small open windows. Slanting shadows of late afternoon shed an ephemeral light across the dingy uncovered floor. His eyes found and rested on the form of a woman aranging a tray on a small table near the center of the room. Yes, it was Ethel. It all came back to him with startling clearness. He sat up quickly on the side of the bed. Ethel, looking up from her preparations of the tray, saw him.

"Come on, William, an' eat yo' dinner while it's hot," she called pleasantly, siding up to him.

"I don't want no dinner," he answered shortly.

"Whut's de mattuh, William?" Ethel asked anxiously, noting his frowning countenance.

"Oh, nothin'. I jes' don't like being here when there's so much work over at the shop to do."

"You just as well eat now, it's all fixed. Dere ain't much you kin do nohow. It's pretty nigh six uh clock."

William ate sullenly and hurried away with a gruff good-bye. He was thankful for once that the usual crowd that blocked the sidewalk in front of Daddy Jenks' place gossiping and telling jokes, had taken a recess.

Slippery looked up from his pressing, as he entered the shop. Neither spoke; but Slippery easily guessing where he had spent the day, felt vaguely uneasy. He realized William was in for a world of trouble getting mixed up with Ethel.

One by one the gang dropped in for their things that had been left for cleaning, and to loll around and talk about William's triumph over the bragging Sugar Kid.

"Boy, oh boy, dat's one snake whut ain't so popular roun' dese diggin'," Cotton Eye laughed. "Ah sho is glad yuh took 'im for his dough, Willyum!"

"Me too," Red Shirt added. "Ah thought sho some uh us was goin' uh hafta step on his head an' flatten 'im out 'fo 'lon', but Ah guess dis'll kind uh cool him off."

"Yeah, but he'll be rarin' up agin, don't you worry!" Slippery reminded them.

The laughter and talk went on about the game of the night before, the boys counting up their small store of change with which they hoped to give Sugar Kid his next battle later that night.

Ten o'clock Daddy Jenks' Juke was crowded. Music and dancing was in full sway. Sweaty bodies pressed close together, moved squirmingly to hot jazz tunes, perspiration running down their faces. Women twisting their bodies, working their hips up and down seductively, dragged themselves around the room, every movement an invitation. If acceptance occasioned an absence of a few moments, each couple boldly returned unashamed.

A close sour odor hung in the room, sickeningly oppressive. There was a heavy smell of bad corn liquor, stale beer, unwashed bodies and dim lights blotted out by the shadows of the dancers, swaying back and forth through the fetid air. Loud tinpanish music was heard from a broken instrument

pushed against the wall on which an overalled in-
dividual beat unmercifully, his feet stamping out
what his hands failed to bang.

Ethel slowly dragged herself around the room in
Sugar Kid's arms, her eyes turned expectantly towards the door every time it opened to admit a
newcomer. Sugar Kid, noticing her agitation, asked
sneeringly.

"Whar's yo' high yaller boy friend?"

"Who you mean, Sugar?" Ethel asked, innocently
looking up into his face.

"Go on gal! You know who Ah means—de high
yaller wid de white folks hair dat took my dough.
Ah seed 'im comin' out uh yo' room late dis afternoon."

"Now look uh heah, nigguh, don't you go med-
dlin' wid my business," Ethel exploded angrily.

"Aw Ah ain't tryin' to queer yuh, kid. Ah laks
yuh an' could do heap more fuh yuh den he kin."

"Fat chance you'll git to do anything for dis sweet
mamma," Ethel laughed in his face.

"Don't be too sho, gal. Yuh may be glad to hang
on to sweet papa Sugar fo' long."

"Don't fool yo'seff. You jes' ain't my style an'
never will be," Ethel taunted.

"No, baby an' you ain't dat boy's style neither
an' nebber will be. He's high falutin' an' gals lak
you is jes' out, far as he's concerned. He thinks he's
a wooden God," Sugar Kid sneered.

"Ah'm good as he is. My brother's uh lawyer
an' uh big man in Chi," Ethel informed him with
spirit.

"An' his sister is whut? Ah'll let you say it."

Ethel jerked away from him angrily. "Yo big

black hunk uh nothin'," she hissed. "Lemme loose
dis minute!"

"Not on yo' life, sister!" Sugar Kid avowed,
taking a firmer grasp on her arm. "Yuh gonna
dance an' lak it!"

Ethel danced on in silence until Sugar Kid pushed
her away in disgust and slouched out of the room.
A few moments later when William appeared in the
dance hall, she nodded her head at him indifferently,
and pulled Cotton Eye, who was standing near her,
finished her dance determinedly.

"Well, Ah see you'se back to try yo' luck again
tonight," Sugar Kid remarked, walking over to
William, who stood looking at the dancers.

"Yeah, I'm sticking around," William answered
nonchalantly.

"Well, yuh know dat luck is a mighty change-
able thing. Take Papa Sugar's advice an' don't try
to ride 'em too hard."

"Don't worry about me—just look out for yourself. I can take care of William."

"Awrite big boy. Whut yuh say we play upstairs in de clubroom tonight?" Sugar Kid asked,
a smile that could have meant anything, wreathing
his smug countenance.

"O.K. by me," William answered, moving towards the stairs.

"Come on, fellows. Let's git de game started.
My hands is itchin' an' dat's de sign uh money."
Sugar Kid called to the fellows scattered around
the room.

"Not so fast," Daddy Jenks remarked from behind the counter. "Eve'body's gotta drink to my
health tonight. I'se jes' become a grandpa. My

daughter done borned uh fine boy an' we gonna celebrate! Come on up, eve'ybody an' have uh drink on de house."

Murmurs of approval came from the crowd, as they rushed eagerly to get their free drink.

"Heah Willyum! Dere's uh glass uh gingerale for you," Daddy Jenks said, handing William the drink.

"Put a nipple on it, daddy"! Sugar Kid shouted.

"Shut up, you big loafer!" Ethel exploded. "Eve'ybody ain't a gin lapper lak you is."

"Atta gal, Ethel. Willyum sho' is got yo' number. You done fell lak de Walls uh Jericho". Cotton Eye laughed.

"Shut up all uh yuh black bastards!" Ethel shouted, her temper getting the better of her. "You ain't no good yourselves an' yuh hate to see anybody that got guts, try to be something."

William, standing at the end of the counter, said nothing. He felt miles above these ignorant riff raffs and their brawls.

"Ah leave de kid alone! He's awrite. Ah don't care much 'bout de stuff myself," Daddy Jenks ended the argument. "Anyhow Ah wants eve'ybody to be happy tonight. I'se got a good cause to be. Ah had uh hard time raisin' dat gal uh mine wid no woman to help me an' me bein' in dis kind uh business. Ah sent hur to Atlanta to school an' she comed out and teached. Den she married Sam an' he's a good, hard wukkin' man. Now dere little home is all paid for, an' my gal's in de best 'society 'roun' heah an' ain't nebber gived me a minute's trouble. Ain't dat somethin'?"

"Ah'll say it is!" the crowd shouted.   "Three cheers for dad's daughter and grandson."

* * *

Sugar Kid finally succeeded in getting his crowd together, and the game was on.

Ethel had had no chance to talk to William. She felt hurt. Daddy Jenks' recital had gotten under her skin in a way that she would not have admitted, as in her mind she turned over the incidents in her childhood. The environment and the advantages that had been given her, which she had thrown away to become a nobody. Walking over to the counter she called for a good stiff liquor which she drank hastily, then another and another. Her conscience numbed by the potent moonshine, she was soon dancing and laughing again. Finally, pushing the other dancers from the floor, she danced in a wild, primitive, sensuous manner. Her hips twisting, her body quivering, her mood changed to savagery. The crowd lining up, around the room, looked on, clapping their hands in delight. She pulled her dress higher and higher above her knees, her head thrown back in defiance. Pausing in the midst of her exhibition, she climbed from a chair to the top of the battered old piano; where she opened her lips to sing one of her course blues.

But the alcohol and dizzy twirling had gotten the better of her and she dropped heavily into the arms of some of the by-standers. Slippery, who had just come into the room, helped to take her upstairs to bed, where she lay in a drunken stupor.

In the clubroom the game went on steadily. The

atmosphere was tense. William was dealing, his small stack of money lay on the table before him. Slippery placed his small pile of change on the table, and took a card. The deal went around. Sugar Kid won. Again the cards were spread out. Each player picked his card. Swish—swish—the cards were turned from the pack. First Slippery then William lost and so on around the table. Sugar Kid swept their money in. Slippery, losing the last of his few pennies, stepped aside.

"You'se out 'fo you'se in," Sugar Kid taunted.

"Whut's it to you? Ah play my own money, don't Ah?" Slippery asked angrily.

"Awrite, Bo. Ah wasn't meanin' no harm. Ah was gonna let yuh have uh blind," Sugar Kid retorted.

"When Ah wants anyt'ing from you, Ah'll whistle!"

"Yeah. Yuh mought git yo' mouth puckered up an' my fist mought keep it dat uh way."

"Ah ain't gonna have no arguin' 'round heah. Dis is gonna be uh peaceful game so both uh yuh shut up!" Daddy Jenks reminded them.

Hour after hour the game went on, Sugar Kid taunting the boys spitefully, as one by one they dropped out, their money disappearing into his pockets. But he wanted to break William and although he was losing at almost every turn, he stuck with him longer than any of the others.

"They call dis game Georgy skin, but Ah'se a Florida boy whut kin teach you Georgy punks uh lot uh points," Sugar Kid grinned.

William was down to his last five dollars. Reaching over, he picked out a nine spot of spades and placed the five dollar bill on top of it.

"Ha! Ha!" Sugar Kid laughed. "De nin uh spades is whut digs de gamblers' grave. Ah'll take de ten uh hearts. An' say Carter, I wanna riffle dem cards."

"All right," William assented, handing him the pack.

The cards riffled and cut were handed to Daddy Jenks, who dealt them slowly. One, two, three, the cards were deftly turned. Sugar Kid glancing over Daddy Jenks' shoulder, said carelessly. "Wanna raise hit, Willyum?"

"No," William answered shortly.

A few more cards and then William's nine. Sugar Kid reached over and picked up the bill.

"Wanna play some mo'?" he asked.

"No. I think I'll go on home. I've got a headache."

"Bes' place in de world for uh headache," Sugar Kid laughed. "Well, Ah ain't got nobody to play me so, ah guess de game is all washed up."

"Aw no it ain't, Sugar Kid!" Daddy Jenks said slowly. "Put yo' money back on de table. Ah feels kinder lucky tonight."

The room was instantly tense. It had been years since any one remembered Daddy Jenks playing Georgia skin. Everybody crowded around as he spread and shuffled the cards. Daddy Jenks won the first bet then Sugar Kid won. Back and forth the money passed for almost an hour. Then Daddy Jenks' luck seemed to forsake him. He lost steadily, sent downstairs to the poolroom for more money, and lost that.

With the last money from the cash register before him, the gang begged him to quit, but Daddy
Jenks was fascinated. A power stronger than himself held him. He played on, sometimes winning
on a card only to lose again more than he had won.
His last dollar lay upon the queen of diamonds,
face up. He lost.

"Yuh wanna quit, dad?" Sugar Kid asked, cun-
ningly gorging him on.

"No, ah ain't nebber seen a meat man on earth
whut could clean ole Daddy Jenks," he answered
testily. "Ah'll write yuh uh check, Sugar Kid.
Let's play."

"Ah don't lak checks, daddy!" Sugar Kid answered. "But Ah'll tell yuh whut, Ah'll play yuh
for dis clubroom, three chances each. If Ah win,
Ah runs it. If Ah lose, Ah pay yuh whutever it's
worth. Whut yuh say?"

"No. Ah won't do that!" Daddy Jenks answered
slowly. "Ah guess Ah'll quit!"

"An dey say dat you was de greatest gambler
'round heah—*was* is de rite word!" Sugar Kid
jeered.

"Whut yuh mean, was? Ah still is de best
gambler 'roun' heah!"

"But you sho is slippin', Daddy!" Sugar Kid
taunted.

"Ah ain't slippin' nothin' uh de kind."

"Well, yuh jes' damn scared den!"

"Ah ain't never been scared uh no man an' Ah
ain't yit. You put up uh hundred dollars an' if Ah
lose, Ah'll make yuh out uh lease for uh year on
de clubroom," Daddy Jenks replied coolly.

"Don't do it, Daddy!" William begged, laying his hand on Daddy Jenks' shoulder.

"Mine yo' business, son. When Ah want advice, ah sees uh lawyer!" Daddy Jenks flashed back.

"All right, Daddy, it's your funeral," William replied.

"Yeah, but Ah ain't buried yit. Whut yuh say, Sugar Kid, let's get started." Daddy turned to Sugar Kid impatiently.

"Sho thing. Let Willyum deal," Sugar suggested.

"No, not me!" William spoke up, quickly.

"Ah'll deal 'em," Slippery offered. "An' Ah'll deal 'em so Sugar Kid can't look through 'em lake he seem to been doin' all night!"

Daddy Jenks' card was the last to fall for the first deal. The crowd was jubilant. Again he and Sugar Kid picked their respective cards. Swish-swish-went the cards to the table. Sugar Kid won. The cards were again shuffled, and spread on the table face up. Each picked their card. Tense silence pervaded the room. It was the last deal. The onlookers scarcely breathed. Slippery held the pack tightly gripped in his hand. Swish-Swish—the card fell to the table. One, another and another. Then Daddy Jenks' card flipped off, as a sigh went around the room. Sugar Kid had won.

Daddy Jenks sat as if in a dream. He had lost his clubroom, where he had reigned for many years, and with it went the best part of his profit. His body slumped in his chair, as his head rested on the table. Sugar Kid had slipped quietly from the room. Slippery examined the cards carefully. Yes, they were all right. The seals had been broken before their eyes. Silently they filed out, leaving the old man alone.

William was the last to leave. The first faint streak of dawn was coloring the sky, as he made his way through the semi-darkened streets. After a ten minute walk he reached his Cousin Sissy's house and let himself into his room, where he lay for hours, thinking of his muddled life in the city.

CHAPTER VIII

Sunday was a great day among the simple farmers
in Byron. They rose early and hurried to and fro,
doing their usual chores before church time when
everyone, saint and sinner, were wont to gather for
worship. People came from far and near in wagons
to which were hitched any kind of animal from
horses to oxen. The settlers, who lived a distance
from the little meeting-house, hitched their con-
veyance to the young saplings that grew in pro-
fusion around the church, and remained all day.
Some brought their dinner in slat baskets and others,
who were more fortunate, ate with neighbors, who
lived nearby.

Between the services they gossiped and enjoyed
the day like a group of children. The day showed
promises of being a fair hot one. Jim and Ruth did
their chores laughing and playing as they worked.
Sara Lou standing on the steps of the back porch
threw out hands full of corn and called the cackling
chickens to their feed. In the distance birds sang
airily. An air of peace pervaded the farm. The
field of snow white cotton stood tall and erect, and
as Jim put it, "nodding" to him to get ready for the
picking.

Putting away the empty pan from which the
chickens had been fed, Sara Lou bustled around the
kitchen preparing breakfast and putting the finishing touches to the dinner, which had been cooked
Saturday. She always entertained for dinner a good

many of the farmers, who lived too far away to
return home until after the last service.

A large cured pork ham lay on the table beside a
fat hen that had been baked for the occasion. Sara
Lou viewed with pride a large iced cake and two
apple pies, as she tried to count her guests—her
hand held before her checking off each one with a
finger pulled down to her palm.

"Ah guess Ah'se got vittels 'nough!" she mused.
"But dere's allus some dat jes' comes in whethur
yuh ask dem uh not. Now lemme see—dere's Hilda
an' hur husbun', Ben, an' dere four chillun, dat make
six altuhgether an' dere's ole man Pettiebone an'
'Riher an' de Dausies. Now how many is dat?
Lawd, Ah'se done lost track. Anyhow dere's de
preacher. Umm, seems lak Ah done count uh
hundred to say nothin' 'bout cousin Ella an' Jerimah
an' dey six young 'uns. Ah guess Ah better let
Ruth put 'em down on paper. Ah sho is sorry
William ain't heah. He's allus such uh help when
my ole brain ain't wukkin' rite."

She gave the big pan of batter bread an impatient
push into the oven, and turned to lift the skillet
from a hook behind the stove, smiling to herself,
as she cut—a small chicken into four parts.

"Ah guess Jim'll purty nigh drop dead at de
thought uh me killin' one uh my best pullets for
Sunday breakfuss but Ah wanted to have somethin'
real nice for Ruth. She's such uh comfort. Wonder
whut could 'er keep Willyum in Macon anyhow?
He done clean forgit dey gonna call uh new preacher
today an' 'ull need his advice."

The chicken was soon frying and sputtering in
the grease. The odor of bread and boiling coffee

filled the kitchen, as Sara Lou moved to and fro
stopping to mop the perspiration from her brow on
the corner of her apron. Taking down three plates
from the shelf, she wiped them carefully and put
them on the table, pausing in her work, as a voice
called from the front of the house.

"Yo hoo, is yuh in, cousin Sara?"

"Yeah, Ah'se heah", she answered loudly.

Turning, she gasped in amazement, as her cousin
Ella appeared in the doorway. On each side of
her clinging to her calico skirt were her two younger
children, her husband Jerimah and the four older
boys close behind her.

"Lawdy, cousin Sara," Ella exclaimed breathlessly, "Ah was dat scared we'un wouldn't git
heah in time for breakfuss. Our ole hoss done took
sick and we done had to leave home dat early we
ain't had no time for vittels so we hurried on heah
to eat wid yuh'all. Ah tole Jerimah it would be
awrite wid you."

"Course it's awrite, Ella," Sara Lou answered
not over enthusiastic at the prospect of having six
more to feed, who would also be on hand for
dinner, and it would be just like Ella to stop by for
a late lunch after the evening services.

Jim and Ruth brought the two pails of fresh
warm milk to the kitchen, and washed up for breakfast. Sara Lou grumbled inaudibly as she added
six more plates to the table. Jim laughed softly
at his mother's chagrin, and cast uneasy eyes toward
the yard, where Ella's boys were playing.

"Yuh better keep yo' eyes on 'em, Ma," he
warned. "De las' time dey was over heah, dey
pulled up nigh all uh my new plants, an' if dey pull

up dem geraniums dat Ruth brung over heah an'
sit out, Ah'll skin 'em alive."

"No son, yuh mustn't do dat. Dis is de Sabbath
an' you mustn't lose yo' temper on de Lawd's day."

"Sabbath or no Sabbath dey better b'have. Look
uh dere!" he exclaimed, as the objects of their discussion were seen in the act of uprooting a plant.

"Hey, you young uns, come out uh dere dis
minute!" Jim called.

Ella ran out and jerked the boys away from the
little patch of plants, and set them down on the
front steps.

"Now yuh'all stay dere," she warned. "You
know yo' cousin Jim is fussy 'bout his ole yard so
don't you young'uns touch uh thing!"

Jim boiled over, but a look from his Mother
stopped the words that were about to pour from his
lips.

At last they were all seated at the table. The
children, hard to be kept quiet, rattled their knives
and forks and fidgeted in their chairs. Sara Lou
bowed her head to pray, but her prayer was brought
abruptly to an end by a scream from one of Ella's
boys.

"Ella, dem chillun is de worse Ah ever seen,"
Sara Lou complained, wiping a stream of milk from
the table cloth, where little Jet had upset the glass
that had been given him.

"Dey ain't no worse den nobody else's," Ella defended, turning on her angrily.

"We won't argue, but Jerimah should take 'em
in hand rite away. You done rotten 'em ontell dey
stincks," Sara Lou retorted, looking at Jerimah,
who sat a little huddled creature afraid to even

breathe when his two hundred and fifty pound wife was with him.

"Huh, Ah jes' wish Jerimah would tech my chillun," Ella remarked, giving him a look that seemed to wither him up like a flower beneath a scorching sun. He opened his mouth to speak, but closed it meekly. Jim looked at Ruth and they turned their heads to hide the laughter that showed in their faces.

"You allus talkin' 'bout my chillun, cousin Sara, but you ain't done sich uh good job uh bringin' up wid Willyum," Ella said, and the next moment realized she had tread on dangerous ground.

"Whut you mean, Ella, talkin' 'bout my Willyum lak dat?" Sara Lou asked sharply.

"Oh, nuthin', cousin Sara, but . . ."

Jim's hostile look cut her off. She changed quickly to:

"Folks says dat he sho is spendin' lot uh time in Macon dese days, not even comin' home most uh de time on Sundays."

"Well, Ah'se satisfied an' it ain't nobody else's business. Dey allus did pick on my Willyum jes' kaise he's got mo' sense dan de rest uh dese ignorant nigguhs 'roun' heah," Sara Lou replied with spirit.

"Dat's zact'ly whut Ah tells 'em," Ella said, looking at Jim sheepishly.

"Jim, we better hurry an' do de dishes for An' Sara," Ruth said, rising, looking down at the side of her dress which one of the boys seated near her had smeared with molasses.

"No, you ain't gonna wash no dishes, Ruth!" Sara Lou spoke up. "You an' Jim git ready for church. Ah can wash dese dishes in no time an

Ah'se ready 'cept for puttin' on my clean apron so yuh'all run on upstairs an' don't be late."

Ruth looked reluctantly at the table filled with dirty dishes and smeared with molasses and crumbs, as Ella gathered her brood and herded them to the back porch to wash them up for the meeting.

Jerimah, eager to get out of his wife's opulent presence, slipped out into the yard to smoke his long stemmed clay pipe.

Jim went quietly upstairs, his thoughts of William, wondering just what Ella had intended saying. He had no doubt that she too had heard some of the talk that drifted into Byron of William's life in Macon. He wondered how long these stories could be kept from their mother whose adoration and faith in William was pitiful. At any rate, if he could prevent it, nothing would ever reach her ears that would tend to lessen that faith, he resolved, hurriedly changing to his Sunday suit. He and Ruth would be walking to church alone today. William was usually along, making him look homelier than ever by comparison.

Ruth in Sara Lou's room across the hall, could hear him moving around. Quietly she slipped across the hall, and tapped lightly on the door of his room.

"Come in," Jim called after a moment's silence.

"Whut you hidin'?" she asked, as he turned from the dresser, where he had shoved something into the half-open drawer.

" 'Tain't nothin'," Jim answered bashfully.

"Ah'm gonna look an' see," Ruth laughed, as she pulled the drawer open. "Why, Jim, whut you

doin' wid dis mail order book?" she questioned,
spreading it open on the side of the bed.

"Lookin' atter uh purtty marryin' dress," Jim
answered, turning the pages.

Ruth looked in rapturous silence at the bridal
array pictured there.

"Ah was jes' thinkin' how purtty yuh'd look in
dis 'un," Jim said, pointing to the sheer white dress
with sweeping train.

"Why Jim, you know we could never git uh dress
lak dat. It'ud cost lotta money but it sho is swell,"
Ruth sighed.

"It's twenty-five dollars an' dat is uh heap uh
money. Does yuh lak it, Ruth?" he asked, putting
his hand caressingly on her shoulder.

" 'Course Ah do, Jim. Ah ain't never had uh
silk dress nohow."

"Well, we'll jes' wait an' see. Maybe some day
yuh'll wear it," Jim promised, taking her hand in
his tenderly.

Sara Lou's voice called from downstairs, interrupted their dream. Ruth and Jim kissed, and ran
downstairs to join her.

"Yuh'all sho does tak uh time to dress," she
grumbled, as they walked briskly to the little log
church nearby.

A low murmur went around the assembled wor-
shippers as they entered the building. William had
not entered with them and they were eager to find
out why.

Reverend Thomas, a small, dried up man with a
shiny bald spot, whom as Sara Lou remembered,
had always conducted the services whenever the
church was without a preacher, stood behind the

rostrum, adjusting his horn rimmed glasses, which
had a habit of sliding far down on his small flat
nose.

"Well, sistuhs and brudders," he wheezed through
his nose. "It's become my duty to take de place
uh our dear departed pastor dis morning."

The congregation peeped at each other sheepishly.
They all knew that Reverend Thomas would preach
at least two hours, if some of the deacons seated on
the rostrum did not stop him or he had to stop from
sheer exhaustion.

"Ah'se gonna take my text in Revelations in de
words uh John—

'An dese are dem, who done washed dere gar-
ments in de blood uh de lamb,' "
he announced, looking over his sliding spectacles.

The congregation settled themselves more comfortably. They knew when Reverend Thomas
chose Revelations, they were in for an all-day
session.

Sister Spencer, a little old dried-up, brown
woman, who, ever since Sara Lou and some of the
older settlers could remember, had held the place
of honor as the best moaner in the amen corner,
settled herself more comfortably, pushed her snuff
brush to a secure corner of her mouth, and started
her plaintive moaning, "Preachee, Brudder Thomas,
preachee!" and kept it up except for the few moments she dozed.

Reverend Thomas preached on. Brave souls
amened and every now and then shouted a loud
"Hallelujah!" "Help 'im Lawd!"

Jim slept faithfully through the long sermon, re-
fusing to awake even to Ruth's nudging. Even Sara

Lou snatched a few nods occasionally. Somebody
started a hymn. The congregation joined in sleepily. Gradually they shook off their drowsiness and
gained in volume in their singing until Reverend
Thomas, no longer able to talk loud enough to be
heard above their blatant voices, sank into his seat,
wearily mopping his brow with his large red cotton
handkerchief. The congregation now fully awake,
sang lustily, swaying to the rhythm of the song.
"In de morning when de Lawd says hurry . . ."
until one of the deacons, Jaffus Simms, raised his
hand, bringing their song to an end.

"Brudders an' Sisters," he began, and after clearing his throat several times continued. "Us done
hearn uh powfull sermon dis mornin', an' 'fo Ah
raise de collection, I wan' to ask yuh'all is anybody
heah present got uh preacher in mind dat we·kin
call to pastor dis church now dat we'se widout uh
leader uh dis flock? 'Course Brudder Thomas heah
is uh ordain preacher, but we done asked him, as
we'se allers done, in de pass when we was widout
uh shepard an' he done refused."

"An' Ah rises to say, brudder Simms, dat de
reason is dat Ah ain't so strong as Ah uster be, an'
Ah couldn't stan' de strain." Thomas interrupted,
rising from his seat, panting from his exertions.

"Thank yuh, Brother Thomas," Simms acknowledged, and continued: "I don't zackley see how
we'se gonna git any whar wid brudder William
Carter not heah, him bein' de junior deacon uh dis
church as well as de clerk. Is dere anythin' wrong
wid 'im, sister Carter?" turning to Sara Lou.

Sara Lou hastened to reply. "Lawd no, brudder
Simms, I guess he done stayed in Macon 'count 'er

'portant business but he'll be heah bright an' early
next Sunday."

"Well, Ah moves eff'en ah kin git uh second, dat
we wait ontell next Sunday when we'ull have brudder Willyum wid us," Simms put to the congregation. After the members gave assent to their willingness to wait, the matter was put aside and the
services closed with the benediction.

Ruth and Jim, taking advantage of Sara Lou's
being besieged on every side with questions about
William's absence, walked home alone.

"You know Ruth," Jim said thoughtfully, after
they had walked a distance in silence, "Ah wish we
could git married right uh way."

"Jim, you sho is for hurryin' up some things an'
slow 'bout other things," Ruth laughed.

"Ah wants you, Ruth. Somethin' insider me is
jes' cryin' for yuh honey."

"An' Ah done tole you it's bad luck to marry
while you're wearin' black for yo' folks!"

"Ah don't b'lieve in dem signs. Ah wants to be
sho uh you, an' 'sides Ah been havin' uh spell uh
mighty bad dreams lately."

"Dat's b'lievin' in signs, Jim," Ruth reminded
him. They both laughed at his contradictory moods
and hurried home to start putting dinner on the table
before Sara Lou's many hungry guests arrived.

Everyone Sara Lou expected for dinner came and
almost as many more. They had to be fed in sec-
tions, the grown-ups first and a second table for
the children. After dinner, the men strolled around
the farm smoking their pipes, while Sara Lou and
the women sat on the front porch stirring their
neatly chewed brushes, deep in their boxes of rail-

road snuff, everybody enjoying themselves and re-
laxing for the big meeting to be held that night
when the much-talked-of "Swamp Angel" would
preach one of his stirring sermons at their own Calvary. Excitedly they talked of the many things they
had heard about his fiery sermons, how he could be
heard for as far as a mile away, and the many souls
he gained for the Lord, how at the climax of his
preaching, he placed the Bible upon his shoulder and
walked the aisles of the Church, the building trembling under his three hundred pound tread.

Thus the afternoon passed and the evening found
them again in the little church, where for more than
three hours the Swamp Angel preached his sermon
of fire and brimstone and lived up to all the things
that had been told about his mighty power to rock
the very depths of a sinner's soul.

Jim, his mother and Ruth walked home after the
meeting in silence, each busy with their own thoughts,
and Sara Lou hurried straight upstairs to bed. Disappointment over William's not coming home or
sending a message to say why, filled her heart but
she would not for the world have let anyone, not
even Jim, know it.

"Come on, Ruth, less you an' me eat some vittels," Jim, who was always hungry, suggested when
he and the girl were alone.

"Ah don't want nothin' to eat but Ah'll come an'
keep yo' company," Ruth consented.

Jim pushed her playfully into a chair at the table,
and placed a glass of milk and a slice of cake before
her, taking his place beside her a moment later
with a plate filled and overflowing with food.

"Ah had dis vittels hid in de stove. Ah was

scared dem starved out old stickin' plasters was gointer eat up everything today," he laughed.

"No wonder you dream all kinds uh dreams," Ruth smiled. "Jes' look whut you goin' to bed on." "Dis ain't nothin' but uh bite. You ought'uh see whut Ah does eat som'times."

"Well, don't complain 'bout bad dreams den, Jim." "Gee, boy, you sho can hug!" Ruth complained a few moments later when Jim, having finished his meal, caught her in his arms.

"Ah loves you so much, Ruth, dat it makes me scared sometimes," Jim whispered, kissing her before he let her go.

"An' Ah loves you more den so much," Ruth returned, playfully pinching his round cheeks, and running lightly upstairs where she lay awake thinking for a long while beside his mother, who was sleeping soundly.

After a day of excitement and bustle, everything was still. Outside firebugs flitted to and fro, making the only light to be seen for miles.

Another Sunday had come and gone in the peaceful village. Everybody had put on their Sunday best and served God in their own simple way. Monday would find them again in their grimy rags —busy, hard working farmers intent on their daily tasks.

CHAPTER IX

To William in Macon, Sunday had not brought the peace his family had enjoyed in Byron. He had crawled into bed in the early hours of dawn broke, discouraged, ashamed of the life he was leading and disgusted with himself for not having the will-power to break away from the thing that was slowly but surely carrying him to disaster.

His cousin Sissy from whom he rented a small shabby room for one dollar a week, had called him in time for church, but receiving no answer, had decided he had worked in his shop late and needed rest. Of all her relatives, William was her favorite.

He had never shown by word or deed that he disapproved of her mode of living, and was always kind and encouraging. The others scorned her and called her a scarlet woman because when a girl of fifteen, she ran away with a man, whom she met during cotton picking time in Byron and had lived with him until he became tired of her and walked out. In the years that followed she had lived with any man who happened to suit her fancy, drinking and fighting her way down to the lowest ebb of morality.

William, on coming to Macon to attend high school, had looked her up, and made his home in her lop-sided hut in one of Macon's dingy alleys to which his mother while not approving, had explained to the rest of the family.

"William's stayin' wid Sissy might help to make de pore loose gal better."

But to Sissy's mind, it was proof that he did not think her so very bad, and she loved him for the thought.

William had dressed to go out Sunday afternoon when Sissy and her latest man, whom she had salvaged from a nearby poolroom, entered. She hastened to set the dinner of stewed chicken and rice on the table, and insisted on his eating dinner with them, but William ate so little she became alarmed and asked:

"Whut's de matter wid you, Willyum? You don't feel well?"

"No, Sissy, I don't. I've got a headache," William answered listlessly.

"Yuh see, Sissy, dat's whut Ah'se allers sayin'," Sissy's man remarked, boastfully slapping his chest. "Eff'en uh body'ud take on uh little liquor now an' den, dey 'ud never know dey had uh head. Look uh me. Ah feels fine, Ah does!"

"Aw shut up, you ole likker head. Willyum ain't yo' kind," Sissy snapped back scornfully.

"But you sho is, gal, an' Ah done brought long uh bottle for us to nibble on." Sissy's man grinned, setting the pint of corn at her elbow. Sissy reached for it eagerly and William, knowing the regular weekend fight would begin as soon as its contents were gulped down, put on his hat and walked out.

Hours later when he returned, the house was dark and silent, and reeking with bad corn liquor. Sissy and her man were asleep, but the over-turned table and broken chairs told a mute story of the battle that had previously raged.

Monday when William awoke, it was raining—
a steady down-pour. The dampness that seethed
through the partly paneless window had awakened
him. He searched around for a few old rags to
shut it out, and crept back into bed.

It was one o'clock when Sissy returned from
gathering up her numerous bundles of washings.
William had fallen into a heavy sleep. Hurriedly
she made a fire in the kitchen stove, and warmed
up the remainder of the Sunday dinner, adding a
batch of butter milk biscuits and setting the table
for two.

"Git up, boy, an' less eat. Lawd Ah ain't never
seed a body dat sleeped de whole day through
'thout' dey was sick," she chided.

William rose, stretching sleepily and soon joined
her in the kitchen.

"You bettuh drink some 'uh dis Sassfrass tea.
It'll bring yuh out," Sissy suggested.

William reached for the tin cup Sissy always
kept on the back of the stove and poured a cup of
the hot tea.

"Willyum, how come you didn't go home Sat-
tiday night?" she asked, setting the plate of hot
biscuits on the table.

"I didn't feel well and I know it would've worried Ma," William replied, busily helping his plate.

"Dat's you, Willyum, never wantin' to worry nobody wid yo' troubles," Sissy agreed, looking at him
fondly and adding: "Ah sho wish som'times dat Ah
had uh thought uh somebody 'sides myself, 'fo Ah
ups an' runs off lak Ah did, but no, Ah jes' hated
tyin' myself down wid lots uh promises to one man
an' kaise Ah was sot on doin' my own choosin' an'

my own quittin', Ah ups an' does it, 'thout' carin'
who it hurt."

"You ain't so bad, Sissy. We all makes mistakes.
There ain't none of us perfect," William consoled.

"Anyhow, jes' you b'lievin' in me makes me
happy; Willyum kaise Ah sho gotta lots uh faith in
you an' some day you gointer make us all proud uh
you."

"I sure hope so, Sissy," William replied, putting
on his coat and hat.

As he walked down the narrow alley, Sissy's
praise kept ringing in his ears. His mother, Sissy,
everybody except Jim perhaps, expected great things
of him, and he was getting deeper and deeper into
trouble—gambling, mixing with a prostitute, even
stealing, for in his heart, he could find no other
word for losing money his mother had given
him to purchase things with and having them
charged when he had no idea where the money
was coming from to pay for them later when the
bills came due.

He walked rapidly down the street trying to still
his accusing conscience but at the pressing shop
trouble awaited him, like a menacing evil. One of
his creditors, John Stevens, a white hardware merchant greeted him with a torrent of abuse, demand-
ing his money immediately with threats of appeal-
ing to his mother if it was not paid before night.

"Give me a few more days, Mr. Stevens, and I'll
pay you the money," he pleaded.

"You been owing me since way last Spring, William, and if I don't get my money by six o'clock, I'll
go to your mother. I know Aunt Sara. She don't
believe in owing nobody. I need my money. Every

week you been telling me the same lie—you'd pay
in a few days and I'm fed up with you," Stevens retorted angrily, shaking his finger under William's
nose.

"Whew!" Slippery grunted, looking after the
merchant when he walked away.   "Dat white man
sho is mad."

"Yeah, and I sure am in a tight place.   Where'm
I gonna get thirty-five dollars?" William groaned.

"Man, is you askin' me?   Yo' goose sho is cooked
kaise dat other white man whut you owes ten dollars done been heah an' said de self-same mournful words dis mornin'," Slippery informed.

"Instead of paying off those debts Saturday morning when I had the money, I had to hold it and lose
it back Saturday night.   I had just as well pack up
and start traveling if Jim ever finds this out."

"Maybe you could borrow de money from Daddy
Jenks," Slippery suggested.

"Not a chance, Slippery.   I owes him now, and
now that he's lost his club room to Sugar Kid, he'll
be tighter than Nick's hat band."

"You think Sugar Kid 'ud loan it to you?" Slippery asked hopefully.

"No, he don't like me.   Maybe I could borrow it
from Ethel," William mused, his face lighting with
hope.

"Don't make me laugh, William.   Dat broad got
pulled in dis morning for fightin'.   'Course Daddy
Jenks got her out but whut li'l' money she did have,
she done turned it over to him for payin' her fine."

"Well, that's that and to tell the truth I don't
wanna get under no obligation to her nohow."

"Dat's one time you is so right.   Ontell you is

perfect, dat gal's pizin. Whutever yuh do, stear
clear uh dat drunken hussy. She'll git you in uh
mess uh trouble," Slippery advised.

"Ah guess Ah'll take a chance and ask Sugar Kid.
He can't say nothing worse than no," William ventured, ignoring his warning.

"Ah b'lieve he'll let yuh have it jes' for biggity.
He's got gobs uh money an' loves notuhriety. He'll
jes' love to brag 'bout havin' to help you out. Ah'll
go over dere an' git 'im." Suiting his words to
action, Slippery was gone, returning in a few moments followed by the swaggering Sugar Kid, who
guessed that the cause of William's sudden desire
to see him was to ask a favor. He was none too
popular with the gang but William was, and it would
be a good thing to have him under obligation to him
so that he could use him to win the confidence of the
boys to continue gambling in the club room he had
won from Daddy Jenks. Yes, he would do whatever William wanted of him, provided it was not
too large a sum, he decided, but he would be sure
to get evidence of the favor in black and white.
Then if William attempted to show off, he could
put him in his place.

"Yuh craves to see me, Carter?" he asked, stepping into the shop, rolling the big black cigar he
was smoking from side to side between his beefy
lips.

"Yes, Sugar Kid," William answered, backed up
by a wink from Slippery, who walked through to
the back of the shop.

"Sit down," William offered, and continued pleasantly. "I want to ask you to lend me some money
for a few days."

"How much money?"

" 'Bout thirty-five dollars."

"Whut's yuh got dat's worth dat much 'cause Ah gotta have some kin'er security for my money, yuh know," Sugar Kid said, shrewdly pulling out a roll of bjlls.

"I'll give you my word that I'll pay you in thirty days," William smiled.

"No suh'ree! Ah ain't dat dumb, Carter. Ah gotta have black an' white dat don't fool nobody, for my hard cash an' you gotta write it out dat effen you don't pay me in thirty days, ah kin take over dis shop," Sugar Kid replied, his eyes running estimatingly over the small stock of pressing equipment in the place.

"All right, Sugar Kid. I'll give you a note promising to pay in thirty days or turn the shop over to you," William consented.

Sugar Kid made himself comfortable, puffing his cigar in hard quick puffs, as William hunted in the drawer of the table for pen and paper, and in a few moments passed the note over for Sugar Kid to read. He studied it carefully, spelling out the words slowly and passed it back to William.

"Now sign it, William, good an' clear in big letters," he directed.

William signed the note, as he laughingly retorted, "You're a good business man, Sugar. I'll grant you that."

"Tries to be, Carter," Sugar Kid admitted, counting out the bills and placing the note carefully in his wallet.

"Ah don't want yuh to think dat Ah don't trust you neithur jes' kaise Ah ask for dis note. Ah jes'

laks to be on de safe side but Ah'm glad jes' de
same to do you uh favor."

"And I sure thanks you," William acknowledged,
almost having to grit his teeth to hold back the
words he would have liked to say to the big brag-
gard.

"Dat's de way to feel, Carter. Ah wants all uh
you boys to feel dat when you plays wid me, everythin' is on de up an' up. Now dat Ah'm de boss over
dere at de club room, Ah'se yo' friend an' Ah wants
you to help me make de boys know dat kaise Ah
b'lieve you for one done been thinkin' diffunt,"
Sugar Kid hinted.

"Forget it, Sugar Kid! That girl's remarks upset me Friday night. You're all right with me."

"Dat's how Ah loves to heah you talk kaise Ah
wouldn't ever thought uh lendin' nobody but you
dat much dough. Ah laks yuh an' dis is gwine tuh
be strickly private 'twix us."

"Mighty nice of you, Sugar Kid," William
acknowledged.

Slippery stepped into the room as soon as Sugar
Kid cleared the door, a broad grin wreathing his
homely red face, struggling to control his laughter
until Sugar Kid was out of hearing. He puffed an
imaginary cigar and imitated the lolling gambler.

"Gee, dat nigguh gives me uh laff, he'll keep it uh
secret. Ha, ha! He kin hardly wait to git cross
de street to spread de news but Ah'm gonna fix 'im.
Ah'm gonna git dat paper off'en him 'fo he kin say
scat an' den let him try an' collect his ole measly
thirty-five dollars," he avowed.

"You better say you reckon," William laughed,
hurrying out of the shop to pay Stevens the money

which would at least save him in that direction, and wondering what would be the next mishap to befall him.

Neither he nor Slippery dreamed how much trouble that small slip of paper would cause them both.

CHAPTER X

John Stevens was surprised when a short time later, William appeared at the store and paid over the thirty-five dollars and said in his usual blunt way.

"I hated to have to be so severe with you, William, about my money, but business is business, and right now it's as bad as it can be, and I need money to carry on. You people are easy going. You jes' live today with no thought of tomorrow, and have to be shaken up to get anything out 'er you."

"That's all right, Mr. Stevens. I'm glad to get it off my mind. I ain't making much money now in my shop, that's why I haven't paid it before," William replied.

"You know I can't see why you don't stay home and help your Ma and Jim with the farming, William?"

"I'm attending school here. That's why, Mr. Stevens."

"Didn't you go to school in Byron? Yo' Pa, John Carter, ain't never went to high school, and he was as good 'er farmer as there was anywhar. You young darkies make me sick, hanging round going to high school, and when youse come out all finished, all you'll do is loaf."

"I'm going to college when I finishes and I'm not going to loaf when I'm all through, neither," William answered shortly, hardly able to hide his anger.

But before he left the store, he and Stevens were laughing and talking pleasantly, and he had accepted

an offer from the merchant to ride to Byron with
him Saturday. The rest of the week he loafed
around his shop while Slippery did the little work
that had been brought in. The days were hot,
bringing thunder storms that did not help the suf-
ferers in any way except to make the streets sloppier
and the air more stifling, and bring in their wake
swarms of mosquitoes that made the long close
nights a torture.

The streets were filled with strangers, their dirty,
sweaty overalls sticking to their bodies, as they
loitered around Broad street, filling up on white
mule, playing pool and Georgia skin or dancing in
Daddy Jenks' back room to rancorous tinpanny
music.

Sure-Foot-Jack, a six foot policeman, who had
been so nick-named because of the fact his foot
never failed to connect with the part of the anatomy
at which it was aimed, was kept on the alert hunt-
ing out vagrants.

William felt sick of the whole thing. Even Slippery's coughing and spitting around the shop, wher-
ever it suited him, got on his nerves, and Sugar Kid
whose greatest fear was the Law, had taken to sitting around the shop almost all day, much to his
displeasure. So he spent most of his time in Ethel's
room laying half clad on the rusty iron bed, pushed
close to the window, while Ethel, happy to have him
around, brought his meals up to him from one of the
many dingy little restaurants.

Saturday came at last and William rode home in
Stevens' car late in the afternoon. His mother and
Ruth were seated on the front porch when he
stepped out of the car.

"Lawd heah's my boy," Sara Lou exclaimed happily, running to the gate as fast as her rheumatic legs could carry her.

"Yea, the prodigal is here," William remarked.

"You ain't no prodigal, son. Kaise yuh ain't done nothin' wrong," his mother laughed. "You jes' comin' home to yo' ole Ma whut loves yuh.

"Howde Mr. Stevens. Ah clean forgot my manners, bein' so glad to see dis heah boy."

"Jes' fine, Aunt Sara. Thought while I was coming out, I'd jes' as well give William a lift."

"An' Ah'se sho thankin' you for it, Mr. Stevens. 'Member me to de misses, when you gits home. Lawd don't look lak Ah helped to nurse her, time done pass so fast."

"No, it don't, Aunt Sara, not with all the six young uns she's got hanging round her skirt tail now. How's your cotton comin' on?" John Stevens asked, looking towards the field in the distance.

"Jes' fine. Jim says dis gointer be de best crop we's had!"

"Wal, I'll be moving on Aunt Sara. You ain't heard nothing from Gordon, is you?" he asked, as he turned the car in the direction of his place two miles further.

"No suh, not uh word since way lass month. Guess he'll be gone a spell." Sara Lou called, to which William added his thanks for the ride.

"Mighty fine uh Mr. Stevens bringin' yuh home, Willyum," Sara Lou said, looking after the fast disappearing car.

"Sure was, Ma," William replied, seating himself on the edge of the porch at Ruth's feet.

"Come on in an' git yo' supper, son, we done

eat but Ah put yuh uns whar it ud keep hot," Sara Lou said, playfully pulling William to his feet.

"Ah'se gotta 'sprize for yuh," she said later as she set a generous portion of ginger bread before him.

"I've got a mind to eat it first," William threatened.

"Dar yuh go jes' lak when yuh was uh little boy, wantin' to eat yo' dessert fust. Mind out or Ah'll take it way from yuh," his mother teased reaching for the plate.

"Ah'll be good Ma, 'clare to goodness I will. See, cross my heart and Ah'll give you a big kiss to boot," William teased, as he caught the hand that held the plate and drawing her to him, smacked a kiss on her cheek.

"Lawd boy, you'se de beatinest for makin' a body do whut you wants done," his mother laughed.

As he ate, his gaze rested on Jim and Ruth, whom he could see through the window, their heads close together, tying a vine that had broken and lay across the path. He could not help a pang of hot jealous anger that gripped his heart. He had been a fool to think that Ruth did not care more for Jim than she did for him. There was a look in her eyes, as she looked up into his face that told plainly that she did.

He felt ashamed of the murderous thoughts the knowledge brought him and wondered could he give up the hope of winning her. One thing he was sure of, he had never liked Jim and at that moment he hated him, and would like to have swept him from his path, no matter how.

He was slowly finishing his meal, absorbed by his

jealous thoughts when his mother sat at the table opposite him.

"You think yuh gointer finish school dis year, William?" she was asking.

With a start he brought his thoughts back to the present, answering, "I'm sure of it, Ma. It won't be hard for me to make two terms when I get started."

"Dat's fine, son, an' Ah'm goin'ter lay by a little money from de cotton dis year for when yuh starts in de preachin' school. Ah jes' knows you goin'ter be de finest preacher dere ever was, Willyum. Ah'se wearin' out my knees prayin' for dat one thing an' Ah gointer keep rite on prayin', an' Ah knows dat God gonna answer my prayers."

"Thank you Ma. I'm going to do my best."

"Dat's all we kin do, our best all de time an' not git too proud an' puffed up kaise God don't want us to be too proud."

"I know Ma but sometimes I don't feel like I really know what I wants and I tries so hard to make myself satisfied with what blessing I have but, oh, I don't know, Ma, it just seems like a lots of different devils fighting inside of me, making me want to do wrong and makin' me not able to do what I really wants to do. Ah! Don't mind me, Ma. I'm kind'er talking crazy now, ain't I?"

Sara Lou, tears filling her eyes, reached over and patted her favorite on the shoulder.

"My pore boy," she murmured. "Ah knows jes' whut yuh means. Dere's lots uh things William dat Ah'se allers prayin' you'll escape. Maybe Ah should tell 'yuh 'bout' 'em, but Ah ain't got de courage."

Tears of remembrance filled Sara Lou's eyes as

her mind traveled back over a past that was filled
with things she would have loved to forget. William caught and squeezed her hand, and rising quickly, walked around the table and placed his arm
around her shoulder.

"Don't Ma," he whispered huskily.

"Don't mind me, Willyum. Ah'm gittin' ole an'
Ah guess sometimes Ah does git crazy ideas. Ah'll
jes' set dese things 'way an we'll go an' sit on de
porch an' sing some hymns. Dat'll cheer us up.
Dere ain't nothin' lak singin' God's praises to cheer
a body up," she whispered, closer to William than
she had ever been, even in the days she had cuddled
his brown curly head on her breast and tried to figure
out what the future would hold for her illegitimate
child, who would always walk in the middle of the
road, not being able to get a firm footing on either
side.

"Yes I guess when you sings you ain't got no time
to think about the things that worries you," William said thoughtfully, but there was no enthusiasm
in his voice and his mother looked at him inquiringly.

"Whut's troublin' yuh, Willyum?" she asked,
placing her hand on his shoulder tenderly.

" 'Tain't nothin' much, Ma. Nothing that you
can help," looking beyond her searching eyes.

"But maybe Ah kin help. Tell me son."

"Well for one thing, Ah needs some money. The
shop ain't been doing so well lately and I owe a
debt I've got to pay right'er way. If you could let
me have the money, I'll pay it back as soon as I
start making money."

" 'Course Ah'll let you have de money. Ah ain't
been botherin' wid lookin' atter things 'round heah

uh late. Ah'se jes' left it all to Jim an' Ah don't
know dat he's got any money left atter de Spring
seed buyin' but Ah knows we'll have some jes' soon
as we sells dis cotton crop."

"But I needs it the first of next month, Ma."

"Den Ah'll find out whut Jim's got. Ah could
allers go to Mr. Gordon when he was heah."

"There ain't much chance of me getting it then
if you expects to get it from Jim," William replied
hopelessly.

"Ah don't know why you two boys is allers 'gainst
one 'nother. It's jes' plum pass understandin', Willyum. Sometime Ah wonder ef'fen yuh loves one
'nother uh tall lak brudders aught to."

"It ain't my fault, Ma. Jim is just so set against
me stayin' in Macon and tryin' to get an education.
Jes' because he don't care for school, he can't see
why anyone else should, and thinks I'm throwing
away lots of money when the fact is I don't have
none to throw away."

"Don't blame him too much, son. He jes' lak his
Pa was, hard-workin' an' no frills but he got uh
good heart an' you is jes' lak Ah was 'fore you was
born, cravin' atter learnin' and wantin' to be somebody. Yuh two is far uh part as de east an' west
but Ah sho wish you'ud try an' git long together,"
Sara Lou sighed.

"I do try, Ma, but Jim is stubborn and don't seem
to even like me," William complained.

Sara Lou shook her head slowly and led the way
to the front porch, where Jim and Ruth were seated
on the steps. Jim turned and looked at his mother
and William as they came out of the house. He
could see from his mother's troubled expression that

something was wrong and wondered what William
could have been saying that disturbed her. He had
not seen William since he came home an hour earlier
and although he was glad to have him home, he
never made a fuss over his visits and now calmly
helloed in his slow, undemonstrative way.

Ruth sat in a low rocker at Sara Lou's side, and
William seated himself on the step she had just va-
cated beside Jim.

The early twilight brought a breath of coolness
after a day that had been hot and sultry. The heavy
odor of honeysuckles that clung to the porch was
sweet with fragrance. Sara Lou, rocking back and
forth, started singing one of her favorite spirituals.
Ruth's soft soprano mingled with the deeper melody
of the two boys as song after song floated upon the
air.

William's thoughts drifted in comparison to the
noisy music of Daddy Jenks' dance hall with its sordid crowd shouting discordant blues. The quiet
peace of his home engulfed him with a mood of
spiritual longing. He hated Macon fiercely for all
of the corruption it had brought into his life during
that brief spell of emotion. He wondered how he
had been able to stand it so long. New resolutions
formed in his heart.

His mother's plaintive singing smote his heart.
"Go find my sheep," her voice crooned soft and
effectively, bringing hot tears to his eyes. He felt
relieved when she rose and announced it was time
to go in and have their usual evening prayer.

Lighting the kerosene lamp that stood on the
little marble topped table in the parlor, Sara Lou

opened the bible to the twenty-third psalm, and
passed it to William to read.

"William, you lead us in prayer dis evening. You
ain't home much an' Ah laks to hear yo' voice in
prayer. It kin'er gives me mo' stren'th to carry
on," she said when he lay the book on the table at
the end of the reading.

William knelt obediently. He knew what his religion meant to his mother and although he did not
feel like praying, after he started, he poured out
his soul to God, tears of repentance flowing down
his face. Sara Lou rose from her knees feeling
better than she had during the two weeks he had
not come home.

"Come on, Ruth chile, less us go on upstairs, an'
leave dese boys to dey seffs. Maybe dey want'uh
talk wid one 'nother widout us womens hangin'
'round," Sara Lou remarked, playfully pushing
Ruth up the narrow stairway before her.

William and Jim talked for a while about the cotton and the Gordon peaches that Jim was busy picking with Luke Brown and Slack Henderson assisting
him.

"What are they bringing, Jim?" William asked
interested.

"Twenty-five cents uh bushel an' it looks lak Ah'm
goin' to have 'bout five hundred bushels," Jim replied proudly.

"We ain't gonna have no peaches this year to
amount to anything I notice," William remarked.

"No Ah jes' set dem trees out lass year an' Ah
didn't 'speck much ud dem dis soon but next year
dey gonna be loaded."

"How 'bout the watermelons and canteloupes?"

William asked, turning the leaves of a book that lay on the table.

"Not so bad but dere ain't gointer be no money but de cotton money dis year an' when we gits uh few things dat we needs to fix up de place, dat'll be all gone. Ah'm doin' all Ah kin dis year so as next year we'll uh have some spare money. Ma's so set on you goin' to Atlanta to dat preachin' school," Jim said, trying hard to keep out of his voice the trace of impatience he felt towards his brother's ambition.

William did not answer. He knew that school was a sore spot with Jim, and he did not want to start an argument, not just now when he needed a favor anyway.

"I'm sleepy. Guess I'll go to bed so that I can get a little rest. Got to be in church all day tomorrow," he said instead.

"You laks bein' in church all day, William but Ah jes' hates to sit dere an' heah dem ole sisters uh moanin' an' de preacher gittin' all het up an' spittin' 'round. Ah don't mind de singin' and prayin' but dey keeps at it too long to suit me," Jim complained.

"Why Jim, anybody to hear you wouldn't think you was brought up in a Christian home an' by a mother like Ma."

"You mean dey'd be sprized to see dat Ah kin tell de truth. Most uh dese folks 'roun' heah would say de same thing ef'fen dey wasn't scared uh whut de others 'ud say ef'fen dey heard 'em, but Ah ain't. Ah'ud heap ruther be home hoein' cotton or somethin'. Ah b'lieves in God same as everybody else does, but Ah knows dat most uh dat loud preachin' is jes' uh bluff to cover up de fact dey don't know nothin' 'tall 'bout de bible an' it makes me sick."

"But don't you ever let Ma hear you talk like that. It would make her sick in bed," William cautioned, adding: "And I don't like to hear you talk like that myself cause some day I intends to be a preacher."

"An' when you gits to be uh preacher, effen yuh ever does, you gointer be plenty learnt an' yuh ain't gointer preach long for fear de folks'll forgit to put plenty in de collection plate," Jim laughed.

William felt a wave of anger rising within him but he hid it with a smile, as he said.

"Never mind, Jim, jes' wait till you get religion. Then we'll see how you feel about it. I bet you'll want 'er be sittin' in church all day."

"Ah'll be jes' lak Ah is now, plain an' strait. Religion or nuthin' ain't gointer change me, an' ef'fen dey ever makes me uh deacon, de fust thing Ah'se gointer do is vote dat ole brudder Thomas don't never be lowed to preach agin long as he lives," Jim declared.

"What has poor brother Thomas done now that you're ready to shut him up forever and break his poor old asthmatic heart?" William asked, laughing heartily at Jim's serious mien.

"He ain't done nothin' but git up lass Sunday an' preach for two solid hours."

"How did they ever stop him?"

"Some uh de folks jes' got to singin' an' he couldn't talk louder den dey could sing so he jes' shut up. Boy it sho was funny."

William could not help joining in the laugh Jim

was enjoying. He could imagine he saw Brother Thomas gasping for breath and preaching on and on.

"But William dat ain't nothin' to de one dey calls de Swamp Angel dat preached lass Sunday night," Jim went on and William listened again to a lengthy description of that preacher.

"Honest Jim, it's a sin to make fun of God's messengers like you do," he said at the end of his recital.

"Ah ain't makin' fun uh dem. Ah b'lieves in dem when dey preach good sound gospel but jes' jumpin' 'roun' makin' lots uh noise don't mean nothin'."

"Well anyhow, we'd better be getting to bed," William said, leading the way. Jim closed the front door and followed.

They undressed in silence. It had been rather pleasant to laugh and talk together without ending in an argument, Jim's thoughts ran. He loved his handsome wayward brother and did not even surmise that deep down in William's heart, he disliked him and always had. He had played his cards well and managed to keep cool for a point and long after Jim had fallen asleep, William lay planning how he would try and get a loan out of Jim by playing up to him pleasantly.

CHAPTER XI

Sunday morning's radiant sunshine brought an exultant feeling to Sara Lou, as she stood in her kitchen door throwing handfuls of corn to the chicken cackling noisily at her feet.

"Ah sho got plenty to be thankful for," she mused, as ripples of laughter reached her from the barn where Ruth and Jim were busy milking. As she hurriedly prepared breakfast, her eyes traveled to the old-fashioned clock on the mantel over the table.

William was still upstairs. She would have to wake him for breakfast. She climbed the stairs slowly, and stood for a moment looking down on him with an indulgent smile upon her face.

"Wake up, lazy bones. You sho is de limit heah sleepin' while Jim an' Ruth an' me does all de work," she said playfully poking him in the side. "Git up an' hurry on down to yo' breakfuss." Hurrying back downstairs, she called Ruth and Jim.

"Ah'll race yuh to de house, Ruth," Jim challenged as her voice reached them from the kitchen.

"Awrite but you gotta give me a little head kaise yo' legs longer den mine," Ruth consented.

Jim reached the house a few paces ahead of Ruth and William found them seated on the back steps, laughing about their race. A few moments later when he came downstairs, he could not suppress the tide of anger and jealousy that swept over him at

the sight of Jim and Ruth's happiness but hid well
his real feeling when he asked pleasantly.

"Who won the race?"

"Jim 'course. His legs is longer den mine an' he
jes' wouldn't gimme uh head start," Ruth laughed.

"I'll race you sometime Ruth an' give you a
whole yard on me," William promised.

"Don't yuh b'lieve dat, Ruth," Jim laughed, as
they seated themselves at the table. "Don't yuh
never b'lieve dat Willyum goin' uh leave anybody
beat him at nothin'; 'member when we'all was kids
how he use 'ter win all de marbles 'roun' heah an'
whut uh time Ma had tryin' to make him give 'em
back?"

"Does Ah 'member? Why William even had
our ole teacher Miss Jimerson scared to look in her
desk after de time he put uh frog in it," Ruth
laughed.

"Ha, Ha! She sho did let out one yell an' ain't
never stop runnin' ontell she was heah tellin' Ma,"
Jim added.

"I wanted to get out early that afternoon to go
fishin' an' I sure got out," William smiled.

"An' yuh got de terriblest tannin' uh yo' life,"
his mother ended, placing the plate of hot bread on
the table, chuckling at the remembrances of William's early tendencies of having his own way at
any cost.

"Now yuh'll jes' quit yo' carryin' on an' git yo'
minds on church. Dis is de Lawd's day," she reminded them, bowing her head for William to pray.

William prayed fervently and her eyes filled with
tears, as he thanked God for having given him such

a wonderful mother. Even Jim felt a catch in his throat as the words poured from his lips.

"Oh Lawd, make me worthy of your blessings and keep my feet in the path of righteousness," he ended.

His mother flashed him a grateful smile when she raised her head.

An hour later, the happy family was seated in church which was filled to its capacity, every inch of the long, backless benches taken. It was going to be an important day—a new preacher had to be called, and a candidate was on hand to preach a sermon for their approval.

The long morning service was over at last and the congregation gathered around the building in bunches to discuss his merit.

The day that had dawned so fair became suddenly over-shadowed with black scurrying clouds. Loud claps of thunder rent the air and a heavy deluge of rain sent them scurrying for shelter. Sara Lou's home, the nearest to the church, became a haven for many of them from the fury of the storm that lasted all afternoon.

Jim, worrying over what the storm might do to the cotton, went back and forth in the rain all afternoon and Sara Lou later that evening, made him take off his wet clothes and go to bed, pouring several cups of scalding herb tea down his unwilling throat.

Services were neglected that night. Most of the farmers hurried home as soon as the storm abated. William prevailed upon his mother to stay home and he and Ruth went to church alone. The business of calling the preacher to pastor their church took up most of the evening and to Ruth's relief, William walked almost the distance home before he said the things she had been praying he would not say.

"Some day when my dreams come true, Ruth," he began, "I wants you to be my wife. Will you promise?"

It was all she could do to keep from telling him that she and Jim were engaged but they had planned to keep it a secret, and she would not tell even William although it would perhaps keep him from forcing his attentions on her. Instead she answered simply.

"Ah can't say whut Ah'll do dat far off, William."

"It don't have to be far off. We can marry now an' while I'm away in Atlanta, you can jes' go on livin' with Ma," William persisted.

"But Ah don't love you dat uh way, William. Ah jes' feels toward you lak uh sister."

"Do you feel the same towards Jim?" William asked, determined to have his answer or know whether Jim was the cause of her evasiveness.

"Let's don't talk uh 'bout it," Ruth evaded, as some of the church members caught up with them.

Martha Green and Sally Ann Peck dropped back beside them to talk about the new preacher.

"Ah b'lieves we all gointer like de new Preacher," Sally was saying. "He don't preach all night lak some uh dem does an' whut he says is de gospel truth."

"Yeah, dat jes' suits you, Sally," Martha broke in. "You don't lak to sit church 'long nohow. As for my part, Ah don't know as Ah'm gonna lak him uh tall. He puts on too much airs."

And the battle was on as usual. Ruth thought of

what her father had had to contend with, how these same people had fought him when he first came to their church and wondered why it should always be so with every new preacher.

William ended the discussion by letting them know he was going to back the new preacher in every way, and Martha, not wanting to oppose any one Brudder William was for, fell to finding many good points in the sermon and decided after all, the new Reverend Hooper was all right.

Sally Ann laughed heartily at her sudden change of heart and they were again off on one of their usual arguments.

"Ruth, think over what I asked you," William said when they were again alone after bidding the two women good-bye.

She did not answer, but quickening her steps, passed into the house and ran lightly up to her room.

* * *

Monday morning Jim realized his fears had been well-founded although the storm had done no serious harm to the cotton except to beat some of it down a bit, which could be fixed by filling in the rows with the dirt that had been washed away. But other damage had been done. The cotton house-roof had been partly blown away and the posts that held the long rails that made the fence around the field were in many places down and needed immediate repairing.

William rose early and helped Jim and Ruth with their work, deciding to stay a few days and help with the repairs, which surprised and pleased Jim.

"Ah'll be mighty glad to have yuh helpin' me, William," he said warmly.

And Sara Lou, always alert to the best in her beloved son, remarked happily.

"Dat'll be jes' fine, Willyum. Ah sho will be happy to have both my boys 'roun' workin' together an' me an' Ruth cookin' hot dinners for yo' hungry mouths. Lawd, it'll mind me uh times when yore pa was livin' an' you an' Jim was helpin' him wid de farmin'."

"An' Ah'll help too. Dere's lots Ah kin do," Ruth added.

"Lawd chile, you can't do nothin' to suit dem two men 'side cook an' wait on 'em," Sara Lou laughed.

"We'll see 'bout that, Ruth. You may be useful in keeping me an' Jim from fightin' before the week is over," William remarked.

"Now don't you two go an' git in no fight kaise ef'fen you does, Ah'll jes' switch yuh both," their mother warned.

They all laughed heartily at the mental picture of her switching them and started the day merrily, working first on the cotton house roof. Sara Lou hummed happily as she worked around the house, a contented smile wreathing her round face.

"Come heah, Ruth an' take dis bucket uh grub an' some milk over to Julie for de new baby she got," she called when the dishes had been washed and dried.

"Ah'se ready An' Sara," Ruth answered, taking the pails.

"You hurry back, Ruth. Ah clean forgot Julie. Her breast done dried up an' dere ain't a blessed thing for dat pore little mite to nurse on. Dat husban' uh hearn is too lazy for anything. Jes' sittin' 'roun' waitin' for cotton pickin' stead 'er gittin' out pickin' up uh nickle or two. Pore Julie is smart uh nouff when she ain't got uh new baby to keep 'er in bed."

"An' dat ain't often she ain't," Ruth said, as she hurried away.

William and Jim worked steadily all morning and returned to their job after the noon day dinner.

That night they sat out on the porch after supper to get a breath of fresh air and Sara Lou laughed and talked and led in hymns until time to retire.

Several times during the next day William tried to get up courage to ask Jim to let him have some money. He felt sure there was none on hand to be had but Jim stood well with everybody around Byron, and could borrow money any time he needed it. Besides he knew he had received some money for the peaches he had already delivered to Mr. Carmicheil, who ran the general store and shipped crates of fruit to northern markets. The money was Owen Gordon's but Jim could lend him some of it if he cared to, and as Gordon would not be home until after the cotton was picked and sold, it certainly could be replaced.

Every now and then William glanced at Jim working a short distance away. They were working in the Gordon orchard stripping the peach trees of their last remaining luscious fruit.

Late that afternoon, William unaccustomed to working so steadily, complained of being tired.

"Go on up to de house an' rest uh spell," Jim advised. "An' close de windows an' lock up while you'se dere," he called, as William walked away.

After closing the windows that had been opened
to air the house out and locking the door, William
stretched himself out on the back porch to rest and
in a few moments was drifting drowsily into a light
sleep. Ruth's voice calling Jim from the back gate
awakened him.

"Come on in Ruth. Jim's in the orchard," he
called to her, sitting up.

"It's really you Ah wants. Ah got uh letter for
you, William," she smiled, handing him the letter.

William glanced quickly at the envelope. It was
from Macon and looked like Slippery's writing.
What on earth could have made him write, he wondered. Certainly nothing that would make him
happy, he decided before tearing the seal.

Ruth was looking toward the peach orchard,
where the outlines of Jim's figure could be seen
moving to and fro among the shadows of the trees.

"Ah'm gointer run over dere an' scare Jim," she
laughed starting towards the orchard.

William read the letter carefully and tore it into
small bits, kicking them under the sand with his
toes. The letter was worse than he had expected.
Creditors hounding the shop and Sugar Kid hanging around bragging to the boys that in a few weeks
he would be running the shop. His heart filled with
anger towards Jim. How easy it would be for him
to help him out. He realized he had made quite a
few mistakes but if Jim would only let him have
enough money to square himself he would not be a
fool again, he promised himself.

He could see Jim and Ruth talking under the
trees. Jim was handing her a large yellow peach
from one of the crates. She was smiling her thanks

prettily. Fierce hatred filled his heart. He resented everything about the homely, ignorant, coolheaded Jim, who although his inferior in looks and learning, possessed the power to make him feel small with his calm, clear vision and busy useful life. Ruth waved a cheery goodbye as she passed through the yard, and he waved back to her listlessly, and sat for a few moments trying to calm the emotions that filled his heart. When he walked over to where Jim was busy sorting peaches, he was coolly smiling.

"Did yuh rest any?" Jim asked.

"Yes, a little but I just received a letter that made me feel more tired than I was before."

"Bad news?"

"Yes, it sure was bad news and I want to ask you to do me a favor."

"Whut is de favor, William?"

"I wants you to loan me some money."

"How much an' whut for, William?" Jim asked, looking for the first time at William.

"Well as much as I dislike asking a favor, Jim, I'm behind in the rent of my shop an' last month I borrowed some money to pay it when it was due and now I've gotta pay the money I borrowed back an' the rent again too. I ain't been makin' nothin' and I gave a fellow a note on the place, and I know it'ud worry Ma if I lose the shop."

"How much money does yuh need?"

"Fifty dollars would square everything and I'd pay you back as soon as I make some money."

"Ah haven't got fifty dollars, Willyum an' besides Ah knows dat you'se lyin'. You borrowed money to pay Mr. Stevens wid at'ter me givin' yuh de money to pay for de things lass Spring," Jim spoke calmly.

William's face turned a dull red, as his temper flared but he bit his lips and tried to control himself.

Jim went on in his same maddening, calm way.

"Mr. Stevens tole Mr. Carmicheil all 'bout you owing him so long an' he havin' to jump on yuh for his money, an' when Ah went to de store yistiddy, Mr. Carmicheil tole me he knows whut yuh done. Yuh gambled de money 'way. Cotton Eye tole me dat when he was heah lass week to see Aunt Sofia."

"It's all a pack of lies, dirty lies!" William almost shouted. "An' I don't b'lieve nobody tole you nothing."

"Have it yo' own way but you got yo'self in dis mess, an' you'll have to git yo'self out. Ah ain't got no money nohow," Jim replied, stooping to raise the crate of peaches to his shoulder.

"You'll have that much an' more when you deliver all these peaches."

Jim placed the crate upon the ground again as he said slowly. "Dat'll be Mr. Gordon's money. You ain't askin' me to steal, is yuh, William?"

"It won't be stealin' and besides you can replace it before Mr. Gordon gets back."

"Well, Ah ain't gointer do it. Ah wouldn't touch uh penny uh dis money lessen Ma was low sick, Willyum."

"Then I'll ask Ma to borrow it from somebody else for me," William answered, turning away but Jim's next words brought him around again angrily.

"Ef'fen you ask Ma for one penny, Ah'll tell 'er

all 'bout yuh gamblin' in Macon an' everything Ah
knows 'bout yo' doin','' Jim threatened.

"And if you do, I'll smash your ugly black face
in, you stingy good-for-nothing fool," William
hissed, and, completely losing control of himself in
face of what he realized was failure to get his aim,
he struck Jim full on the mouth, taking him by surprise, but not for long.

Jim's fist shot out catching him on the point of
the chin, and William reeled, almost falling to the
ground. The fight was on. Back and forth blows
rained. They fought like mad beasts until a hard
blow from Jim, the stronger of the two, sent William to the ground. Jim stood over him for a
moment undecided whether to pull him to his feet
and knock him down again or to walk away and
leave him where he had fallen, but as William lay
still, realization dawned upon him that he was not
faking but unconscious. Quicky drawing water
from the well nearby, he bathed his face and lifting
him to his shoulder, carried him to the Gordon
porch, where he worked over him until he regained
consciousness and was able to stand. Jim felt sick
and ashamed of what had happened and tried to
tell William how sorry he was but William gave him
no answer, as he carefully brushed the sand from his
clothes, and walked out of the gate, his head high,
hate and anger raging in his heart. All the pent-
up feelings he had had against Jim for years filled
his heart. He would make hi.n pay for beating
him that afternoon. There were several ways. He
knew them all. He had taken over the farm which
was as much his and his mother's and ran it, spend-

ing the money as he saw fit.   He would put an end
to that, he vowed.

Jim sat where William had left him.   His head
bowed in his hands.   It was the first real fight they
had had since they had grown to manhood and although William had struck him first, he blamed himself for losing his temper to the extent he had.   It
had been so pleasant the last two days working and
talking together.

It was a relief to them both when Ruth told them
on reaching home that their mother had gone over
to Sally Brown's cabin, as Sally was sick and alone.

"She sayd for yuh to bring me over dere soon as
supper's over, Jim," she said.

And as soon as the dishes were washed and put
away, Jim and Ruth went over to Sally's, leaving
William sulking at home.

Sara Lou looked up as they entered, a wave of
disappointment passing over her face.

"Whar's Willyum?" she asked anxiously.

"You didn't say for him to come so he stayed to
home," Ruth answered, sensing something had happened between the brothers.

"No.   Ah ain't sayd but Ah thou't him hearin'
dis pore chile was so low sick, he'ud want to pray
wid her."

"He's jes' tired, Ma.   You know Willyum ain't
use'ter workin' hard all day lak we'uns," Jim ex-
cused.

The long, hot night passed slowly.   Jim sat with
his mother while Ruth dozed in a chair nearby.
Neighbors dropped in from time to time, and Sara
Lou cared for the sick woman and prayed for her
recovery but deep in her heart, she was worried.

Something had gone wrong at home. She felt it, but said nothing.

Martha Green and Sally Ann Peck came during the early dawn and relieved the others, and Sara Lou, Ruth and Jim hurried home, but William had gone, leaving a note for his mother that he would be home early Saturday afternoon.

CHAPTER XII

During the next few days William sulked around
the shop planning in his mind some way of hurting
Jim severely for his imagined wrongs. His two
years in Macon had changed his entire outlook on
life and brought out all of the worst there was in
his twisted make-up. At first he had enjoyed spending most of the Summer on his mother's farm, not
that he helped any with the work if he could get
around it, and contrived most of the time to get
around it, leaving it entirely to Jim, while he lay
under some tall leafy tree on the smooth green grass
and read or dozed in the welcome coolness of its
shade.

But each year he found excuses to stay more and
more in town, where the lights and laughter suited
him better, and the convention of the staid farmers
could not reach him. Even if the hot mid-summer
days with sudden drenching thunder storms did de-
press and madden him, as he sat around his little
windowless shop playing cards with the boys, there
was always Daddy Jenks' place, where there was
music, cold soda pop, cards and dice and an occa-
sional game of pool to liven things up.

During July and August, the city was filled with
riff-raff that drifted in to prey upon the farmers,
who drove in daily from nearby farms to sell their
products. With their small proceeds they would
make straight for some place of amusement, and

fill up on bad moonshine while their hard-earned money disappeared over the gambling tables.

Sugar Kid profited nightly by their losses and strutted around days, his bead-like eyes shining, as his hands jingled the silver that lined his pockets, very much pleased with himself, but frightened at the interest the law was taking in his and other gambling places. A general cleaning up was in progress and his place might be raided at any time but he made up his mind to get his while the getting was good.

Every time William entered the club room, he patted his pocket affectionately, and felt an exultant joy in the fact that in another week the thirty-five dollars William owed him would be due. He would either have to pay it or pass over his little shop. But William, apparently not aware of his presence, was coolly aloof and indifferent.

Sugar Kid's arrogant attitude nor Ethel's amorous advances interested him in the least. In fact, Ethel made him sick and he frankly told her so, and proceeded to ignore her entirely.

Ethel, more in love with him than ever, tried every known trick imaginable to win him back but in vain.

Sugar Kid watched the little drama with a keen feeling of satisfaction. He liked Ethel for himself and told her so and she laughed in his face, but he felt that sooner or later she would realize that William would have no more to do with her and turn to him.

"See yo' high yaller is givin' yuh de gate, gal," he taunted, as they danced around Daddy's back room.

"Whut's dat to you, ole fat head," Ethel snapped back.

"It ain't nuthin' to me but it jes' goes to prove whut Ah done tole yuh. He thinks he's too good for de sun to shine on. 'Roun' heah puttin' on airs, goin' to school, jes' kaise his mammy's got little cotton growin' an' is fool 'nough to let him lay 'roun' wid his lazy seff."

"Huh. De pot's callin' de kettle black," Ethel laughed. "You ain't done uh day's work in yo' life, Sugar Kid."

"But Ah ain't puttin' on no airs an' makin' out how great Ah am when all de time Ah'm jes' uh gambler."

"Dat's kaise you ain't got no education. As for gamblin', Ah don't see no harm in William playin' cards ef'fen he wants to. He don't smoke nor drink."

"But he hangs out wid you an' dat's bad 'nough," Sugar Kid sneered.

"It sho is kaise he ou'ter stop it an' give you uh chance," Ethel came back.

"Aw well, Ah ain't doin' no worryin'. He done borrowed money from me an' ef'fen he don't pay me back, Ah'm goin' uh take dat shop uh his or collect my money from dat dotin' ma uh his'n," Sugar Kid said, walking away.

Sugar Kid's remark about William owing him money worried Ethel. She knew that William would not want his mother to know about his having to borrow money or losing his shop. A little later she decided to go over to the shop and offer to help William pay off the debt. It would be a good excuse

to have a talk with him and if she did him a favor,
it would also win him back to her.

The front door of the shop was open and she
walked in and started through to the back room,
where she could hear William and Slippery talking.
She stopped for a moment at the door. She could
not catch their softly spoken conversation. William
was talking rapidly and Slippery was saying little
but agreeing to what William was saying. A chair
creaked across the floor as one of them stood up
and not wanting them to find her trying to eavesdrop, she slipped out of the front door and across
the street again.

"Say gal, why don't yuh git wise to yoseff an' stay
on dis side uh de street," Sugar Kid grinned, as she
reached the other side.

"Shut up an' mind yo' own black business," she
retorted with spirit.

"Come on in an' have a drink on me," Sugar Kid
invited, and seating themselves at a table with a
pint of corn before them, they were soon laughing
and talking, the best of friends.

Later when William went to his room out at
Sissy's. Slippery dropped into Daddy's to play a
game of pool. Ethel's pent-up anger for William,
inflamed by bad liquor, flared up at the sight of the
little sickly red man.

"Come on over heah, William's lakey, an' have a
drink wid decent folks," she called.

Slippery ignored her remark but sat down at the
table gulping down a big drink as a bracer. As the
liquor began to take effect Sugar Kid became very
talkative and bragged about having lent William
thirty-five dollars, pulling out the note William had

given him to prove it. Waving it in Ethel's and Slippery's faces, they were compelled to read and reread it to please him. Fumbling he pushed it back into his pocket and continued pouring drink after drink down his throat. The night wore on. Slippery left them and Sugar Kid staggered upstairs to his room.

The next day when he looked for the note it was gone. Vaguely he remembered taking it out of his pocket the night before to show it to Ethel and Slippery. Slippery had stolen it, no doubt to protect William, he decided, and would give himself away, and then he would be justified in beating him up for picking his pocket.

But that night fresh disaster came to the gambler. His place filled with players was raided. Few escaped but most of them were taken to jail and released the next morning with light fines.

He, himself, did not fare so well and was held without bail for running a gambling house.

"Dey liable to keep dat nigguh in jail all Summer," Slippery remarked, when William returned to Macon and they talked of the luck that had made them two of the few that had not been caught in the police net.

"That sure will be a break for me," William declared.

"An' Ah b'lieves yuh gointer git dat break kaise dat ole judge don't care much for 'im kaise he don't b'long in Macon and de way he done looked at dat darky was lak he'ud jes' soon keep 'im in jail forever."

"I know Daddy Jenks is glad. Now he'll have his clubroom back agin."

"You know, William since Ah comes to think
'bout it, Ah b'lieves Daddy done put de white folks
on dat nigguh anyhow kaise dey tells me dat Daddy
was upstairs in de club room an' as soon as he went
downstairs, de white folks rushed in," Slippery said
with conviction. He had meant to tell William that
he had stolen his note from Sugar Kid the night before but decided, as William had outlined a plan
by which they both could profit, he would not mention the note, as William might get cold feet and
abandon their plan so William, with no knowledge
of Sugar Kid's being helpless to harm him, rejoiced
that at least the day of reckoning was delayed.

Things were once more normal over at Daddy
Jenks', who again took over the club room and ran
it full sway.

Ethel, peeved over William's indifference, went
on a wild spree, keeping the dance hall lively with
her songs and squirming dances, but gradually the
old passion she had awakened in William flared into
life again and he was once more spending his nights
in her room.

Two weeks had passed since he and Jim's fight.
William had not been home. He dreaded facing
Jim, and stayed away. Saturday came again. William rose early and helped Slippery finish what work
there was on hand, determined he would go home,
Jim or no Jim and he would take Slippery with him,
as he had done several times during their acquaintance.

Saturday night he and Slippery rode to Byron
with a farmer, who was returning home.

His mother welcomed Slippery, and tried in every
way to make him feel at home but Jim, who had

never liked him, could not entirely hide his resentment and Ruth kept out of his way as politely as possible.

Sunday was by no means a pleasant day for anyone and William, who felt the hostility, appealed to his mother.

"Ma, I'd think you'd teach Jim to be at least civil to folks," he began.

"Lawd, son, whut Jim gone an' done now?" she asked in alarm.

"Well, I invited Slippery out here so he could attend church seeing he won't in Macon an' Jim acts like he's afraid he'll steal the doors off the house."

"Ah thought Jim was treatin' 'im real nice, seein' dat he don't lak him," his mother replied.

William said no more but when the time came for them to go to evening services, the strain of watching and praying all day that Jim in his outspoken way would say nothing that would start an argument, proved too great for her and instead of going to church, she went to bed with a severe headache.

All day Monday after William and Slippery had gone, she bustled around in a state of excitement and by evening she was worn out and again ill.

"It sho is uh shame how Willyum does things to upset Ma, bringing dat no count Slippery out heah," Jim complained.

"Ah don't b'lieve he means to upset her. He's jes' tryin' to be kind to Slippery seein' he's uh stranger an' sick," Ruth defended.

"Ah guess he got you fooled lak everybody else,

Ruth, but as for me, Ah don't b'lieve dere's no good in him," Jim replied.

"Why Jim, Ah'm 'sprized at you, speakin' lak dat 'bout yo' own brother," Ruth exclaimed, looking at Jim, who stood calmly regarding his feet.

"Ah can't help it, Ruth, and brother or no brother, yuh gointer find out Willyum is uh bad lot, someday."

"When we gointer start pickin' cotton?" Ruth asked, anxious to change the subject which she realized was embarrassing to Jim.

"Nex' week, Ah got lots dis year an' Ah gotta start early kaise Ah ain't able to hire nobody but Luke to help. Ma's so determined to let William have some money to put side for his schoolin' in Atlanta."

"Ah'm gointer help you Jim, an' Ah kin pick uh lot an' you don't need to pay me nothin'," Ruth said, putting her arms around Jim's neck and laying her cheek against his.

"Ah sho'll need yo' help, Ruth, but Ah hate to have you pickin' cotton in de hot sun."

"Shame on you, Jim. Ah'm useter pickin'. Ah done picked for pay since Ah was eight years ole. How is it gointer hurt me?"

"Awrite, we ain't gointer argue 'bout it honey."

"Is William comin' heah to pick any, Jim?"

"Lawd no, he jes' goin'ter sit an' wait ontell us gits it ginned an' sold an' den hold out his purtty yaller hands for his share."

Ruth laughed heartily. "Jim," she said, "Ah know whut's de matter wid you. Youse jes' jealous uh William kaise he so light-skinned and you ain't."

"No, Ah ain't but he's so biggity an' stuck up.
Ma's fair as he is an' look how sweet she is."

Ruth gave him a poke between the ribs, and ran
away to do some unfinished work in the house. Jim
turned to his garden that needed his care and worked
until dark with it. Work and routine meant everything to him.

Friday he received the balance of the money for
the peaches. He felt proud and happy knowing he
had done better than even Owen Gordon had expected. His mother was surprised when he gave
her the twenty dollars he had taken out for his labor
but Ruth refused his offer to buy her a dress. Later
that evening Sara Lou trudged down to the village
general store and bought it for her anyway.

"An' Sara, you'all shouldn't uh done dat. Ah'se
'nough expense as it is to y'all," Ruth pleaded.

"Chile, you does 'nough work 'roun' heah to pay
for uh little ole calico frock," Sara Lou assured her.

The week passed happily. Even with the many
duties that filled each day, Jim and Ruth found time
several afternoons when the sun disappeared beyond the western horizon to wander hand in hand
over the flat fragrant woodland, saying little, content and ready to burst into childish laughter at the
little nothings that amused them.

Most of these excursions ended at the old hickory
nut tree, where with a few strands of hair they had
become engaged. Sitting there, they would plan
their future and return home swinging hands and
singing songs.

Monday proved an ideal day to start picking
cotton. Bright with cloudless skies, long before

sunrise, Jim was in the field, his long sack slung
across his shoulders.

The cotton seemed ready to burst from its bowls.
Sara Lou busied herself with cooking and household
duties but late that afternoon she shouldered her
sack and laughingly teased.

"Lawdy, you youngsters is slow. Heah Ah done
filled my sack in no time."

"Dis my fourth, An' Sara an' Jim not wantin'
me to pick," Ruth smiled proudly.

"Well at dis rate we'all 'ull be through 'fo' de
rest uh de folks 'roun' heah gits started," Jim
bragged.

All around busy people were laughing and working. Bits of song floated upon the air. Wagons
of cotton passed down the red clay road on their
way to the gin. Happy children picked at their
parents' sides. At night men gathered at the general store to discuss how many sacks they had
picked during the day. Everybody was busy and
happy.

Sara Lou's home was the happiest of them all
for this year there would be more money than there
had been since John Carter's death. She breathed a
prayer of thankfulness for her many blessings, and
smiled as she remembered how even Marshall Bailey
had complimented her on having two such fine sons.

Saturday came round again and Sara Lou having
finished her Sunday cooking, stood on the front
porch waiting for a glimpse of her darling boy,
her face brightened with a smile. But she was
doomed to be disappointed. A farmer returning
from Macon handed her a letter sent by William
explaining he would not be home this week-end as

his cousin Sissy had been seriously injured and he would have to stay in Macon with her.

"Huh, dat's jes' lak Willyum, takin' on everybody's troubles," she remarked when later she showed the letter to Jim.

CHAPTER XIII

August passed swiftly. Soft fluffy cotton held the attention of the farmers, who worked from sun-up until darkness gathered, making their task impossible.

Sara Lou's little cotton house was fast being filled but William did not come home, not even for the usual week-end. Jim said nothing, as his mother querulously complained about his absence.

To his mind the excuse William gave in the letters his mother received from him, of having to stay with Sissy, were just lies. But for once William was telling the truth. He had gone to his room late one night and found Sissy lying on the floor bleeding profusely from several long gashes inflicted by one of her latest men friends, a strapling six-footer. William had hurriedly summoned a doctor and for weeks the wounded woman had hovered between life and death.

She had few friends in the dismal little alley she made her home. Most of the women hated her because she kept to herself. The few, who had wormed their way into her home, remembered her sharp tongue and ready fists, and stayed away henceforth. When William appealed to some of the women to come to his assistance in caring for her, they laughed in his face.

"Let some uh dem injun folks she done bragged 'bout she comed from look at'ter her," one fat, jet-black woman taunted, remembering how Sissy had bragged about her long straight hair and copper colored skin having come from Indian ancestry.

"Yeah, yuh bettuh ask ole chief squattin' in de corner to sit wid 'er," another chimed in and William turned away disgusted to start what proved a trying four weeks at Sissy's bedside, relieved at times by Ethel, who on hearing the news of his cousin's injury, rushed to his aid.

But even the nearness of death did not soften William's heart towards Jim. Instead he had plenty of time while sitting idle through the long nights to conjure up the smallest grievances of his childhood when their father, John Carter, had taken Jim's part against him. He brooded over imaginary and real wrongs until his heart filled with hate and seemed almost bursting with longing for revenge, but no one, who saw him daily, would have believed beneath his suave smiling personality, a tumult of rage and hate burned fiercely.

To Sissy he was perfection. "Lawd, William, Ah jes' kain't figure how come you is so diffunt from the rest uh yo' folks," she said, as she and William ate breakfast the first morning she was able to be up.

"Ma offered to come an' see you, Sissy, but I begged her not to, cause they pickin' cotton an' Jim needs her home," William said.

"Yeah, An' Sara is kind lak you is. Ah kin'er glad she didn't com' to see me in de fix Ah was in."

"Now that you're better, Sissy, I'm gonna ask Ethel to stay with you while I run out home Saturday."

"Sho William, you go see 'bout An' Sara, but

don't bother askin' Ethel.   Ah kin take care uh my-
seff now."

So William wrote his mother he would be home
Saturday and all day Friday he and Slippery worked
steadily finishing up the work that had been left in
the shop.   Late that evening Slippery donned the
one good suit he possessed, and slipping his well-
oiled, shiny pistol in his pocket, departed for a visit
to a nearby village, where as he put it, "De gamblin' was good."

Saturday afternoon William closed the shop, and
took a late afternoon train for Byron.

Sara Lou saw him, as he came swinging down the
road, smiling brightly.   Throwing his bag on the
porch, he caught her in his arms and kissed her
affectionately, and holding her at arms' length looked
at her admiringly.

"Go 'lon' boy, whut yuh doin' 'zamin' yo' ole Ma
to see if she done growd uglier?" she asked, chuckling happily.

"Uglier?   Why, you're the prettiest girl in the
world to me, Ma," he answered, hugging her close.

"Lawd, William, Ah sho don't see how any gal
in de world kin resist you, effen yuh makes love to
dem lak yuh does to me."

"I ain't tried it out on any gal yet, Ma.   Ah'm
practising on you first," William laughed.

"Well, you is purtty nigh purfect," she smiled, as
she hurried in to complete preparations for his
supper.

William walked out on the back porch just as
Ruth came up with an armful of kindling.

"Hey William, how'se you feelin' after yo' sick
nursin' job all dese weeks?" she greeted.

"Fine an' how's the old cotton picker gettin' on?"
he replied.

"Back's nigh 'bout broke but outsid-er dat, Ah'm
on de up and up," she laughed. But more seriously
—"Ain't you glad Sissy didn't go an' git hurt after
yo' school had started?"

"I sure am, cause I've got to make two terms in
one this year."

"Ah wish Ah could go to high school," Ruth
sighed, dropping the kindling into the wood box at
the kitchen door.

"Why, Ruth, I never thought you wanted to go
back to school. Maybe I could help you," William
replied, taking her hand and looking fondly into
her upturned face.

Ruth slowly withdrew her hand and hurried into
the kitchen. Jim was standing on the steps and
William realizing what had caused Ruth to hurry
away, burned with quick, hot anger.

Sunday Sara Lou was happy. William was in
Church sitting on the little rostrum, where she could
look at him, while the neighbors paid him the
homage she felt was his due. William beamed on
them all, and accepted their tribute as his rightful
due.

"Us don't never git de scripture read so as we'all
kin understand it ontill you'se heah, Brudder Willyum," Martha Green commented after the service,
as they all walked home together.

"Well, Brudder Simms does de best he knows
how an' dat's always 'ceptible in de sight uh God.
Everybody ain't edercated lak Brudder William,"
Sally Ann remarked.

And she and Martha entered one of their usual

arguments in the midst of which William and his
Mother left them at their gate.

The day passed uneventfully but pleasantly.
When time for the evening service came, Jim com-
plaining of being tired, stayed home.

"Dere's uh 'Vangelist preacher gonna preach tonight, Jim. Ah sho wanted you to heah 'im kaise
it's high time you try gittin' some religion," his
mother remarked, hoping to change his mind.

But changing Jim's mind was no small task and
to her pleading, he simply answered: "Ah jes'
don't feel good an' Ah don't want 'er sit up half de
night when Ah'se got so much work to do early in
de mornin'."

And she, William and Ruth departed without
him. In Ruth's mind there was a doubt as to
Jim's not wanting to attend the service. She was
sure he had overheard the conversation between
William and herself when she had expressed a desire to attend high school, and the knowledge that
she was not entirely satisfied had disturbed him.
She heartily wished she had not said anything about
school. After all she was content as things were.
It was just William's presence that brought it to
her mind. William's presence always disturbed their
quiet peace, she remembered.

Jim sat for a while on the front porch thinking
of Ruth, William and the future. He had never
dreamed that she was not contented to just become
a farmer's wife. The bit of conversation he had
overheard, disturbed him. She was young. Perhaps after they married, she would rebel against
the monotony of the only life she had ever known.
William would be preaching, going from place to

place. Wouldn't a life of that kind suit her better, he asked himself over and over. He would rather die than see her unhappy.

Slowly he rose and walked down the narrow path that led to the big road.

The skies were clear and starlit. A gentle breeze fanned his cheeks. A good long walk alone would do him good, he decided, as his feet struck the hard clay road, and from force of habit, propelled him towards the Gordon place, a mile away.

"Lawd, Ah jes' goes dere so much ontell my feets jes' natu'ly turn dat uh way when Ah ain't thinkin'," he laughed. It would be a good chance to make sure that the place was well locked up and secure, he thought, his mind on the tracks he had seen around the back of the house when he went over to do some work earlier in the week.

The moon shining brightly through the long branches of trees threw ghostly shadows across the road. Firebugs flew close to his face. Now and then he caught one in his hand, turning it loose later to watch it flicker through the air like the tail light of a small machine and disappear in the distance.

He was within a few feet of the house when a sudden cracking of dry leaves in the thick growth of young trees frightened him for a moment, but as he drew nearer, the cause of his agitation caused him to laugh heartily.

"Lawd, dat's jes' Marshall Bailey's old mare an' heah Ah was scared stiff. Come heah Josie," he coaxed softly, holding out his hand as if offering some tid-bit to the animal who shied away and bounded to the back of the place.

Thinking of the harm she had once done to the place, he tried to catch her but failed.

"Ef'fen she's still 'roun' heah when Ah goes home, Ah'll catch de critter an' take 'er home to de Marshall. Ah bet he's huntin' every whar for dat crazy onery fool dis minute," he thought, going through the back gate.

The house, built several yards back from the low picket fence, looked like some deserted castle, its large, colonial pillars gleaming white against the dark foliage of oleander bushes. Vine covered, its veranda extended the length of two sides of the house. The dining room at the back with its numerous long, green blinds added to the ghostly aspect of the place.

Jim walked around the kitchen. Suddenly he stopped and could have declared he saw a dim light moving about in the dining room, but tried to dismiss the idea as only imagination.

"Huh!" he grunted, "De next thing ah'll be b'lievin' in ghosts," trying to shake off the uneasy feeling that possessed him.

There it was again. He was sure this time. Someone was moving around in the room. He could see the light, first on one side, then on the other. For a moment, he stood stark still, watching the window, fascinated. His first feeling of fright soon passed, and gliding up to the porch cautiously, he picked up an old lantern, he had left there, lighted it, and moved noiselessly to the back door, slipping the key he always carried into the lock. He turned it slowly. A rasping sound came from within. Someone had gone out through the side window that opened on the veranda.

Rushing quickly into the now empty room, holding his lantern high, he dashed for the window, which the intruder had left open. There was no one there. The oleander bushes obstructed his view beyond when he tried to pierce the darkness of the grounds.

Giving up the effort as fruitless, he re-entered the room. Something white near the window caught his eye. Stooping he picked it up. Just a small piece of soiled paper, he decided, and started to throw it away. A jumble of figures were written across its creased surface. Nine stood out clearly, followed by the word right. Another number that looked like five. He spelt out the word—left.

There was something strangely familiar about the writing. His heart almost stopped beating. It was the combination of the safe in William's handwriting. He had seen it all his life, and had copied pages of words and figures he had written in an effort to help him learn.

Walking over to the safe he noticed for the first time that it was standing wide open. He ran his hand into its depths. The money he had so recently put there, was gone! He remembered William had wanted that money. He had copied that combination and gave it to someone to steal it for him. He could easily guess who—Slippery. Well, they would not get away with it. Brother or no brother, he would have them arrested. He decided—but even as he made the decision, thoughts of his mother filled his mind. William was her idol. She would never survive the blow. It would break her heart, and William was not worth it. Hastily before he had a chance to change his mind, he tore the paper into small bits. He would just have to replace the money and not let her know anything about it. Of course, William would have to answer to him for this night's work. He would not be as easy on him as he had been when they last had an encounter.

Suddenly he thought about the small bag of antique jewelry that Owen Gordon kept in a secret drawer in the safe. If that was gone, it would be a different story.

Reaching again into the safe, he felt for and pressed a small spring. Trembling he pulled out a small shammy bag that contained nearly one hundred pieces of old jewelry, heirlooms of several generations. Breathing a sigh of relief, he dropped it into his coat pocket, and stood so absorbed with his thoughts that he did not hear soft footsteps, as someone entered the room.

Marshall Bailey and his wife returning home from Macon where they had spent the day, saw their old mare grazing at Owen Gordon's back gate. The marshall got out, intent on trying to coax her home. He noticed the figure of a man emerge through the window, look around, and enter the house again. Cautiously he slipped to the porch and peeped through the blinds. He was amazed to see Jim take something from the safe and slip it into his pocket. Slipping into the room, he faced the startled boy.

"Jim, will you tell me whut you's doin' snoopin' 'roun' Gordon's house this time 'er night?" he asked sternly.

"Why, Mr. Bailey, Ah jes' happened to walk over heah an' while Ah was heah, Ah thought Ah'd see dat everything was locked up good, an' den Ah

seed uh light in dis room so Ah comed on in, but
whoever it was in heah dey had done got out 'er
dat window," Jim replied, indicating the window
through which the Marshall had just stepped. An
incredulous look in the Marshall's eyes brought to
his realization the seriousness of the situation.

"Well, go on! Whut else happened?" the Marshall asked testily.

"Nothin', but Ah ain't seed uh livin' soul an'
when Ah looked in de safe, Mr. Gordon's money
dat Ah put in dere from de sale uh his peaches was
gone."

"How was the safe opened?"

"Wid de combination, Mr. Bailey."

"Who knew the combination?"

"Nobody but me an' Mr. Gordon. He done tole
me to put his money in dere an' mine too in case Ah
had any."

"Are you sho nobody knew it but you two?"

"Dead sho. Ma ain't even knowed it."

"So you thought you'd come heah and take the
money out tonight and pretend it was stolen, is that
it?"

"Ah 'clare 'fo de Lawd Ah didn't take de money,
Mr. Bailey," Jim answered, almost sobbing.

"Was that all that was in the safe, Jim?"

"Yes suh," Jim answered, forgetting in his agitation the bag of jewelry he had slipped into his
pocket.

"A likely story," the Marshall said, his voice
hard with disbelief. "But Ah been watching you
ever since you came in here from the porch, where
you no doubt went to make sure there was no one
around." Walking over to Jim, he ran his hand

quickly into his coat pocket and drew out the bag of jewelry. Opening it on the table, he poured out its glittering contents.

"Huh, larceny after trust is whut Ah calls it," he said, sweeping the jewelry back into the bag and catching Jim by the arm, he pushed him through the door before him.

CHAPTER XIV

Jim's arrest was the biggest shock the little settlement had ever had. For months nothing else was talked of. Cotton and even church receded far into the background, as the farmers discussed the surprise of it and the outcome of the trial set for early November.

Sara Lou engaged one of Macon's best lawyers, John Hayden, a former partner of Owen Gordon's, to defend Jim, who through the lawyer's efforts, had been released on bail the Wednesday following his arrest.

There had been a very tearful scene at the Carter home when his mother, William and Ruth had returned from Church and found him in Marshall Bailey's custody. The Marshall had been waiting to question them, but there was nothing they could say that would help Jim, and amidst his mother's tears and prayers and Ruth's pitiful sobs, he had been taken away. Ruth had torn aside the secrecy of their engagement and begged to be taken to jail with him. Marshall Bailey had been glad when it was over, and Jim was landed safely in the little leanto jail.

But Lawyer Hayden was hopeful. The evidence to his mind was too flimsy to win a conviction. He also felt sure that Jim, although not guilty, knew who had committed the robbery, and was trying to shield the guilty party. But as time passed, he found that getting him to talk would be a harder job than he had anticipated.

Jim refused to talk, persisting that he knew nothing but the bare facts he had already stated to the marshall.

"Is there anyone who visits your home that you have reason to suspect?" the lawyer asked him.

"No, suh, not uh soul," Jim answered positively.

"Could anyone except yourself have at any time seen that combination without your knowledge?"

"No, suh. Ah kept it hid all de time an' Ah ain't never recollecked it bein' missin'."

"Did your brother know you had that combination?" the lawyer asked, looking straight into Jim's eyes to see the effect his question would have on him. But if Jim was taken by surprise he did not show it, as he calmly answered.

"Yes, Mr. Hayden, William knowed Ah had it, but he ain't never seed it."

"Well, Jim, ain't that slick nigger that works 'round his shop in Macon been visiting your home?"

"Yes, suh. He done been dere lots uh times, but Ah watched him an' he ain't never been upstairs whar Ah keeped de combination," Jim answered, without batting an eye. After a moment he continued: "Anyhow, he was in Spring Valley, William tole me, dat Sunday night."

"Yes, I know he has a trip to Spring Valley as an alibi, but I'm investigating its authenticity," Lawyer Hayden said, rising to indicate the interview was over.

Jim realized, as he rode back to Macon that he was throwing away the only chance he had of clearing himself, and would perhaps have to suffer for a

crime he had not even thought of committing, but
it was the only way to save his mother from a life-
time of suffering. She knew that he was not guilty,
but if he told what he knew, William could easily
be proven the culprit, and break her adoring heart.

His blood boiled to think that even now, William
was again in school posing as a martyr to the stu-
dents, who sympathized with him for having a
brother under suspicion of robbery.

Through the remaining days of October, Jim
worked doggedly up and down the rows of cotton,
cleaning up the last fragments. Ruth worked tear-
fully at his side, blaming herself for the tragedy.
Had it not been for her remarks to William about
school which Jim had overheard, and worried about,
he would have been in church with them that night.
He had stayed home because he felt angry and hurt.

One evening she sobbed out her self accusation
to Sara Lou, as she helped with supper.

"Don't you feel dat'uh way chile. Dey would 'er
'cused Jim anyhow, ef'fen he had uh been in church
jes' kaise he's de only pusson dat knows dat ole combination," Sara Lou comforted, tears filling her eyes.
"Anyhow, dese white folks is mad 'roun' heah
kaise Mr. Gordon done left Jim in charge uh his
place, but don't you worry, honey, he gointer come
out uh it 'thout uh bit uh trouble."

But Ruth did worry, and as days passed into
weeks, she became just a shadow of herself. Black
circles appeared under her eyes. Her shoulders
drooped and she grew years older. And Sara Lou
for all her assurance of the outcome of Jim's trial
being acquittal, worried herself sick in bed. The
once happy home became sad and silent. No more

songs floated out upon the still night air. The
family retired almost at dusk, to lay and restlessly
toss throughout the long night. Neighbors, who
loved them, not wanting to see the sorrow that had
befallen them, stayed away as much as possible.

William, conscience-stricken, did not come home
Saturday, making excuses of having to study hard
to keep up with his school work; while in Macon
he and Slippery spent sparingly the fruits of their
crime for fear of detection.

As the time for the trial drew near, speculation
as to its outcome was rife among the farmers. Sally
Ann Peck and Martha Green nearly came to blows
because of their difference of opinion. Martha had
said as they walked home from church:

"Lawd, Ah jes' kain't see how Jim kin be so innocent uh dat robbin' when don't nobody else know
dat combination but him."

"You shut yo wide mouth up 'oman. Dey ain't
nobody found out whut went wid de church money
you was keepin'. You is de lass one whut aught'er
go layin' blame on folks," Sally came back hotly.

"Is you 'sinuatin' dat Ah ain't tole de truth when
Ah said dat de money was stole out 'uh my house,"
Martha asked threateningly, shaking her fist under
Sally's nose.

"Ah ain't 'sinuatin' 'nothin' but Ah is sayin' dat
folks whut lives in glass houses gotta watch out
when dey throws stones."

"Yeah, you is somebody to talk. You ain't got
no husban' uh yo' own an' you'se allers sneakin'
'roun' at'ter somebody else's. Folks is talkin' 'bout
running you out'er Byron right now," Martha
snorted.

"Ah sho ain't sneakin' at'ter yo's, Martha, kaise
he done left you years ago 'bout dat Jones boy an'
you readin' de Bible down by de branch in de moonlight," Sally laughed.

"Ah gotta good mind to wring yo' neck for dat
remark, Sally Ann Peck," Martha retorted beside
herself with rage.

"Don't let yo' wooden God an' cornstalk Jesus
fool yuh, 'oman nor yo' good mind, neither, no
matter how good it is," Sally retorted.

Martha gritted her teeth and walked away, throwing over her shoulder. "Don't you never speak to
me agin long as yuh lives."

And although the two shared the same two room
log cabin, Jim's trial was over before they spoke
to each other again.

Jim, the subject of all their discussions, worked
on silently, as the days swiftly passed. There was
no malice in his heart for the brother who had wan-
tonly placed him in the shadow of the chain gang—
only pity for his weakness and for his mother, trying so hard to hide her real anguish from him.

Bright sunshine, warm and cheering, the morning
of the trial, mocked the anguish within the hearts
of Sara Lou, Ruth and Jim, as they rode the ten
miles to the county seat of Peach County. William,
silent and making a fine effort of grieved concern, rode beside Jim on the front seat of the
wagon while Sara Lou and Ruth sat behind on a
board laid across its body.

Sara Lou's cousin, Ella, Jerimah and their six
children drove in their team behind them and almost of the entire population of Byron greeted them

when they rode up to the one story frame court-
house.

When the, doors were opened at nine o'clock,
the building was soon packed, and the trial started
by Lawyer Hayden's insisting that a jury be im-
panelled instead of the customary judge presiding
and deciding the case. After many objections and
discussions, a jury of twelve sturdy farmers was
selected, and the case proceeded.

William, the first witness called, could tell nothing except he and his mother and Ruth were in
church the night of the robbery. He knew nothing
of the money paid Jim for the peaches and had
never seen the combination of the safe. His
mother, next called, proved a difficult witness. Her
testimony collaborated with William's exactly, but
the judge and lawyer had a hard time keeping her
to the point, as she insisted on telling how Mr.
Gordon trusted Jim and how she had brought him
up in the fear of God.

"We ain't askin' you aller that, An' Sara. We'all
knows that Gordon done gone off and left a par-
sel'er you niggers running over his place instead'er
a good, honest, white man and this is what has come
of him doing it," Judge Graham, a former resident
of Byron and a friend of Owen Gordon's informed
her.

Sara Lou's sobs became louder and louder, until
the Judge dismissed her from the witness stand and
asked that she be taken from the court-room.

Ruth was next called. She proved the most
damaging witness of the trio. The judge determined to establish a reason for the usually trust-

worthy Jim turning thief, questioned her relentlessly.

"Didn't Jim always take you to church?" she was
asked.

"Yes, suh," the answer came soft and quivering.

"Were you two in love with each other?"

"Yes, suh. We is."

"Were you engaged to be married?"

"Yes, suh, we is."

"Didn't he promise to buy you pretty clothes?"

Ruth raised her eyes and looked around the
court-room as if seeking someone to aid her, and
the Judge had to repeat the question.

"We jes' looked in uh catalogue an' was admirin'
uh dress," came hesitatingly.

"And he promised to buy it for you, eh?"

"Not zackly, suh, he sayd it'ud look mighty nice
on me."

"What else did he say?"

"Dat some day Ah might wear it."

"That's just the same as promising it to you,
ain't it?"

"Yes, suh. Ah mean, no suh," Ruth sobbed dis-
tractedly.

"Well at any rate, there was a reason for Jim
wanting this money desperately," her persecutor
announced.

And Ruth, realizing that her testimony had been
unknowingly damaging to Jim, burst into a torrent
of uncontrollable weeping.

Lawyer Hayden was on his feet, his face red, his
eyes blazing. "Judge, your honor," he shouted.
"This is no love affair. This Jim Carter is on trial
for robbery not for being in love."

"All right, Attorney," the Judge replied, looking over his glasses. "Proceed with the case! Call the next witness!"

Marshall Bailey told without interruption his story of finding Jim in the Gordon dining-room, where the safe stood empty and of finding Owen Gordon's jewelry in his pocket, and all the incidents leading up to his going in to investigate.

" 'Bout what time was that, Bailey?" he was asked.

" 'Round ten o'clock," the answer came promptly.

After a few more pointed questions, the Marshall was dismissed, and Jim called to the stand in his own defence. He told how he happened to walk over to the Gordon place but could tell nothing about the robbery but what he had told the Marshall. He admitted he alone knew the combination of the safe, but could give no excuse for having the jewelry in his pocket, except that he was so glad it had not been taken. He slipped it there, and forgot all about it in the excitement of the Marshall's appearing on the scene which the persecution claimed was a sure sign he planned to steal it.

After a torrid examination, his testimony ended. Lawyer Hayden used every argument he knew in his summary to try and clear the frightened boy. The hour then being late, court was adjourned until the next morning at nine o'clock.

All through Jim's testimony, William sat, his eyes averted, avoiding his brother's haunted face. It was a joy and relief when they were again on their way home.

CHAPTER XV

On the evening of the next day Sara Lou sat in her bare, clean dining room. Her cane bottom rocker swayed back and forth in even rhythm with her sobs. Her friends, Sally Ann, Martha, Ella, Sally Brown, Reverend Hooper, and a few others sat grim-faced and sympathetic trying to console her. They had just returned from the County seat, where Jim had been convicted and sentenced to five years in the chain-gang.

Reverend Hooper rose and bade them kneel while he carried Jim's case to a greater judge than Judge Graham. For almost an hour he prayed, and as they rose from their knees, Martha Green sang softly, helped by the others. "Ah'm leanin' on de Lawd."

"Dat's jes' whut Ah'm doin'," Sara Lou declared, as the song ended.

"He's uh good one to lean on, An' Sara, but ef'fen yuh could 'ford to git dat Lawyer Hayden to git uh 'nother trial for Jim an' have it in Macon, it might help de leanin'," Sally Ann remarked earnestly.

"Lan' sakes, Sally Ann, you don't trust de Lawd for nothin'," Martha chided.

"Course Ah trusts him but sometimes he kind 'er slow to act. Lak de time my ole man Joe was 'cused uh stealin' in Macon. Ef'fen Ah hadn't been workin' for dat big lawyer man dat took up Joe's case, he'ud been in de gang till now."

All eyes were turned on Sally Ann in horror but undaunted, she continued. "To tell de truth, Ah should 'er let 'im gone to de gang kaise Ah had to work uh whole year to pay de lawyer an' 'fo Ah was throu' payin' 'im, Joe he ups an' runs off wid uh trifflin' gal dat was stayin' wid us."

"Huh, served yuh right," Martha grunted, and to avoid further discussion of the matter, Sally Brown started another song.

William, who had been walking around to get away from the sight of his mother's suffering, came into the room and hinted that his mother needed rest, and they bade goodnight and hurried away. William assisted his mother up to her room, where Ruth, who had been preparing the evening meal, served her, and for the first time in Sara Lou's busy life she was unable to leave her room for a week. As strength came back to her during the week that followed, her first concern was William.

"You must git back to yo' school, son," she said, as they sat around downstairs for the first time since Jim had been sent away.

"I will, Ma, soon as you feels all right again, but I'm in no mood for study," he replied obediently.

"You jes' git in de mood. Dere ain't nuthin' heah to do an' us jes' kain't give up. We jes' gotta trust in de Lawd. He's gointer make everything all right an' bring de guilty to judgment."

"Ah sho wish Ah could b'lieve lak dat, An' Sara," Ruth remarked sadly. "But things lak dis makes me b'lieve sometime dat de Lawd ain't much bothered 'bout whut comes to us folks."

"Why, Ruth, dat ain't no way for you to talk!"
Sara Lou exclaimed in surprise.

"It sure ain't no way for a Christian to talk.
Maybe if Jim had got religion instead of making
fun of preachers and the church, this might not
have happened to him," William said with an air
of pious dignity.

"Religion ain't got nothin' to do wid it.   Ole
Judge Graham is uh deacon in his church an' Ah
ain't never seed nobody act any more unfair den
he did tryin' Jim," Ruth exploded angrily.

"When is you seen them act fair when there's
one uh us on trial?" William asked quietly.

"Dey jes' takes it for granted dat we'se guilty
'fo we'se tried, but Ah thank God dey ain't de
judge when it comes to gittin' to heaven," Sara
Lou smiled, happy with the prospect of that far off
reward.

Ruth's reply filled with defiance shocked them
both.   "Shucks, Ah ain't wantin' to have to wait
ontill Ah gits to heaven to have uh little happiness," she said, walking out of the room.

Later that evening some of Sara Lou's neighbors dropped in to see if there was anything they
could do for her, and for a while they all sat
around talking, trying to forget the tragedy that
had befallen them.

"William, Ah want yuh to write Mr. Gordon a
letter an' tell him whut done happened," Sara Lou
said when she, William and Ruth were again alone.

"All right, Ma.   That's a good idea!   Do you
know his address?"

"Ah jes' know dat he done write Jim from a
place called London.   Ah got de letter heah so

send it dere," handing the letter to William, who wrote the long, rambling letter his mother dictated, telling Owen Gordon the details of the robbery and begging him not to believe Jim guilty.

"I'll mail it first thing in the morning, Ma," William promised, sealing the missive.

"Awrite son, an' tomorrow is Tuesday, you go back to school."

"I will, Ma," William promised, glad to get away from home, where everything reminded him of the crime he had committed. Things had turned out far different from what he had planned. He had had Slippery take the money because he needed it to pay the debts he owed and to spite Jim, whom he knew would have to replace it, but he had not dreamed that the outcome would be as it was. In fact, he blamed Jim for going to Gordon's house that night when he might have been in church, and wondered why Fate had sent Marshall Bailey by just at that time. But now that it had happened, he could not find one spark of pity in his heart for Jim. If it had not been for the suffering the whole thing caused his mother, he would have been happier than he had been in years.

"Ah wonder ef'fen Lawyer Hayden could git my boy uh new trial?" his mother's voice brought him back to the present.

"Maybe so, Ma, but it'ud cost a lot of money," he answered without enthusiasm.

"Lawd, Ah'd sell de roof from over my head to git Jim out'uh dat prison!" Sara Lou declared.

"Let's wait a while and see what Mr. Gordon says when he writes," William suggested.

"Ah sho' hopes he answers right 'er way," Ruth breathed hopefully.

Sara Lou rose reluctantly and stretched her arms above her head. She had been sleepy and on the verge of going to bed for some time, but the prospects of lying awake thinking until far into the night had kept her putting it off.

"Ah'm goin'ter carry my ole bones to bed, chillun," she said, moving towards the stairs.

"Ah'm goin' too, An' Sara," Ruth said, rising.

William caught her hand and pleaded. "Please don't go, Ruth. I've got a new book I want to tell you about and it's only eight o'clock anyhow."

Ruth reluctantly resumed her seat. She did not want to hurt William's feelings but would rather have been anywhere than alone with him in her present state of mind.

"Why didn't you tell me you and Jim was engaged?" his first question brought an uneasy flush to her face.

" 'Cause Jim an' me promised to keep it uh secret an' we wasn't goin'ter marry nohow ontill Ah was out uh mourning."

"Now that Jim's in prison for five years, you ain't aiming to wait for him that long, are you?"

"Sho' Ah am! Ah'ud wait twenty years for Jim."

"But you're young and I loves you, Ruth. Would you rather sacrifice five years waiting for him than marry me?"

"Please William, don't talk lak dat. It ain't fair to yo' brother when you knows dat Ah done promised him, an' anyhow Ah ain't goin' to listen to yuh," Ruth answered, rising.

"Jim ain't selfish enough to want you to wait that long for him nohow, Ruth."

"Leave go my hand, William," Ruth begged, trying to free herself from the grasp William had on her hand. "Ah want to go to bed anyhow. Ah'm sleepy," she pleaded.

"Let me kiss you good night. I ain't kissed you since we were children," William begged, drawing her to him.

Ruth shrank as far away as possible, but William drew her struggling into his arms. She placed her hand over her mouth but William gently removed it and held her close, pressing his lips to hers in a long passionate kiss. Again and again his lips pressed hers, despite her desperate struggles to free herself from his embrace. When she finally pushed him aside and ran to the stairway, her limbs were trembling so violently, they could hardly carry her weight.

CHAPTER XVI

The next morning, William left Byron to return
to his studies. He tried to get a chance to speak
to Ruth alone before leaving, but she steadfastly
avoided him and greatly disappointed, he left to
catch his train.

He had lost considerable time; but it would mean
nothing. Studies had never even been an effort to
his alert brain, and before the week was over, he
had caught up with his classes, and was again spending his leisure time over at Daddy Jenks' with Ethel.

For long hours she would sit beside the bed and
watch him as he lay stretched full length upon it,
his eyes closed, one arm thrown carelessly above his
head, letting her fingers linger for a moment upon
his face as they glided on through his soft curly
hair. As she waited for him to open his eyes or in
some way respond to her caresses, she loved him
with all the love of her starved warped soul.

William stirred uneasily and pushing her hand
aside, sat up on the side of the bed.

"Whut's de matter, William, did Ah wake you
up?" Ethel asked softly.

"No."

"Are you angry wid me, honey?"

"No."

"Well den, Ah got something Ah wants to talk to
yuh 'bout," she persisted, sitting on the side of the
bed beside him. "Ah been thinkin' long time, William, dis ain't no place for you. Why don't you

come on up north wid me whar you kin 'mount to
somethin' some day. You kain't ever be nothin'
heah. You may finish school an' become uh stomp
knockin' preacher, but dat ain't no good for you
when you could do so much better."

"I'm not leaving Georgia, Ethel, now or no time!
I belong here, and I'm gonna stay here. I guess you
think because I hangs out 'round you, I ain't never
gonna be no good. Well, I'll show you, I'll stay
away!" William retorted sharply and dashed angrily from the room.

Ethel's harsh laughter followed him until he was
out of hearing.

Once again he swore he would keep away from
Daddy Jenks' gang and Ethel. He loved Ruth mad-
ly. Her clean, sweet beauty, fascinated him. With
her as his wife he would be safe from himself, his
weakness and passion; and able to make of himself the great man his mother wanted him to be.

He went straight to his room and was thankful
that Sissy was out. For several hours he studied
and read, and before getting into bed, knelt and
prayed that God would give him strength to do the
things he wanted to do.

But getting rid of Ethel was no small task. She
hung around his shop night and day, sometimes
sober, but more often drunk and in an ugly mood.

"Yuh think you kin ditch me jes' lak dat?" she
said—snapping her finger under William's nose the
next afternoon.

"Ethel, I've got to study and I've got lots of re-
sponsibility and can't be bothered," William explained.

"Aw, yeah? Well, you gonna be worried uh

hell'eva lot an' before Ah'm through, Ah won't be de only one botherin' yuh, neither," she returned, rushing out of the shop.

But William continued to stay away and she drank more and more, and tore things up in general.

Jim had been in prison two weeks when William got sufficient courage to visit him. He hated the trip. The chain gang held a horror for him that made his visit a torture, but his mother had asked him to go, and he could not refuse.

Jim had intended telling him what he had found in the Gordon dining room, the night of the robbery, and make him promise by holding the knowledge of his criminality over his head, to stop being a hypocrite and live right for their mother's sake, but the presence of the guards prevented him from doing so, and he treated William civil in their presence—not because he wanted to.

It was almost time for him to leave when he said casually: "It sure is a shame the way Ruth is worrying, Jim."

"Whut's she worryin' 'bout more den usual?"

"Well, she's young and realizes five years is a long time to be engaged."

"Did she say dat?"

"No, she wouldn't say it for the world, but she thinks it, and she did say something like that to me when I was home last."

"Ah don't want 'er to wait five years for me, William. It jes' wouldn't be fair nohow."

"Well, don't be too hasty, Jim, in tellin' her that you don't. Mr. Gordon may come home, if he gets

Ma's letter.   And get worried 'bout his place, and
he may get you out."

"Less don't talk uh 'bout it."

"Just as you say, Jim," William answered, uneasy because of the look he saw in Jim's eyes.

He felt he was treading on dangerous ground
and bidding Jim goodbye, left the prison.   Later
when he told his mother the events of his trip she
said:

"Me an' Ruth jes' dyin' to see de boy an' we
goin'ter take him lots uh vittels when we goes out
dere, ain't we honey?" turning to Ruth.

"We sho is, An' Sara, an' we goin'ter be jes'
dat cheerful, dat he goin'ter be laughin' 'fo we
leaves."

Ruth was all excitement as the holidays drew
near—the time she and Sara Lou were to visit the
chain gang.   Jim had scribbled a few short letters
and every morning she ran down to the post office
to see if there was anything for her or Sara
Lou.

Two days before Christmas Eve she returned,
her steps lagging as if they were lead.   In her hand
she held a letter tightly clutched.   Sara Lou heard
her enter the house and start upstairs and called
her into the kitchen, where she was putting away
a cake she had baked for Jim.

"Lawd chile, whut's de matter wid you?   Is
yuh seen uh ghost?" she exclaimed when she saw
Ruth's drawn face.

For answer Ruth handed her the letter she had
received from Jim.   Sara Lou spelt out the few lines
carefully.

"Dear Ruth:

Dis is jes' to tell yuh dat Ah ain't holdin' yuh to our engagement kaise five years is too long to ask you to wait. Jim."

"Shucks, Ruth, dat boy is crazy! Don't yuh pay dis no' 'tention," Sara Lou said, drawing Ruth into her arms.

"Ah don't know whut maked him write me lak dat, An' Sara," Ruth sobbed.

"He jes' scared he gointer have to stay in dat place five years sho' 'nough an' dat's worryin' him," Sara Lou consoled. "When we goes out dere, he goin'ter take dat all back."

"Ah don't know ef'fen Ah'm goin' out dere, An' Sara, not rite uh way nohow. Ah knows Jim well 'nough to know he don't never joke. Ef'fen he say our engagement is broke, he means it, an' Ah ain't gointer worry him 'bout it, kaise he got 'nough to worry 'bout as it is."

Ruth spent the rest of the afternoon wandering in the woods that surrounded the farm. For a long time she stood looking at her and Jim's hickory nut tree, where their hair had been buried years back. When she returned home she found William, who had come home as usual to spend Sunday, sitting with his mother. He had brought her a new book, and a box of candy for his mother to share with her. His witty jokes soon had them both laughing and in a measure feeling better than earlier in the afternoon when Jim's letter had so cruelly hurt her.

William was diplomatic and took sides with Jim, excusing his action with the hopelessness of facing years in the terrible confinement of prison. After Ruth had gone to bed, he and his mother sat for a while talking.

"Ah goin'ter bring dat boy to his senses when Ah goes out to dat prison," she declared.

"If I was you, Ma, I'd let them settle it themselves. You know how stubborn Jim is. He might not like you interfering."

"Dat's rite, son," Sara Lou agreed. "Ah won't say uh livin' word, less'n he mentions it hisseff."

William went to sleep that night relieved and pleased with the progress he had made in breaking up Jim's engagement. He was now removed as a rival, and with time and the many ways he would use to win Ruth, everything would be in his favor. He had feared more than anything else his mother's asking Jim why he had written that letter, and Jim, in turn, telling her and Ruth what he had said during his visit.

CHAPTER XVII

The Christmas holidays passed quickly, but not happily for the Carter household. A gloom hovered over the house that the visit to the chain gang seemed to intensify; instead of dispel. At the time of year when many people visited their friends and relatives in prison and extra care was taken to guard the place, Ruth had had no chance to say the things to Jim she had wanted to, and returned home sadder and more hopeless than ever.

William was glad when time came for him to return to school, and spent more time than usual studying. He saw little of Ethel or the boys, but Sugar Kid's release from prison caused him many sleepless nights, as he worried him daily for his thirty-five dollars.

January and February passed and he had not paid the debt because Sugar Kid had failed to produce the note. It was Saturday afternoon early in March, and William was helping Slippery to finish the work in the shop when Sugar Kid walked in.

"Say, listen heah, William," he began.

"I knows just whut you're going to say, Sugar Kid," William interrupted. "That you want yo' money, and I'm going to say what I've told you before—that you can have it when you give me back the note I gave you so save yo' breath, if you ain't got the note with you."

"Yeah, Ah gonna say jes' dat an' Ah'm goin'ter say something else. Ef'fen yuh don't give me my money right now, Ah'm goin'ter scatter you all over de state uh Georgy," Sugar Kid retorted angrily.

"Not so fast!" Slippery spoke up, reaching for his gun that he kept in a drawer nearby, and walking over to the door where Sugar Kid was standing, he continued: "You is one snake, Sugar Kid dat Ah's jes' dyin' to step on an' flatten out, so yuh better git out uh heah an' stay out 'fo' Ah does jes' dat!"

Sugar Kid backed out of the door quickly, and walked across the street cursing the two of them roundly under his breath, his mind made up to get even with Slippery, if it was the last thing he ever did.

"Ah guess dat's de last uh dat snake, askin' for dat thirty-five bucks," Slippery laughed.

"I don't know about that, Slippery. Sometimes I feels that I aught'er give him that money. It might cause lots of trouble yet," William replied, thoughtfully.

"Aw you'se jes' uh tender, William. Ah knows how to handle dese darkies 'roun' heah. Dey don't scare me."

" 'Course I'm in my rights. He insisted on me writing a note that I owed him the money and if I pay him without getting it back, he can produce it later and make me pay him again."

"Well, whut yuh worryin' 'bout den? Jes' forgit it!" Slippery advised.

"Gee, whut's all de commotion over at Daddy Jenks'?" Slippery exclaimed a moment later, when a loud scream carried him to the door.

A large crowd had congregated in front of Daddy's place and several policemen were struggling with someone as they dragged them towards the patrol wagons standing near the sidewalk. William and Slippery looking on from their door, tried to make out who the struggling culprit was. Slippery no longer able to control his curiosity, crossed the street, returning in a short time with the news of the fracas.

Ethel, who had gone on a drunken rampage, had been the unwilling struggling prisoner. Daddy Jenks had tried to keep her quiet and had almost succeeded when Sugar Kid came in and started raving about what he was going to do to William and she had broken loose again, and grabbing Daddy's ice pick, had gone for Sugar Kid. The police had to be called, finally, to keep her from committing murder.

"Ef'fen dat gal ain't careful she goin'ter git runned out'uh dis town! She done been in court four Mondays hand running," Slippery remarked.

"She sure can raise Cain, all right. I don't see how she gets away with it," William said, worried over the outcome of the trial, when mention of him might get him into an unpleasant situation.

"Well, she stands in wid de deputy sheriff. Dat's how she gits way wid it. Ef'fen yuh don't know," Slippery was glad to inform him, hoping it might keep him away from Ethel henceforth.

But William ignored the remark and turned the subject to other things. Later that evening, he left the shop to catch a train home remarking laughingly to Slippery, as he went out of the door.

"See you Monday. Be careful of Sugar Kid. Don't let him get the drop on you."

"Don't worry. Ah been wantin' to bump dat

bird off long time an eff'en he starts anythin' dat'll
jes' be my chance," Slippery called cheerfully.

Late customers started dropping in to get their
clothes and Slippery had his hands too full to think
further of Sugar Kid. Cotton Eye, among the last
to call, was in a particularly talkative mood, when he
flopped down on a box to wait while Slippery put
the finishing touches to his one and only suit.

"Gee boy," he said between mouthfuls of peanuts,
he crammed into his mouth from his overall pockets.
"Dere sho is been some tall doin's 'roun' heah today.
Dey tells me dat Ethel done gone to jail an' dat
Sugar Kid is raisin' hell over at Daddy Jenks."

"Whut's he raisin' hell 'bout?" Slippery asked.

"Well, for one thing, he swears dat he goin'ter
plug you full uh holes de fust time yuh steps foot in
Daddy's place, an' dat's got Daddy all hot an' bothered kaise he don't lak nobody startin' nothin' in his
joint."

"Daddy needn't be kaise Ah ain't scared uh Sugar
Kid. Ah'm goin' in de place any time Ah gits good
an' ready. Ain't nothin' to dat bag uh wind nohow."

"All Ah gotta say, Slippery, is jes' watch yo'
step!"

"Ah kin take care'uh myself. Don't you worry."

"Ah ain't gonna, but Ah jes' hopes Ah be dere
when de fun start. Ah wouldn't miss it for nothin',"
Cotton Eye grinned, handing Slippery the money
for his suit.

It was almost eleven o'clock when Slippery closed
the shop for the night and walked slowly over to
Daddy Jenks. A tremor of excitement passed over
the crowd standing around when he entered the

door. Sugar Kid, his back towards the door, was not aware of his presence until he called for a drink. Everybody expected a fight or even gun play when the two men faced each other. A sigh of relief and disappointment went around the room when instead, Sugar Kid walked over to Slippery and said casually.

"How's de boy, Slippery?"

"Ah ain't so bad off, Sugar Kid. How's you?" Slippery replied, his eyes on Sugar Kid's hand fumbling in his pockets.

"Ah awrite. Now dat Ah'se kind'er cooled off, less have uh drink. Daddy sit up uh bottle," Sugar Kid answered.

Bottle after bottle was placed on the counter, and Sugar Kid and Slippery drank. It was near midnight when Slippery walking somewhat unsteadily, followed Sugar Kid and the boys upstairs to gamble. For all the liquor he had consumed, he played carefully and in fairly good luck. Someone suggested they put the cards aside and shoot dice instead and he readily consented.

As the game progressed, Sugar Kid became quarrelsome and the boys realized he was trying to pick a fight with Slippery. One by one they dropped out of the game, leaving him and Slippery facing each other. Slippery had won several passes when Sugar Kid suddenly reached for the dice.

"Why, yuh dirty crook!" he shouted. "Whut yuh mean puttin' dese crooked dice in de game?"

Slippery looked on in surprise as Sugar Kid threw the dice to one of the boys standing near.

"Look at 'em! Ain't dey loaded?" Sugar Kid demanded.

"Sho is!" the reply came, as the dice went down the line from hand to hand.

"Ah didn't put 'em in, Sugar Kid, an' you know it!" Slippery denied hotly, realizing he was being accused of a deed that was considered the lowest among gamblers.

"Yuh did an' Ah'm goin'ter git yuh for it, tryin' to rob me right 'fo' eve'ybody," Sugar Kid snarled, making a dash for him.

"Git back dere," Slippery warned, reaching for his hip pocket, but Sugar Kid came on slowly advancing around the table towards him, shaking his arm. Slippery saw something shiny drop from his sleeve and backed away until he was against the opposite wall. Still Sugar Kid advanced slowly like a cat ready to spring, his gums drawn back from his teeth in an ugly snarl.

"Git back, Sugar Kid!" Slippery begged, trying in vain to slide beyond his reach, one large hand reached out, almost touching his throat.

Slippery wiggled along the wall; shouted again to the advancing man to keep away. Suddenly his hand came out of his pocket. In it his pistol was tightly grasped.

"Look out—he's got a gun!" someone yelled.

But Sugar Kid gave one lunge and as Slippery jumped aside, his hand ripped the collar from his shirt. A shot rang out, found its mark. Sugar Kid paused for a second, his hand clutching at the weapon, his eyes wide and bulging as he swayed dizzily; his knees sagged and carried him crashing to the floor.

Slippery leaped over his prostrate body and before anyone could recover sufficiently to stop him, was gone.

Pandemonium reigned. Men fought to get out and soon the club room was as clean as if no one had been there. Sugar Kid lay still upon the floor, killed by a single bullet from Slippery's gun.

* * *

William, just seventeen miles away from the tragedy, slept peacefully through the night. He had set up late with his mother, who was almost overcome with the joy of having received a letter from Owen Gordon, who had just reached London, and found her letter awaiting him.

"Jes' to think, Willyum, Mr. Gordon goin'ter be home soon, an' he goin'ter git my Jim right out'er dat chain gang," she had said, her eyes filled with tears of joy.

"Don't get yo' hopes too high, Ma, cause after all, maybe Mr. Gordon won't be able to get Jim out, and maybe he won't want to nohow. After all, he's white, and he might believe like the other white folks, that Jim did steal his money," William replied, avoiding his mother's happy face.

" 'Deed he ain't goin'ter think dat Jim did no stealin' an' 'nother thin', he ain't lak no other white folks. He's jes' Mr. Gordon lak hisseff an' de smartest lawyer dere ever was an' he laks Jim an' he goin'ter git him out, yuh'll see."

"I hope so," William assented, bidding his mother good-night. Until after midnight he lay wondering whether Owen Gordon's home-coming would in any way affect his secret of the robbery which he felt was safe between Slippery and himself.

Ruth, who had gone to Ella's to help care for one of her boys, who had been taken suddenly very ill, returned early Sunday morning. The child was worse and Ella wanted Sara Lou to come and see what she could do for him.

"Land sakes, why don't dey git uh doctor? Ah ain't no doctor!" Sara Lou grumbled, putting on her clean white Sunday apron to go to Ella. "You chillun jes' go on to church. Dinner's cooked an' ef'fen Ah don't git back by night, William you bring Ruth over to Ella's at'ter de night services."

"Ah may come over dere 'fo' dat An' Sara," Ruth replied anxiously, as she did not like being left at home alone with William all day.

Sara Lou was on her way happily trudging the distance between her and Ella's home, her thoughts on the end of her trouble being near. Snatches of happy songs burst from her lips every now and then. Between the prayers of thankfulness she murmured:

"My boy gonna soon be home. I kno it Lawd."

Later William and Ruth, after attending morning services, stopped by to see Deacon Simmons, who had been sick for several weeks and then came home to have their dinner.

"Lord, William, it jes' beats me how dese pore igno'ant folks 'roun' heah kin lay sick an' not git de doctor—jes' leavin' An' Salisbury stew up roots for dem an' makin' 'em think dey's conjured," Ruth remarked, as they cleared the table.

"Yes, Ruth, it is a shame. You know sometimes I get so tired of this place, I can hardly stand it. I'd like to go up north some place where things are different and our people gets somewhere. Wouldn't

you like to live where our folks are educated and
livin' like white folks."

"Ah don't know, William. Sometimes Ah dream
uh livin' in uh big city an' enjoyin' life but Ah'ud be
so scared an' lonely," Ruth answered thoughtfully.

"You wouldn't be if you was my wife. Some day
I'm going to have a big church and folks would just
worship you, Ruth, as their preacher's wife. You
are so pretty and refined," William said softly,
placing his arm around her shoulder and trying to
lift her head so that he could look into her eyes but
Ruth moved away quietly, as she said evasively:

"Yuh know Ah ain't promised to marry you yet,
William. Ah still loves Jim an ef'fen Mr. Gordon
gits him out, we's goin'ter marry yet."

"But he's broke your engagement. What you
goin'ter do—beg him to take you back?"

"Ah won't have to beg him, William. He still
loves me. It's jes' dat ole prison dat made him
write whut he did."

"But, Ruth, honey, I loves you, loves you 'till it
makes me hurt all over. Marry me. I'll make you
so happy. I needs you, Ruth. Jim don't."

Ruth sank into a chair. William, who had stood,
his arms around her, could feel her body trembling
violently as he pressed her unwillingly to him.
Dropping to his knees beside her, he continued
pleading softly, tears gathering in his eyes. He lay
his head in her lap, sobs shaking his frame, as he
told her how weak he was, and how much he needed
her to strengthen and encourage him.

There was something about him that fascinated
her. She felt unable to resist his pleading. As she
looked down upon his bowed head, she wondered

if it was love that made her feel so sorry for him. She didn't want to promise him anything but when he rose and sat beside her and gently drew her to his lap, she did not resist but lay pensively in his arms. As he covered her face with kisses she felt dizzy and weak and afraid to stand, fearing her limbs would not support her.

"Honey, you do love me," he whispered close to her ear.

Trying to release herself, she pleaded feebly. "Oh, Ah don't know, William. Ah want to think. Please let me go!"

Gently assisting her to stand, he watched her as she staggered haltingly upstairs to her room, where she fell upon her knees before her bed, trying to close her eyes and shut out the memory of his face but she could not. She could still hear his soft pleading voice whispering in her ears. She did like the way he took her into his arms. His passionate kisses still smarted her lips. A thrill crept deliciously over her body, as she remembered the way he held her close.

Suddenly her thoughts frightened her. She was just a wicked sinner and out of wickedness could come nothing but sorrow and disgrace. Clasping her hands she prayed for guidance, tears flowing down her cheeks, as she silently rocked herself back and forth in agony and repentance.

CHAPTER XVIII

William walked back and forth in the room down-stairs, where Ruth had left him. In the grip of alternating hope and despair, his passionate love for Ruth and the desire to have her for his wife so filled his mind, he did not hear the light taps on the back door until they were repeated several times. Mechanically he passed through the short hall, opened the back door and started as if he had seen a ghost, as Slippery ducked quietly by him into the room and sank into the nearest chair.

"What on earth are you doing here?" William whispered, looking around the room as if expecting to see someone spring out from behind the furniture.

"Keep yo' shirt on, bo, an' Ah'll tell yuh," Slippery answered shortly. "Ah'm in trouble an' wants you to help me git 'way."

"What kind'er trouble—been raided for gambling?"

"God. Ah wish it was jes' dat. No William, it's serious dis time. Ah killed Sugar Kid."

"My God, Slippery, that's awful!" William exclaimed paling.

"Yuh tellin' me? But Ah'll git out uh dis. Ah been in tighter places den dis an' got out," Slippery bragged.

"But spose the marshall sees you coming out'er my house? Don't you see what a mess you'll get me in?" William asked, taking a cautious peep from the half-opened door.

"Dat's all you ever think of—yo' own yaller skin. Ain't Ah in uh worse mess an' whose de cause uh it all? You, if yuh ask me—helpin' you out. Dat's what got me in dis spot and yuh know it. Wasn't for you, Sugar Kid wouldn't uh picked on me," Slippery rattled off, for the first time in his life angry with William.

"How come you to kill Sugar Kid is all I wants to know and it ain't no need'er you getting mad because I'm worried 'bout the outcome," William replied, frightened at the attitude Slippery had taken.

"He picked uh fuss wid me in uh crap game. Ah begged him to keep way but he comed on an' Ah saw uh razor drop from his sleeve. He put de crooked dice in jes' to git uh chance to cut me. Ah didn't want to shoot him. Ah swear Ah didn't but Ah had to. Ah jes' had to. It was his life or mine. You know why he was mad wid me? 'Twas 'bout dat money you owed him an' Ah had to shoot." Slippery whimpered on and on almost breaking under the strain of fear.

"Well, it's done and here's all the money I've got," William interrupted, handing him a small roll of bills and assisting him to his feet. "Suppose they catch you, Slippery?" he asked when they reached the door.

"Effen dey do, put dis down in yo' little red book. Ah won't bring you into it even if dey string me. Ah swear it, William. Heah," he added, as he stood in the doorway, handing William the note he had stolen from Sugar Kid's pocket.

"When did you get this?" William asked, looking hard at the crumbled piece of paper.

"Ah took it of'fen Sugar Kid sometime ago."

"Why didn't you tell me you had it, Slippery?"

"Ah didn't want to, not den," Slippery answered, slipping out the door and sliding around the house towards the back fence. William tore the note into small bits and turned to go back into the parlor but drew back. Ruth was standing in the hall door.

"You scared me Ruth. How long have you been there?" he asked.

"Soon after Slippery came in," she answered calmly.

"Then you heard?"

"Yes every word Slippery and you said. Ah didn't want to eavesdrop yuh'all but Ah jes' couldn't help it, William," she answered wearily.

"Poor fellow, he's in trouble, Ruth."

"Yes, because of something you've done. He's uh murderer an' you'se jes' as bad."

"Why Ruth!" William started.

"Keep still, William. You'se jes' uh mean, low hypocrite gittin' people into trouble. Dat's whut you is."

"Ruth, you don't know what you're sayin'."

"Aw yes, Ah do. Ah heard Slippery promise yuh not to tell on yuh, no matter whut happens. He must know something dat you'se scared stiff he'll tell. Ah see through you now William. Dat's why Ah was al'lers scared uh you an' to think Ah almost made myself b'lieve Ah loved you," Ruth cried almost in tears.

"But you do love me, Ruth. I'm not as bad as you think," William pleaded, trying to take her hand.

"Don't yuh touch me, William Carter," she screamed, shrinking from his touch.

"I'm going to touch you," William said slowly
through clenched teeth. "I love you and I'm gonna
make you love me and even if you don't, you'll be
glad to marry me."

Ruth, frightened by the look she saw in his eyes,
backed away, her hands before her face. William
pulled her into his arms and pinning her hands
behind her back, kissed her lips, her neck, her
shoulders, pressing her to him in a close suffocating
embrace, his breath coming in short quick gasps, as
his hand slid over her throat and down the neck
of her dress until they touched her round full breast,
the touch of her warm flesh firing the passion of
his body until he trembled violently from head to
foot. His usual calm was gone. In its place a
savage passion swept all else aside. Ruth, weak
and exhausted, felt her strength failing her, as she
fought to free herself.

"William! Aunt Sara!" a loud voice called from
the gate.

William came to his senses with a start. His arms
dropped to his side, as he straightened himself and
ran his hand over his rumpled hair, trying to collect
his scattered wits and finally stumbling to the door.
He faced Kenneth Bailey, the marshall.

"See you been sleep, William. Sorry to disturb
yuh but has you seen dat fellow dat works in that
shop in Macon with you, this afternoon?" the marshall greeted.

"Why no, Mr. Bailey," William answered slowly,
almost afraid to hear the sound of his own voice.

"Wal, he done killed 'er nigger in Macon an' I
thought maybe seeing he worked for you dere, he

might'er come to you for help," the marshall said, eyeing William uncertainly.

"I'm sorry to hear he's got himself in trouble, Mr. Bailey, but I'd be the last one he'd expect to harbor him," William said firmly, unaware of the fact that Ruth had stepped into the doorway behind him. Her voice came like an electric shock to him when she said:

"Mr. Bailey, Ah b'lieve Ah done seed de man you lookin' for."

William looked straight before him. He was sure Ruth was going to tell all she knew about Slippery's recent visit to the marshall which would put him in a desperate spot.

"Gee, I'm glad you can help out, Ruth. Where did you see him?" the marshall asked eagerly.

Ruth hesitated a moment. A vision of Aunt Sara's face rose before her. If she told all she knew about the afternoon visit it might cause William's arrest and a world of sorrow to his mother. William had treated her shamefully but he was not worth the sorrow his mother would suffer. No, she could not do it, she decided as she said:

"He was sneaking down de road back uh de barn. Ah was lookin' after de cows when he looked over de fence at me, den sneaked on down de road in de direction uh de ole school house."

"Thanks, Ruth. Ah got'er man station over dat'er way. Ah guess he was tryin' to see you, William, an' seeing Ruth scared him 'way."

The marshall hurried away and William too relieved to speak, walked over to Ruth and held out his hand which she ignored.

"Thank you Ruth," he stammered brokenly.

Ruth turned to enter the house and at the door, turned and faced him leaning heavily against the wall.

"Ah didn't lie to save yo' skin. Ah did it because of An' Sara. She loves an' trusts you. It's all she lives for. You're her wooden God an' Ah couldn't even to save my own life hurt her."

"But Ruth, I want to beg you to forgive me," William pleaded, following her into the room. "Please forgive me. I wasn't myself this afternoon. I wants to be good. I swear I do but sometimes there's something inside'er me, I jes' can't control. I wants to be a Christian and do all the great things Ma expects of me but I don't know why. There's so many different parts of me. I can't understand myself. I swear I wish I was different."

Tears were running down his cheeks as he dropped into a chair and covered his face with his hands. She could not help a feeling of pity that filled her heart.

"Ah'm going to church. Ah don't know whar from dere," she said simply turning away to go upstairs.

"Now, I've lost you forever, Ruth. I can't go on livin' knowin' that. Before God I can't," William's voice sounded so hopeless and desperate it frightened her, as she walked up the stairs. When she returned to the room a moment later, Marshall Bailey was again at the gate talking to William, who sat on the steps of the porch. As she came out, he was saying:

"Yas siree. We caught that fellow slick as grease over dar by the school house. My man's done took 'im to jail and locked him up by now till they can send from Macon to fetch 'im. Thanks to you, Ruth," he added, smiling at the stunned girl standing in the door.

She had not meant to tell the marshall where Slippery really was and had just said the old school house at random but he would have been caught anyway, she reassured herself for Bailey had stationed a man over there before he came to the house.

To William the news was a blow. More than anything else he wanted Slippery to escape and never to come back to Macon again. Ruth walked past him and out of the gate but he scarcely saw her. Fear of what might happen next clutched his heart.

CHAPTER XIX

Several hours later Sara Lou came home, after making Ella's boy comfortable and leaving instructions for his care during the night. When she lighted a lamp in the darkened dining room, an exclamation of surprise fell from her lips, as a ray of light fell upon William crouched down in a large horse-hair rocking chair.

"Lan' sakes, William, you sho did scare me. Whut's de matter wid you, sittin' dere in de dark lak you done lost yo' lass friend?" she asked.

"Nothing, Ma," William replied, straightening himself up.

"Yes, dere is. You can't fool yo' ole Ma. Youse worried." Seating herself beside him, she drew his head to her shoulder and patted it tenderly.

His eyes filled with tears. He would have given his life to have been able to tell her everything but he was afraid. She would not understand and he would thereby cause her sorrow and anxiety. Instead he answered, gaining a small amount of his usual cool composure.

"It ain't nuthin' much Ma, only Slippery's got hisself in trouble. He killed a man in Macon and they've got him in jail."

"De Lawd!" his mother whispered shocked.

"I guess I'm jes' sap' enough to feel sorry for him—seeing he worked for me in the shop."

"Dat's jes' de Christian spirit in you, William. You jes' kaint help feelin' bad for de pore sinner but uh murderer is bad kaise God says, 'Thou shall

not kill,' so don't you worry 'bout no sinner kaise
dey ain't worth yo' tears."

"That's right, Ma."

"Whar's Ruth?" she asked, looking around the
room.

"She's gone to church. I didn't feel like goin'
after what happened to Slippery."

"Ah guess Ah better go fetch'er home," Sara Lou
decided and hurried in the direction of the church.
As she came in sight of it, she could see the wor-
shippers standing around outside, gossiping. The
services were over. They all greeted her warmly
and inquired why William had not attended the
service. Sara Lou made excuses for him and hurried to where Ruth stood, talking with Aunt Salisbury, who had whispered to her during the meeting that she wanted to speak to her outside.

"Heah, Ruth," she had whispered when Ruth
joined her, holding out a small red flannel bag.
"Dis uh good luck charm. Pin it inside yo' dress."

And Ruth had obediently pinned the bag to her
dress and listened while Aunt Salisbury instructed
her to wet it in vinegar every morning. She and
Sara Lou walked home together discussing the
plight Slippery had gotten himself into, Sara Lou
bewailing the fact that it had worried her William
so he couldn't attend church. Ruth listened and
wondered when would she wake up to find her
idol fallen and demolished, and breathed a silent
prayer that it would never happen.

When they reached home, William had gone,
leaving a note that he had caught a late train for
Macon to be there early Monday for school. But
he had really gone to Macon to be on hand when

Slippery was brought in. He wanted to satisfy himself once more by hearing it from Slippery's lips that he would not be involved.

Monday afternoon he visited the jail and offered to get a lawyer for him but Slippery flatly refused to let him and went on trial a few days later undefended, except for defense given him by the State. He flatly refused to tell anything of his former life, and at the start was handicapped. The State was bitterly arrayed against the stranger who came from God knows where, to commit a crime within its bounds. There were many witnesses to the crime, but none could swear Sugar Kid had a weapon. The razor found near his body went unidentified and could have belonged to any of the two dozen men who were in the room at the time. It did not take long for Slippery to be found guilty of manslaughter and the judge in sentencing him to twenty years in the chain gang, lectured him on how lucky he was not to have drawn a first degree murder sentence.

Ethel Myers, who had been arrested for drunkenness and disorderly conduct, fared better and was let off with a suspended sentence and ordered to leave town at once.

At one stroke William found himself rid of the two people he feared most and made up his mind henceforth to settle down to school and business and live a better life. For the rest of the term he made greater strides in his studies than ever.

* * *

Life in Byron had also taken on greater interest. Sara Lou's outlook on life had changed now that Mr. Gordon was coming home, and she hoped he was going to get Jim out of prison. She was again happy and cheerful as of old, working around the place with a song on her lips and a bright smile on her face.

Ruth had also been made happier than she had been since her father's death by going to work for Mrs. Carmicheil, the wife of the proprietor of the general store. She helped with the housework and cooking each week-end when the four grown daughters of the family came home from Macon, where they attended high school, with a bevy of young friends.

Ruth wanted to divide the dollar and a half she received for her work each week with Sara Lou, but she would not accept it.

"No chile, you buy yuh some clothes," she advised.

Ruth made up her mind she would buy her a present. She could not refuse to accept that. She felt happy and relieved that she would now be away while William visited his mother, returning home every Monday afternoon when he had gone to school.

"Lawd honey, Ah sho does miss you an' Ah hates to think'er you dere slavin' all day Sunday sted'uh tending de services wid me an' William," Sara Lou greeted her when she came over to visit.

"Ah don't mind An' Sara 'sides it's 'bout time Ah earned my keep stead'uh livin' on you," Ruth smiled.

It wouldn't last long anyway, she thought, and tried to plan some way she could try and get work that would last all summer.

The Spring was with them at last. The green blooming things around them made them feel in accord with the joys of the season. Ruth's steps regained some of the elasticity they had lost.

The first week of April passed and the Monday for the Church Aid meeting that had been so sadly neglected, came around again.

Ruth was busy setting the chairs around in the dining room while Sara Lou supervised Luke's work in the field when looking up she saw Aunt Salisbury standing in the door.

"Lawd yuh sho scared me," she exclaimed laughing. "It was jes' as quiet an' heah Ah looks up an' you'se standin' dere lak uh ghost."

"Dis ain't no time for sounds nor words nuther, Ruth," Aunt Salisbury said grimly. "Ah done had uh bad dream las' night—on dat means death to dis house so Ah done fetched yuh dis charm to keep bad dreams from comin' true." And Aunt Salisbury solemnly held out the little bag which Ruth took grimly and promised to bury it under the front steps as directed. The shriveled-up old woman hobbled away grumbling to herself, her once tall, bony figure bent almost double, her jet-black face hardly visible beneath the numerous bandannas wrapped around her head.

The church aid sisters arrived early, anxious to hear if An' Sara had any news of interest to tell them, and were soon laughing and gossiping like a group of children. Sara Lou laughed and joked as she had before the dark days of Jim's imprisonment.

"Chillun," she said, "we jes' gotta live closer to
de Lawd den we'se been livin'. Ah jes' keeps uh
prayin' dat my boy'll git out uh dat prison an' Ah'm
sho God goin'ter answer my prayer in his own
time."

"Well, An' Sara, wid faith lak youse, God jes'
gotta heah yuh," Sally Ann agreed.

"An it'ud pay us all to have mo' faith den we'se
got," Martha Green said, casting a meaning look in
Sally's direction.

"Dere yuh go, Martha, sweepin' fo' somebody
else's door when de dirt is knee deep 'fo yo' own,"
Sally came back hotly.

"Now den sisters, less don't have no cross words,"
Sara Lou begged.

"You sho is right, An' Sara," Sadie Smith ap-
proved, looking with disgust at the two women, who
could never be together long without a battle of
words.

Ella Brown read the minutes of the last meeting
and plans were discussed for the coming big camp
meeting to be held at Calvary Church in which Sara
Lou was again taking an active part. Long after
the meeting was over and the women had gone home
to attend to their many duties, Sara Lou sat alone
thinking, wondering whether Owen Gordon's home-
coming would really mean her boy's release from
prison. He had been very good to her in the past
years, sharing with her a secret she had never di-
vulged to any other living soul. Through all the
years of her life he had befriended her but after all,
time and his trip might have changed him. At any
rate, she made up her mind she would pray and hope
and wait, and let the future take care of itself.

CHAPTER XX

All day Monday in Macon a steady downpour of misty rain had fallen. By afternoon the streets were covered with soft sticky mud. The air was close and murky.

William had spent a restless night and felt nervous and doubtful of the outcome of his examinations that were to begin that day. Contrary to his usual custom, he was bewildered and confused on the very subjects that during the term he had been so sure of. The buzz of voices irritated him and kept his mind wandering from his books. He had tried to study at home but his mother's information about Owen Gordon's return had upset him. School would be closing soon, and if Jim really was pardoned and returned to the farm, all the humiliation he felt he had endured before, would be heaped upon him again. He longed to get away from it all to some place where he could live his life like he pleased and not with his mother's expectant eyes upon him. He didn't want to be a preacher anyway, he decided. Thoughts of Slippery in the same prison with Jim and Ruth's reproachful eyes kept annoying him.

The teacher called his name several times before he realized he was again holding up the class, but at last the long April day was over. School was dismissed. He passed out of the room hardly seeing the smiling faces around him. Their cheery goodbyes were answered with an absent grunt.

He wanted to be alone. He hurried to the shop, forgetting that on the Saturday before he left for Byron, Cotton Eye had said:

"William, yuh don't know much 'bout dis kind 'uh work. An' even if yuh did, youse too busy in school to do it so why don't yuh leave me help you? Ah ain't got no job an' no place to stay an' if yuh lemme stay heah an' gimme 'nough to feed me, Ah'll take care uh dis place for yuh. Whut yuh say?"

And thinking it a good idea, he had consented, glad to be rid of the work he disliked.

Cotton Eye moved in and with him most of the gang from over at Daddy Jenks' whose place the law had closed because of Sugar Kid's murder. His back room had immediately been turned into a gambling joint. He profited by the few pennies cut from the games but he had promised himself he would not play. Gambling had already cost him too much trouble.

For several weeks things had been bad for him. Very little work came to the shop, and at home it was even worse. The money received from the cotton crop had been spent. The place had become run down and fences needed fixing. Nothing was the same as when Jim was there. His mother had not complained, but he knew by the scarcity of food she placed on the table, things were almost desperate.

As he stepped into the open door of the shop, his hat pulled low upon his eyes, the odor of frying bacon reminded him that he had not eaten all day.

"Come on in, boy, yuh jes' in time for dinner," Cotton Eye called.

He stood in the door uncertain.

"Stick yo' feet under de table an' try some uh dese taters an' fried bacon."

"I don't b'lieve I want anything to eat, Cotton Eye," he answered, not wanting Cotton Eye to know how hungry and miserable he felt.

"Say whut's de mattuh wid you anyhow, William? Yuh sho is in de dumps."

"There's nothing wrong with me. I'm just anxious about my examinations."

"Yeah, dat's whut comes uh folks tryin' to learn all dere is in books. It jes' causes yuh double worry. Look'er me. Ah jes' takes things easy. Ain't got uh care in de world. Jes' come day—go day."

"I wish I was like that, Cotton, but there's always something insider me planning and planning. I jes' can't help it."

"Well folks don't git nowhar plannin'. De plans allers goes wrong. Ah'm jes' gointer take it easy an' let life take care uh me. Come on sit down an' eat. Whut yuh needs is vittels."

William drew a box to the table and ate the hot food with relish, washing it down with a strong cup of black coffee. After the meal, the dirty dishes were stuck away in a pan and a game of cards started, as the gang one by one dropped in and sprawled around on boxes and broken chairs, smoking and talking.

For a while William looked on. Then put on his coat and left the shop, saying to Cotton Eye, as he walked out of the door:

"I won't be back today. I've got some studying to do at home."

"Sho is too bad dat boy ain't white. It beats all

how he kin put on airs when he gits ready," Red
Shirt commented, as he walked away.

"Dat's de trouble. He ain't nuther one thing
nor de other an' he's always 'twix' an' between in
his mind. Jes' studyin' an' plannin' to 'stonish de
world some day wid his learnin' an' sometime
wantin' to give it all up an' jes' be nacherel. Dat's
how he 'pears to me," Snake declared with a shake
of his bullet-shaped head.

Cotton Eye looked up from the hand he was laboriously trying to make win him a few pennies. He
was proud of the fact that he was the only one of
the boys that knew William's history and said:

"It's dat boy's Ma dat keeps him all upsot wantin'
him to be uh preacher an' him not wantin' to be
kaise it jes' ain't in 'im but dat's de way wid de
whole family. Dey allers wanted to be somethin'
dey wasn't. Den at'ter dey all had done borned
half white bastards, dey'd marry some preacher
man an' put on mo' airs den de law allows. His
grandma done it an' den his ma followed suit.
Dey's uh mess."

"Who's dis man Gordon whut William's brother
Jim is in de gang for robbin'?" Snake asked.

"He's de finest white man whut ever lived. He
sho is done lots for An' Sara, William's Ma.
'Course de folks says dat his son was William's Pa.
Ah don't know nothin' 'bout dat but Ah does know
he mighty good to her," Cotton Eye explained.

"Dere's somethin' funny 'bout de whole thing,"
Snake remarked.

Cotton Eye turned to look up and down at Snake,
who was seated behind him before he replied: "You
bet yo' life dere is. But don't yuh try to figure it

out kaise it's way over us nigguh's heads an' al'lers
will be."

Conversation turned to other subjects as the boys
played on, and William sat at Sissy's house trying
to work out some of his most difficult problems. It
was near midnight when Sissy and her latest man
friend came home much the worse for moonshine.
Entering she spied William deeply absorbed in his
studies.

"See dere, whut smart folks Ah'se got," she said
turning to her companion.

"Dere ain't nothin' smart 'bout folks worryin'
dey heads night an' day wid uh pile uh books. Ah
calls dat dumb. When deys smart dey does lak Ah
does—leave dem books for de white folks to worry
over," he grinned.

William laughed and began gathering up his
books. Sissy's men were a joke with him. They
lasted as long as they pleased her fancy. When she
tired of them, they were kicked out and she was
free to choose another. As she often remarked,
"They fit like a loose garment." William looked
at her standing in the door unsteadily, her tall
angular form filling the doorway, her straight
features and high cheek bones set in a face of rich
brown, her straight long black hair wound in a knot
at the nape of her neck, making her look more Indian than negress which fitted her heathen and utter
disregard for principle.

Swaying over to his side, she placed her hand
affectionately on his arm, and asked:

"Does yuh want me to fix yuh some vittels,
William?"

"No, Sissy. I think I'll go to bed. I'm not hungry," he answered, starting to his room.

"Dat's right, boy. Stop bustin' yo' head open wid dem books," her man advised.

"Thanks I will," William replied, closing the door behind him.

Until late that night he could hear Sissy and her man arguing about his learning. Finally all was quiet, and he slept.

When he awoke Sissy had cooked breakfast and was waiting for him to come to eat. As they were seated at the table, she talked of the good time she had had the night before.

"Lawd, dat man sho is de limit when it comes to makin' uh body laugh," she chuckled.

"He's a brand new one, ain't he, Sissy?" William asked.

"He's kind uh new. Ah had him 'bout three weeks now but Ah b'lieve he's awrite. Ah might settle down to jes' him ef'fen he does good as he been doin'," she answered thoughtfully.

"That will be big news," William laughed.

"Sho will but ef'fen he carries on any, dere's mo' whar he comed from an' Ah'm de gal whut'll send him on his way."

"Well, let's hope you won't have to," William said, rising and hurrying off to school, feeling better than he had for several days.

The examinations did not prove such a problem after all and William hurried to the shop after school, feeling that his papers would bring good marks. Cotton Eye met him outside the door of the shop, where he had been eagerly watching for him.

"William, ole man Hopkins from out Byron done been heah lookin' for yuh. He say yo' folks done say for you to come home at once," he greeted.

"How come?" William asked anxiously.

"Ah don't know. He gone to de store to git some seed and say for yuh to be ready byance de time he gits back."

"How long ago was he here?"

"Not so long. While you'se waitin' come on in an' eat."

"No thanks. I'm too worried now for anything. Ma may be sick."

"Don't git all excited. It ain't nothin' serious. Ah don't b'lieve. Dere he comes now," Cotton Eye exclaimed, as a wagon with a bent form came in sight.

Old man Hopkins, his dried up brown face looking more like a mummy than a human being, stopped at the curb and William rushed forward.

"Is dere anything wrong with Ma?" he asked eagerly.

"Well, dere is an' den agin, dere ain't. Dat is 'cordin' to how yuh looks at it."

"Why does she want me to come home, Uncle Hiram?" William persisted.

"Yuh bettuh come on out dere an' see. Git in. My ole 'oman done tole me to fetch her uh box uh railroad snuff. Ah'm gonna git it, den Ah'll be ready," Hiram Hopkins stated, starting to climb down from the wagon.

"Wait'er minute. I'll get it for you," William interposed quickly. "You'll take too long," and William bought the snuff in the little dingy grocery store near his shop and climbed into the wagon.

All the way to Byron he tried to get information from Hiram as to why he had been sent for so hurriedly but each time he evaded the subject, and William bade him goodbye at his gate as much in the dark as when he left Macon.

William rushed into the house. There was no one downstairs but at the head of the stairs he was met by Ruth coming out of his mother's room, her eyes red with weeping. He grasped her arm anxiously.

"What's the matter with Ma?" he asked, a frightened sob catching in his throat.

She drew him into his room and closed the door softly before answering.

"An' Sara is mighty sick, William. Doctor Clarke jes' left an' he say he gonna be back toreckly," she explained between sobs.

"What's the matter with her, Ruth?"

"Well, day 'fore yistiddy she was out tryin' to fix de fence 'round back uh de field an' she gits all tired an' worn out. Den she 'sides she'ud walk down to de post office to see if dere was any mo' mail from Mr. Gordon. Ah begged her not to go kaise uh storm was comin' up but she went anyhow, an' comin' back, she got wringin' wet. Ah tried to git her to take off her wet clothes but right den somebody comed by an' sayd dat Deacon Simmons was dyin', an' she lites right out an' stays wid him ontell almost midnight in dem wet clothes, an' when she comed home, de chills set in an' dis morning she was out'er her head wid fever."

"Oh Lawd!" William groaned.

"Doctor Clarke sayd if she was strong lak she

use'ter be, dere wouldn't be much danger but she
done grieved so inside an' ain't eat right in so long,
he 'fraid it's serious. She's restin' right now. He
gived her something to keep her quiet."

But William was gone. He stood looking down
on his mother, who in her delirium, tossed and
called his name. All through the long night he sat
motionless, moving only when some of the neighbors
asked him to so that they could attend the sick
woman.

Doctor Clarke had returned and found her worse,
her fever rising rapidly, and held out scant hope to
the distracted man who, as he sat and watched at
his mother's bedside, blamed himself for her illness. His lies and sins had brought about her illness and might cause her death. Remorse ate at
his heart. He had sent Jim away to prison—Jim,
who slaved about the place, saving her steps and
worry. A battle raged within him. A silent prayer
trembled upon his lips, asking God to spare her
life. Repentance filled his soul, as he pleaded with
the Lord for a chance to right the wrong he had
done. He felt sick and ashamed of the past. If
she lived, he would tell her all and on his knees beg
forgiveness—he promised himself. Quietly he
slipped from the room just after midnight, and
wandered into the dark, silent woods beyond the
farm. Driven relentlessly on and on by the tumult
of black despair that engulfed his wretched soul.

Early the next morning Ella's husband, Jerimah
and the minister found him on his knees, his body
bent double until his head rested upon the damp
ground, moaning and praying, as tears streamed

down his cheeks. They lifted him to his feet and
led him back to the house, up to his room, where he
lay all morning. The soft voices of the church aid
sisters' songs finally brought soothing sleep to his
tortured brain.

CHAPTER XXI

Six months of long, hard, drab days of toil in sun
and rain passed slowly for Jim, shut away from the
things he had always loved.

May, the most beautiful month of the year,
brought little cheer to the boy, who had lived the
happy-go-lucky outdoor life of the farm. Watching
flowers, birds and green things grow and breathing
in the fresh fragrant air of the flat fertile fields had
been his very life. Came times when he felt he
could not endure another day, the torture of the
close smelly prison, the grumbling, grouchy companions that surrounded him, but each morning
found him in his usual place ready to start another
day of work and struggle.

Slippery's incarceration had not surprised him.
He wondered how he had escaped as long as he had.
He had never liked Slippery and had resented his
visits to his home, and the thought of having to
work day by day beside the man he felt sure was
the cause of his imprisonment, maddened him. Not
that he altogether blamed Slippery. William had
taken him in, sick and penniless, for just the purpose he had later used him for.

As day after day they worked along the road, a
feeling of pity filled his heart for the man, who was
dying with consumption. Sometimes he was hardly
able to move from place to place, but was driven
on by the guards who disliked his stubborn, sullen
ways.

Jim tried to ease over to him and help in some way to lighten his work but the guard checked him and sent him to the further side of the road.

"Hey, you lazy red nigger, get to work and quit stalling," Jim heard the guard call to Slippery as he moved away. Looking back, he saw Slippery knocked to the ground.

"Now Carter, you kin get him 'way from heah," the guard called.

A half hour later, Slippery opened his eyes. Jim was kneeling beside him, bathing his head. He looked up stunned.

"How's yuh feelin' now, Slippery?" Jim asked kindly.

"Ah'm awrite," he answered gruffly turning his head away.

That night Jim lay awake thinking of the day of horror that had just passed. It made his blood boil to think anyone could so cruelly strike a dying man. He was puzzled as to why Slippery had taken the attitude he had towards him. He seemed friendly with all the other prisoners, but he scarcely spoke to him and tried to avoid him at every turn. He fell asleep thinking of his mother and Ruth and dreamed that Slippery and William with long whips, one on each arm, were chasing him towards a deep ravine filled with long, wriggling snakes. He awoke, weak and perspiring.

It was Sunday and many visitors would visit the prison. Almost everyone would have a relative or friend who would call except Slippery. No one during the few months he had been in prison had come to see him. William had made one joint visit to him and Jim—but that was all. Slippery did not

seem to care, and as he often expressed himself,
"Ah'se glad dere ain't nobody to come heah moanin'
over me. Dey'd make me sick'er den Ah ez."

"But ain't you got no folks uh tall?" someone had
asked.

"None dat knows whar Ah is or would miss me
if Ah was planted," he answered with no trace of
regret in his voice.

Jim wondered as he glanced at him, lying on his
bunk gasping for breath whether there had ever
been anyone who had cared for him. The guard
brought his reveries to an end. His visitors had
arrived. He rose quickly and followed him to the
room where they were waiting. He noted with a
sinking heart that his mother was not with Ruth and
the preacher, Reverend Hooper.

"Ah'm sorry, Jim, but An' Sara ain't comin'.
She ain't feelin' so well," Ruth explained. "William
done stayed home wid'er so de Rev. heah comed
'long wid me."

"Howdee Jim," Reverend Hooper greeted cheer-
ily.

"Ah'm all right, Rev. It was mighty good 'er
you to come out heah wid Ruth but Ah hopes Ma
ain't serious," he continued, turning to Ruth, who
avoided his eyes as she answered.

"No, she's jes' feelin' kind uh down, but Ah got
good news for yuh, Jim. She done hearn from Mr.
Gordon an' he'll be home soon an' goin'ter git you
out uh heah."

"Dat's good news, sho 'nough. Ef'fen he jes'
don't b'lieve Ah stole dat money an' tried to steal
his jewelry," Jim remarked hopelessly.

"You knows Mr. Gordon knows you bettah den

dat an' he's de smartest lawyer dat ever was. An'
Sara says dat he kin git yuh right out," Ruth replied
earnestly.

"Now ain't dat somethin' to be thankful for,
Jim?" Reverend Hooper asked.

"Yeah, it sho' is, but Ah ain't gointer git too
thankful ontell it done happens," Jim insisted.

For the rest of the visit Ruth talked cheerfully
about the farm and related the gossip of the settlement, careful to make no mention of William. Ella
had a new baby girl, and one of the Jones' girls had
gotten into trouble, and the man had refused to
marry her.

They laughed heartily, at the picture she vividly
portrayed of the girl's father roaming around with
his double barrel shot gun under his arm, looking
for the guilty man to make him marry her.

Sally Ann had married the Reverend Hanson,
who pastored a church in a small village a few
miles from Byron and had gone there to live, returning every few days to visit Martha Green and
have their usual verbal battle.

For the first time since his imprisonment Jim
laughed and talked unrestrainedly, and enjoyed
their visit which came to an end too soon. Ruth
was gone before he realized it. He had had no opportunity to ask her how she and William were getting along or if she had wanted to break off their
engagement, as William had led him to think.

William had always gotten what he wanted in
the past, he thought bitterly, and there was no doubt
he had succeeded in getting Ruth's consent to marry
him.

A short time later, as he sat on the side of his

bunk thinking of the happy times he and Ruth had enjoyed at home, one of the guards called him to assist in moving Slippery, who had grown worse, to another part of the camp. After they had made him comfortable and Jim turned to go, Slippery stirred and opened his eyes. He asked in a voice scarcely louder than a whisper.

"Will you pray for me, Jim?"

"Ef'fen Mr. Myers say Ah kin. Ah'll do my best," Jim replied, turning to the guard standing nearby.

"Go uh head, Jim. Prayers ain't goin'ter hurt him nohow, Ah reckon," the guard consented.

And Jim, frightened and bewildered, knelt beside the cot, and for the first time in his life, prayed aloud. The guard had walked to the other side of the room, and stood waiting to take Jim back to his side of the prison. As he started to rise, Slippery touched his arm and Jim leaned closer to hear what he wanted to say.

"Ah'm goin'ter git you out 'uh heah, Jim. Me an' William done dat stealin' an' Ah'm goin'ter tell 'um so," he whispered.

"For God's sake, don't do it, Slippery. It'ud kill Ma. Promise me yuh won't never tell," Jim pleaded, glancing fugitively to where the guard stood looking out of the window.

Slippery looked up at him unable to understand his wanting to turn down a chance of getting out of prison. Slowly, with great effort, he tried to raise himself. He would call the guard and tell him anyway. He opened his mouth to speak, but a long stream of blood gushed forth. He fell back, weak and exhausted.

Jim was hustled quickly back to his place, and through the long night he lay awake, his heart filled with the fear of Slippery's reviving and telling the guard the story of his brother's guilt—the revelation of which would bring new sorrow to his mother.

* * *

Sara Lou was again able to come downstairs and watch Luke work in the field, planting and caring for the farm, but for two weeks she had hung between life and death. William, his ambitions and struggles forgotten, had scarcely left her bedside, turning over in his mind plans of the many ways he intended telling her the sins he had committed, which had brought sorrow to their home and begging her forgiveness so that he could start all over with a clear conscience to live a better life. As days went by, he put it off until she was entirely recovered.

Sara Lou's thoughts were as usual for his welfare.

"Lawd, William, yuh ain't goin'ter finish school dis year effen yuh don't git back to Macon," she moaned.

"I ain't worryin' 'bout school, Ma, long as you needs me," he assured her, patting her shoulder tenderly.

Several days later he left for Macon, determined when he next visited home, he would without hesitation tell her everything. During the few weeks before commencement, he worked hard, and seldom went near Daddy Jenks' or saw the old gang. Each week, he received a letter from Ethel, but they went unanswered. He was through with all of that! She was out of his life forever, he told himself.

But in that particular, he was mistaken, for Ethel's return to Chicago had been met with little enthusiasm from her brother, a lawyer and one of the city's most respected citizens. Ethel had disgraced him in the past, and he did not try to hide his annoyance at her return to disgrace him again, and told her so in no gentle manner. For a while, the girl was on her guard and tried to do right but years of wild living and her love for liquor soon drew her back to her old South side haunts and before a month had passed, she was in jail again. Her brother paid her fine and demanded that she leave Chicago but Ethel, older and wiser, made her demands also that he send her money each week, if he wanted her to stay away from Chicago. In the end, he agreed and Ethel boarded a train for Atlanta deciding that after all, her trip had done some good. William had not written her, but she was determined that being in Atlanta where he would be attending school during the next winter, she would make him renew his friendship with her.

On reaching Atlanta, she wrote him again, but receiving no answer from her letter, she became blue and disappointed, and went on one of her prolonged sprees, laying for days in a drunken stupor. A thought formed in her mind. It would be good to steal into Macon and demand a show down with him, and she boarded a train immediately for Macon.

Daddy Jenks, who was again running his place

at full swing, was surprised when she swaggered in that night.

"Look'er heah gal, yuh sho' is doing uh dangerous thing comin' back heah when de white folks done tole yuh to stay 'way," he said.

"But dey ain't goin'ter know Ah'se back less'en some uh you nigguhs tell 'em," Ethel sneered.

"Far as Ah'm concerned, dey ain't goin'ter know but Ah kain't swear for de rest uh de boys dat hangs out heah," Daddy assured her.

But she got her old room back and her meals sent to her room each day. William heard of her return with grave misgivings. He had sincerely hoped she had passed out of his life forever. Her return threatened to again ensnare him into the life he was trying to put behind him.

He stayed away from Daddy Jenks, and even his own shop, but Ethel, who had been good to Sissy when she was laid up badly cut, became a welcome visitor at her home and little by little wormed her way back into William's life.

As soon as school closed, he hurried to Byron, promising to run into town to see her often—a promise he failed to keep so Ethel ranted to Daddy Jenks of how she would get even with William for all she had suffered through their sordid love affair.

"Gal, why don't yuh leave dat boy uh alone? He don't want to be mixed up wid you, nohow," was all the consolation he gave her.

"He done took uh mighty long time to find dat out," Ethel would reply, and for days would drink, brood and plan.

William had not graduated, as he had hoped. Due to the many weeks he missed from his studies, he would have to spend another winter in Macon, but he made up his mind that for the present he would just be a farmer and show his mother he could take care of the place, with Luke's help. He threw himself into caring for and building up the farm, which had become a wreck since Jim's imprisonment.

Everybody was busy and more contented than they had been for months. The garden was again doing nicely. Jim's flowers of myriad colors were again blooming and filling the air with their sweet fragrance. Even his old dog Towser showed an agility in accordance with the Spring lightness which belied his eight years of dog life.

Byron was beautiful with its velvet-like green grass in which nestled wild pansies and violets. The smell of young pines filled the air with a clean sweetness, as the busy farmers tilled their soil, stopping in the heat of the day to sprawl beneath the welcome shade of trees.

Sara Lou, a hopeful smile illuminating her face, moved about, her favorite song on her lips. Owen Gordon's expectant return was a ray of light in her troubled life. To her mind, he had only to say the word and Jim would walk out of the chain gang free.

Ruth was again smiling and cheerful and working around the house and in the field from sun up to dusk. Even William's presence did not upset her as it had. She had become accustomed to having him to talk with evenings. When the work was done at night the family sat out on the front porch to blow a spell and sing spirituals again.

A month had passed since Mr. Gordon had written and at times Sara Lou would think with a sinking heart that perhaps after all, he had decided to prolong his stay abroad. On occasions when she passed his plantation, the sight of its dilapidated condition made her heart sick. The house had been nailed up, but grass and weeds over-ran the place.

"Po' Mr. Gordon," she would mumble. "He sot so much store by his orchard. Now look at it— weeds an' eve'ythin' jes' chokin' dem trees."

Tears would burn her eyes, as she remembered how her husband, John, and later her son, Jim, had worked so hard to make his the finest orchard around the country.

"My Jim would'uh been heah now keepin' dat place spick an' span ef'fen some low life skunkin' thief didn't git 'im in prison."

Trudging on, the many kind deeds Owen Gordon had done for her family and herself would fill her mind, and her confidence thus restored in his helping Jim to freedom, would make her happy and content to wait.

She had wanted to visit Jim, but her illness had left her weak and emaciated. She did not want him to see her that way as she felt sure it would worry and upset him. Ruth's trips to the prison always brought her the news of Jim's cheerfulness, and with that she had to be content.

William had accompanied Ruth on her last visit there and had returned home silent and morose. His mother wondered what had happened to worry him, but William had told her nothing. He had long ago made up his mind that his confessing to her the many slips he had made, during his two years in Macon could not do any good, and would only worry her. The information he received at the prison concerning Slippery's condition frightened him. For days the sick man had laid in a coma, but if at any time he revived, William felt sure he would tell the truth about the robbery and he would be made to suffer for his deed after all. He fervently prayed that Slippery would die before regaining consciousness and trembled every time he saw Marshall Bailey approaching the house. His mother noticed his agitation, but said nothing, trying in every way to dispell whatever there was worrying him with thoughtful kindness, which like coals of fire, burned into his soul.

CHAPTER XXII

It was a beautiful morning early in June when Owen Gordon stepped from the pullman car to the station platform in Macon. Macon had not changed much during the year he had spent abroad. After all, it was good to be home again.

He removed his light felt hat and ran his hand slowly over his fast, thinning gray hair that had once been a luxuriant dark brown. His face round and smooth, showed little signs of his sixty odd years.

An anxious porter ran forward to assist him with his bags. Yes, it was the same old darky, who had carried his bags when he went away. With a merry twinkle in his eyes he pressed a dollar bill into his wrinkled black hand. Old Sam nearly dropped the bags when he saw the bill and looking up to see who the liberal white man was, who could afford to give him a whole dollar, he recognized Owen Gordon.

"Lawdy mussy, if it ain't Mr. Gordon hisseff!" he exclaimed. "Ah sho is glad to see yuh, boss."

"Glad to see me or the bill, Sam?"

"No, suh! Ah's dat glad to see yuh—ah 'clare Ah is."

"All right, Sam. See how quickly you can get me a taxi then," Gordon smiled.

"Yess suh. Thank yuh, suh. Ah gits one 'fo yuh kin say scat," Sam replied, gesticulating wildly to a passing taxi.

Owen Gordon leaned back meditatively, as he rode to one of the Macon's prominent hotels. There was business he would have to attend to before going out to Byron. The year he had spent in Europe passed pleasantly through his mind. He had been sick and almost hopeless during the few days he had spent in New York consulting specialists about the ailment that had worried him for years. They had advised a trip abroad and complete rest, and he had continued his journey. His sojourn in London had lasted only long enough to attend to business, and to leave strict orders with his solicitors that no mail from the United States be forwarded to him. He wanted to be free to wander and rest. He smiled as he thought of the peaceful weeks spent in Northern France followed by a month in Switzerland— happy weeks near the Alps, and the ideal spot he had finally found in Southern Italy, where the climate and quiet peace had restored his health and peace of mind. He had spent the greater part of the year there, eating plain, wholesome food, dressing simply and spending most of his time out-of-doors.

His physician had finally pronounced him cured, and he had taken the first boat home, glad to be back in the quiet of his Byron home, where his plans to live peacefully with Sara Lou to take care of his house and Jim Carter to look after his orchard, stretched before him pleasantly.

On reaching London, Sara Lou's letter had given him quite a shock. There was no doubt in his mind of Jim's innocence and that he had been made the victim of some smart criminal. He made up his

mind that Jim would at least get another chance to
prove his innocence, as he would do all he could to
have the guilty party brought to justice.

At his hotel he unexpectedly ran into Richard
Hayden, an old friend and associate.

"Gordon, you're the very man I've been wanting
to see. When did you get in town?" the lawyer
asked in greeting.

"Just arrived this morning, Hayden."

"I guess you've heard about the little affair out
at your place?"

"Yes, Sara Lou wrote me. Her boy's in prison."

"That's what I want to talk with you about, Owen.
That boy got the rawest deal I've ever seen. I defended him and Judge Graham convicted him in his
mind before a witness was heard. Why, the boy
knows no more about that money being stolen than
I do. I thought at first he was trying to shield somebody but I found out I was wrong. He's been rail-
roaded to the chain gang simply because you left
him in charge of your place when some of those
Byron crackers thought they should have had the
job."

Owen Gordon listened attentively to the lawyer's
lcng explanation, his eyes studying the point of his
shoes, but his mind drawing a mental picture of the
trial that had sent Jim away for five years' hard
labor. When he spoke, he had made up his mind
as to what would be the best move to make under
the circumstances.

"Think I'll be calling on Graham day after tomorrow," he said simply.

Richard Hayden told him all the details of the
trial adding his belief that the thief could be found

if a plan he had worked out came through as he
expected, and before they parted, a meeting a few
days later had been arranged.

Owen spent several days quietly at home in Byron.
Sara Lou had her hands full trying to set the house
to rights as she expressed it, and preparing his
meals. They talked a great deal about Jim and
Owen made a few round about inquiries concerning
William's activities during the past winter. Sara
Lou glowed with pleasure, as she told him how
hard he had studied, what a wonderful son he was,
and her plans for his future.

Then one afternoon, he visited Judge Graham.
It was not until after they had dined and talked of
old times that Owen mentioned Jim's case and explained his belief of the boy's innocence.

"Innocent, bosh! A jury of twelve men found
him guilty, didn't they? And Ah knows he's guilty.
It's jes' in niggers to steal," the Judge exploded
hotly.

"That's just it, Graham. You tried the boy only
looking at it from the standpoint of his color, but I
know him. He's as honest as any white man alive!
His father before him worked for me twenty years
and was as straight as a string. His grandmother,
his mother and the whole mess of 'em have always
been around my house and they are all honest. I'm
gonna get that boy out of the chain gang. He'd
never been there had I been home," Owen ended
convincingly.

"And if you'd left a decent white man in charge'er
your place, there wouldn't have been a robbery,"
the Judge declared.

"It's my business who I leave in charge of my

place, but I'm gonna find out what you failed to
find—who really robbed my safe."

"Go 'er head! Personally, I'm not interested.
I ain't no nigger lover an' it don't matter to me
what becomes of 'em."

Owen Gordon's eyes flashed angrily, as he turned
to the Judge.

"Now you listen to me, Graham, your father and
I were partners. He died a real Southern gentle-
man and out of respect for him, I'll take what
you're insinuating, but don't you forget that I am
every inch a white man, the same as you are, but
unlike you, I want to see everybody get justice.
Even if Jim was found in my house with my jewelry
in his pocket, the money taken from my safe he had
put there, and had he wanted to, he could have kept
it. He knew that, and as for that old jewelry, he
had had every opportunity to take it for the past
four years, had he wanted to. I've owned more
niggers than anyone else around here, but I've never
been accused of being unjust to 'em or of loving 'em
either."

"I'm sorry, Gordon. Maybe I have been too
hasty in my words," the Judge apologized.

Memories of indiscretions of his own youth which
had somehow never been discovered, passed through
his mind and shamed his declarations of hatred of
negroes. They parted good friends and he decided
that although he would do nothing to help him get
Jim pardoned, he would do nothing to hinder it.

A few days later when Gordon again conferred
with Hayden he was surprised to find how closely
the lawyer had checked up on William's activities
right after the robbery.

"You don't suspect William, do you Hayden?"
he asked looking at him quickly, a startled expression in his eyes.

Something in his voice brought back to the lawyer's mind bits of gossip he had heard concerning
Gordon's son Franklyn at William's birth. He
answered cautiously.

"Well no, but a nigger called Slippery that
worked around his shop, has since been sent up for
murder and I've been checking up on his movements.
The night of the robbery he could have easily
slipped out to Byron from Spring Valley between
the time he was seen in a game there, and returned."

"Maybe you're right, but who is he in the mean-
time?"

"An all around bad character. He visited the
Carter home several times, and I've got a fellow
over at the shop now trying to find out something
about his past."

"Who've you got there?"

"They call him Cotton Eye."

"Yes, I know him. He's a slick thief—will steal
anything he can lay hands on, was born and raised
in Byron. Have him here tomorrow morning and
we'll question him," Gordon said in parting.

Early the next morning a frightened Cotton Eye
was ushered into the office where Owen Gordon
and Hayden sat.

"There ain't nothing against you this time, Cotton
Eye. Mr. Hayden and I want some information
about this fellow Slippery," Gordon greeted to put
him at ease.

"Ah ain't found out nothin' 'bout him 'ceptin' dat
he comed from Chicago an' dat his fust name is

Jessie. A gal named Ethel Myers done tole me dat," Cotton Eye answered sheepishly.

"That's good. I've got a friend in Chicago who's one of the best detectives in the country. I'll get him on the wire and in a few days we'll know all there is to know about this Slippery," Gordon commented.

"By the way, Cotton Eye, where is this Ethel Myers you spoke of, now?" Lawyer Hayden asked, turning to Cotton Eye, who was edging towards the door eager to get away, before Owen Gordon remembered. His last encounter with him had been in court where he was being tried for stealing one of his best hogs.

"She puttin' up at Daddy Jenks' when she heah," he answered hastily.

"You can go now, Cotton Eye. Keep your eyes open and if you find out anything else, let Hayden or I know," Gordon said dismissing him and pressing a five dollar bill into his hand. He pocketed the bill and backed, grinning, out of the door.

Their call to Chicago brought plenty of information concerning Slippery's checkered past and Lawyer Hayden and Owen Gordon pinned their hope of getting Jim out of prison on Slippery's forced confession, if he really did do the robbery.

A few days later with the information in their briefcases, they visited the chain gang for an interview with their suspect. But on arrival, to their disappointment, they found they were a day too late. Slippery had died during the night without making a statement of any kind that would in any way help their case.

CHAPTER XXIII

Although Owen Gordon and Lawyer Hayden tried in every way to get Jim's case before the Board of Pardons during the next few months, it was never brought up, and Jim, always a model prisoner, resigned himself to serve his alloted time.

Sara Lou aged rapidly when the realization that Owen Gordon, the best and smartest man on earth to her mind, was powerless before the merciless men who held Jim's freedom in their hands.

William finished school that winter and came home happily displaying his diploma. Sara Lou was happy and to add to her good fortune, Owen Gordon finally got the board to consider Jim's case.

She would not allow herself to hope too much for fear of again being disappointed but went about her work with a constant prayer on her lips for Jim's eventual release.

The Winter had been made miserable for Ruth. William's constant pleas and protestations of love had worried the tenderhearted girl.

Sara Lou had also unwittingly added to her dilemna as afternoons when they sat sewing, she too had added her plea for William.

"Yuh know, Ruth," she had said one evening, "Ah ain't never said nuthin' to you, 'bout my boys seein' dey both loves yuh and Ah loves yuh too, but Ah kind uh scared for my William goin' to dat Atlanta. If he'd up an' marry de wrong kind uh woman it 'ud ruin his life kaise he allers is been kind uh restless an' it'ud break my heart. You is de only purson dat kin save him kaise wid you for his wife, he'ud be settled an' happy."

Ruth had made no answer. Sara Lou's tired eyes filled with tears had touched her heart as William's pleas had never done. She loved her and could not bear the thought of the sorrow that would come into her life if William disappointed her.

That evening she had slipped away to sit under her hickory nut tree and prayed for strength to do the right thing, but as the weeks wore on, her resistance had become weaker until finally to please and comfort his mother, she had promised to marry William before he entered college.

And now with the knowledge of Jim, perhaps being pardoned, and at home again; she wondered how she would ever be able to face him now that she was engaged to William.

But none of their problems worried William. His first scare of Owen Gordon's finding out he had his safe robbed over, he had become his old confident self, had learned much about farming, even taking over Jim's work in the Gordon Orchard, becoming very friendly with—Owen Gordon whom he had always thought disliked him. There had been times when his restless nature had cried out against the monotony of the dull drab life of the farm and times when he had longed for the soft, sensual caresses Ethel had lavished so freely. But he had fought hard against his passions and prayed for strength to overcome them, spending most of his time in church. He had become a senior Deacon, and in the pastor's absence, conducted the services.

It was a late afternoon in June. Sara Lou wiped

her hands on her apron, as she hurried around the
house in answer to Gordon's call from the gate.

"I just got a letter from Hayden, Sara," he
greeted, "and he says the Board has signed Jim's
pardon."

"Lawdy, Mr. Gordon, my prayers done been
answered! Oh my Lawd!" she cried, tears of joy
running down her cheeks.

"Well, you can look for him any day now," he
called; riding away quickly, keenly touched by her
overwhelming joy.

The news spread over Byron by night causing
much joy among Sara Lou's friends. A special
meeting of thanksgiving at the Calvary Church was
called for Sunday, and everybody in the little village
turned out to show their sympathy for the best
loved family among them—singing, praying and
shouting the whole afternoon.

"We sho' is got tuh thank God, for dis blessing,"
Martha Green commented as she and Sally Ann,
who was visiting her, walked home from the meeting.

"Yeah, an' we got to thank dat Mr. Gordon some
too," Sally Ann remarked dryly.

"Dat's jes' lak yuh, Sally Ann, tryin' to take some
uh de credit from de Lawd," Martha retorted.

"Ah ain't tryin' to take de credit from God, but
dat's uh white man and de way he done worked to
git Jim out, yuh'uh thought he was his blood kin,"
Sally came back.

"You aught'er know kaise God ain't had nothin'
to do wid you gittin' dat Reverend Hanson for yo'

husband. Dat was An' Salisbury's mojo' dat you used on him," Martha laughed.

"Ah ain't used no mojo but whut God gine me. It's too bad you don't try usin' some to git Slack Henderson dat's been hangin' 'roun' yuh for de lass six years," Sally hinted.

Aunt Salisbury's overtaking them, ended what would have been a heated argument and the conversation turned to other things, for they all feared Aunt Salisbury whose charms were supposed to make snakes and lizards crawl about under the skin of her victims often causing their death.

Ruth still loved Jim and realized it would be difficult for her to face him. She was unhappy as the days passed, watching Sara Lou working around the house preparing little things for Jim's return. She realized her only escape from the situation she found herself facing would be to run away. Mrs. Carmicheil had asked her to go with the family to Valdosta. She would go. It would only be for a few months, but it would afford her time to think clearly away from the overwhelming influence of William's love-making.

But trouble was brewing for William from another source. Ethel, who had seen him seldom since his graduation, had not given up hopes of having him again as her lover. She was now living in Atlanta and had managed trips to Macon where he had at times joined her for a few days. It was on one of these trips he told her of his approaching marriage and firmly dismissed her from his life, but it was not her idea to let it remain so. She wrote him again and again, begging him to come to Macon, but her letters remained unanswered. He did not show up.

After a night of hard drinking, she borrowed Daddy Jenks' car and with Kongo driving, set out for Byron. During the seventeen miles ride, she drank frequently from the flask of corn whiskey she carried, plying Kongo with big drinks at intervals. Late that afternoon the car was parked at the back of the Carter cotton field.

William's mother and Ruth had gone to spend the afternoon with Ella and William, left alone, planned a quiet few hours' reading. Comfortably seating himself in a large chair with his book resting on his knees, his thoughts drifted to the events of the past few years.

His mother standing at the fork of the road, as if uncertain about leaving him alone, brought an indulgent smile to his lips.

"Poor Ma. She makes me feel like a baby the way she worries and fusses over me," he mused sinking into the depths of his chair and brushing an inquisitive fly away from his face.

The cool afternoon breeze enveloped him like a curtain. Far out in the field he could hear the faint droning of bees and a bird's shrill call. The tall stalks of corn growing near the house waved to him lazily. A drowsy feeling stole over him, his eyelids felt like iron pressing down—down. His hands relaxed and the book slid to the floor as he dozed. He had slept almost an hour when a hand shaking him and a persistent voice calling his name, awakened him. He opened his eyes slowly and rubbed them in an effort to dispel the drowsiness that clung to them, making it hard to realize that Ethel, who stood looking down upon him, was not an unpleasant dream.

"Yeah, it's me in de flesh an' not uh ghost," she said stepping back unsteadily.

"What're you doin' here, Ethel?" William asked realizing that she was drunk, and would be hard to handle in that condition.

"Ah'm heah cause Ah'm fool 'nough to still love you and wanted to see you," she answered shortly.

"But I asked you never to come to my home," William said angrily.

"Ah know yuh did but ah ain't payin' dat no 'tention," Ethel laughed harshly.

"Now that you're here, what do you want?"

"Ah want you to go to Macon wid me."

"And I say I'm not going."

"Well, in dat case, Ah'll stay rite heah an' meet you' Ma an' dat country wench, you goin' ter marry an' tell 'em 'bout us an' lots'uh other things yuh might not want 'em to hear."

"You can't scare me, Ethel, into doing anything I don't want to do. You should know that so get outer here this minute," William retorted, advancing threateningly towards her.

Ethel threw her head back and laughed heartily, and when her laughter died, said coolly:

"Ah ain't goin'ter budge uh God damn step less'en you go wid me, William, an' when Ah gits through tellin' yo' folks whut Ah knows 'bout you, dey'll drive you out lak uh dog—you damn gamblin', lying, cheatin', yaller bastard."

Her voice rose higher and higher as anger and

whiskey swayed her emotions, frightening William
to the extent that he would have done anything—
even murder to get her away from his home. He
decided there was nothing to do but go with her, if
only a short distance from the house, and get rid of
her and come back. Placing his hand on her arm,
he said calmly:

"There's no need'er carryin' on like that, Ethel.
I'll go to Macon with you. Wait till I leave a note
for Ma."

A few moments later, they were seated in the
car speeding towards Macon. William seated in
the back of the car, looked on in disgust as Ethel
reached under the seat, drew out a pint of corn
liquor, placed it to her lips, and took a big drink,
leaning back crazily, passing the bottle to Kongo,
who drank and grinned up at her. Then leaning
low over the wheel, he let the car out to its limit—
faster and faster they raced over the smoothed red
clay road. The car swerving crazily from side to
side, at times the wheels hung dangerously over the
edge of the narrow road, threatening to topple over
into the deep ditches dug on either sides.

Once they miraculously missed colliding with a
passing truck, and a few yards further missed by
inches running over a low stone wall on a bridge
built over a narrow stream.

At each narrow escape, Ethel and Kongo laughed
with glee, but William, seated in the back of the car
with his eyes closed—to shut out the sight of his
drunken companions and the nearness of death,
breathed a prayer. His life of sin and selfishness
passed in vivid clearness through his mind; as they
raced on through the gathering dusk.

Once he cried out in desperation, "For God's sake, Ethel, don't let Kongo drive so fast!"

And Ethel's voice came back harsh and bitter above the noise of the motor.

"Whut de hell difference does it make? I'm bound to go to hell anyhow some day so why keep de devil waitin'?"

William remained quiet and bewildered, the rest of the journey—as the car with its three strange occupants shot like a streak through the night.

* * *

In the meanwhile, Sara Lou and Ruth had walked in the opposite direction almost to Ella's house, when the older woman stopped and stood for a moment thinking.

"Whut is it, An' Sara?" Ruth asked, noting her troubled expression.

"Ah don't know, Ruth, but Ah jes' feel lak turnin' 'roun' and goin' back. Jes' uh funny feelin' done run up an' down my spine lak dey say yuh feels when uh rabbit done jumped over yo' grave."

"Oh, tain't nothin' An' Sara. Jes' yo' nerves," Ruth assured her.

"All de same Ah'm goin' back. You jes' keep on to Ella's. Maybe me an' William'll come over dere later on to-night."

And Ruth watched her, as she turned and started back towards her home that she had just left. Then walking slowly she continued in the direction of Ella's home.

Sara Lou gathered speed as soon as she was out of sight of Ruth and stumbled along as fast as her legs would carry her, never slackening her pace until she was in sight of her home, where a car parked at her door, attracted her attention. She looked at it quizzically.

"Ah wonder whose car dat is," she murmured walking around it, as Owen Gordon and Marshall Bailey stepped into her open doorway.

"Hello, Sara!" Gordon greeted cheerfully.

"Land sakes, Mr. Gordon! My mind jes' kept tellin' me to turn 'roun' an' come on back home. Now Ah knows why, you was heah lookin' for me," she laughed, hurrying to the house.

"Wal, we thought we'ud surprise you, Sara," the Marshall chuckled, motioning to someone in the house to come out.

"An yuh sho done 'sprised me. Who dat in de house?" Sara Lou questioned, coming up on the porch and trying to look beyond them into the room.

"It's Jim, Sara. I just brought him from Macon. He's been pardoned and is home to stay." Owen Gordon smiled.

"No, Mr. Gordon, you don't mean it," Sara Lou cried, taking Jim, who had rushed from the room into her arms, laughing and crying in her excitement.

"Oh, thank de Lawd! Praise His name!" she sobbed, tears flowing down her cheeks.

"Lawd, Mr. Gordon, Ah sho thanks you wid all my heart. De Lawd knows Ah does! Ah done knowed all de time my poor boy 'ud git out uh dat awful place. Ah knowed God in His own time would make it awrite. Ah jes' kain't help cryin', Ah'se so happy." Her words rushed out in a happy jumble.

"We'll be going, Sara," Owen Gordon said, motioning to the marshall to leave them alone.

"Jim, there'll be lots of work over at my place waiting for you, as soon as you've rested up," he called back.

"Ah'll be ready to start in de morning, Ah ain't uh bit tired," Jim answered.

"Come on in, son, an' let's find Willyum," his mother said tenderly, leading the way into the house and looking out of the back door where she had left William seated on the porch.

"He ain't heah!" she exclaimed disappointed at not finding him. Raising her voice, she called loudly: "Yuh, Willyum! Willyum! Ah guess he done gone for uh walk an' 'ull be back tuhrechly," she explained, as she bustled into the kitchen to fix Jim some food. "Ah know youse jes' starved at'ter eatin' dat prison mess all dat long time. Law sakes, ain't yo' brother Willyum goin'ter be 'sprised to find you home an' Ruth de pore chile goin'ter nigh 'bout die wid happiness. She gone over to Ella's. As Ella's kind'er porely. We all goin'ter be happier den we ever was now dat our trouble is over," she rattled on happily.

Jim sat silent at the table, pleased to be home and happy to hear his mother's voice again. His hand rested on a closed book lying on the table. Taking it up, William's note fell to the floor. It was written on a small scrap of paper, and as Jim reached down to get it, William's handwriting caught his eyes.

"Heah's uh note William done rite," he called to his mother, busy in the kitchen.

At the mention of William's name she appeared promptly in the doorway.

"Whut he say, Jim?" she asked, a shade of anxiety in her voice.

"Dat he been called away on business, dat's all," Jim read.

"Well, Ah feels better knowin' whar he is," she said relieved.

The table soon resembled a feast.

"Dis heah is my Sunday dinner but you kin eat it all an' Ah'll cook more if yuh wants to," she laughed, seating herself opposite Jim who ate sparingly while she talked on and on about William, Ruth and the new preacher; how the members had begun to fight him and wanted him sent away because he had not been able to get his wife to move to Byron. Everything she could think of she related.

"Lawd, Ah jes' bout talk yuh to death, Jim," she laughed.

"Ah enjoys jes' hearin' yo' voice, Ma," Jim replied, a little tremble in his voice. He lowered his head over his plate to keep her from seeing the tears that sprang quickly to his eyes.

"Yeah, but you jes' wait ontell de neighbors heahs youse home, den dey goin'ter rush over heah an' 'tween Sally Ann Peck whut done married dat Reverend Hansom an' Martha Green an' An' Salisbury an' Ella an' de rest uh dem, dey goin'ter talk yo' head off."

The evening passed pleasantly. Ruth did not return from Ella's because a storm came up suddenly, and continued furiously until after midnight. Jim and his mother planned the work to be done around

the farm, and chatted happily, glad the rain had
kept their neighbors away. Jim wanted to be alone
with her, his first night home, but much of the happiness he had enjoyed was spoiled for him by his
mother unknowingly when she said earnestly just
before they retired:

"Jim, dere's one thing Ah wants to ask yuh to
do for me an' dat is try an' have uh little more pa-
tience wid yo' brother Willyum. He's been kind'er
restless heah uh late, an' Ah don't want him to up
an' leave home lak Ah scared he'll do, if you'all gits
to auguin' lak you did 'fo you went uh way. Will
yuh promise me you'll try, Jim?"

Jim turned his head aside. Fear and anger
burned in his eyes which he would not for the world
have had her see. William had sent him to prison.
He had suffered two long years and now his mother
was asking him to kiss the hand that had betrayed
him. It hurt and crushed him, but he murmured his
promise.

"An' Jim, dere's something else, Ah want to talk
to you 'bout. It's Ruth. She done promised to
marry William. That goin'ter be de best thing dat
could ever happen, kaise William loves her an' she
kin make him happy an' contented. 'Course Ah
knows you thought dat you loved Ruth when yuh'all
was chillun, but you done tole her in dat letter dat
you changed yo' mind 'bout marrying her so now dat
her an' William goin'ter git married, you ain't goin'ter do anything to make dem feel bad, is yuh
son?" she pleaded, laying her hand affectionately
on his arm.

Jim shook his head in the negative, not even

daring to answer in words what might expose the
anguish her words had caused him.   His first night
at home turned out more torturous than any he had
experienced, during the long, miserable years he had
spent in the chain gang.

CHAPTER XXIV

When William reached Macon in spite of Ethel's entreaties that he accompany her up to her room, he went straight out to his cousin Sissy's home and to his old room. Sissy, surprised and worried over his unexpected visit and the strange strained expression on his face, tried to find out what had happened to cause his sudden appearance.

"Is anythin' happened to Cousin Sara?" she asked, as William threw himself across the rickety iron bed in a corner of the room.

"No, Ma's all right," William answered wearily.

"Is Jim done comed home? Ah heard he was to git out dis week."

"He hadn't come home when Ah left, Sissy."

"Well Ah guess Ah'll be on my way. Ah'se goin' to some kind uh shinding wid my new man. Ah sho hopes he's uh good spender caise ain't nothin' makes me as mad as uh cheap skate hangin' round showin' off."

Sissy looked at William expectantly as she talked, but for once the mention of a new man brought no kidding smile to his lips. Wrapping her snuff box in her handkerchief and shoving it into her pocket, she shook her head doubtfully as she closed the door and stood for a moment thinking.

"Dere's somethin' done happened to dat boy," she decided walking slowly away from the house.

Left alone, William lay for several hours looking

up into the rotten rafters that held the leaky roof
in place, his thoughts a tumult of jumbled memories.
His wild ride from Byron to Macon with two
drunken companions, his nearness to death and disaster, and association with the sordid creature, who
would in time complete the wreck he was making
of his life, frightened and awakened him. He saw
himself as he had never seen himself before, selfish,
weak, mercenary—a thief. The thought sickened
him. The spoils of his crime had done him no good,
but had sent his brother to prison branded for life.

A dry choking sob rose in his throat. What had
Jim ever done to deserve the sin he had committed
against him, he asked himself. Why had he hated
him so unjustly. In his heart he could find no
answer. He was just rotten, unworthy of pity or
the confidence his mother had in him.

Slowly he slipped to his knees, sobs shaking his
shoulders, a torrent of tears smarting and blinding
his eyes as a prayer for forgiveness tumbled from
his lips.

Throughout the long Spring night he prayed
stripping his soul in humble repentance, putting from
him all the excuses he had used in life to cover his
sins.

It was almost dawn when he arose and stumbled
from the house. The sight of the squalor of dirty
streets and slovenly kept houses as he stumbled
along, reminded him of his own life. Something
within him rose in rebellion. Why should he remain
shackled to the past? He would get away from it
all, and prove the truth of his mother's often repeated remark.

"Son, yuh done comed from good stock, yuh jes'

different from dese folks round heah an' yuh kaint help showin' it."

He would show it—he would get away from everyone he had ever known and work out his own future without even the help of his worshipping mother.

The sun rose hot and glaring. He did not feel it as he trudged wearily on. His throat became dry and parched but he did not slacken his pace until he reached the dense woodland beyond the city limits where he sank to the grass under a tall leafy tree. Afternoon faded into twilight, and darkness with it's relieving coolness ushered in the night as plan after plan passed through his troubled brain.

It was near midnight when he retraced his steps towards the city, but his mind was made up, and a new peace filled his soul.

Early Monday morning he wrote Ruth a long letter expressing his regrets of not being able to see her before she left for Valdosta. One phrase he had written in his letter puzzled her. "It will be a long time before you see me again and when you do, it will not be the William you have always known."

She could find no meaning for his words, it sounded so different from the self-confident boasting William she knew. Of one thing she was glad —he had not asked her to answer his letter so she need not worry about hurting him, as she knew she would some day when she told him definitely she could not keep her promise to marry him.

On his way to mail Ruth's letter, he met a farmer from Byron who told him of Jim's being home. He was glad and thanked God in his heart for settling

the only problem that worried him. Now he could
go away feeling his mother would be well taken care
of. Stopping by the pressing shop he had sold to
Cotton Eye, he wrote his mother a long letter in
which he told her he would not be home for several
months—he was going to find himself a job, and
earn enough money to pay his way through college.

Sara Lou beamed with pride when she read his
letter, and later that day she showed it to Owen
Gordon. "You see, Mister Gordon, Ah done told
yuh Willyum was differunt from de rest uh us folks.
He goin'ter be uh great preacher some uh dese
days," she bragged.

"I certainly hope you're right, Sara," he commented a shade of doubt in his voice.

Jim said nothing when he read the letter but
hoped for his mother's sake, William was for once
telling the truth.

Later that afternoon when William saw Ethel at
Daddy Jenks' place, her contrite pleading that he
forgive her for coming to his home and acting as
she had that Saturday afternoon, was ignored.
"It's all past and forgotten," was the only answer
she could get from him, and something in his de-
meanor frightened and repelled her, so she decided
to let his anger cool off before trying to make friends
with him again.

Daddy Jenks looked at William with unveiled surprise a short time later when they were seated in
Daddy's little private office and he asked: "Daddy,
do you know of any public work going on around
here?"

"Boy, you ain't strong uh nough to do dat kind uh

work," he countered, "and furthermore you got a
bad cough now dat ought'er be tended to."

"Yes, I am, Daddy, and I wants to. I've just
been lazy, that's all," William replied with conviction.

"But maybe yuh could git something lak store
work whut ain't so hard, Willyum."

"No, Daddy, I don't want no easy job. I wants
to sweat, and work so hard, I won't have time to
think," William replied earnestly.

Daddy was puzzled. It just did not sound like
William. What had come over the boy, he wondered, trying to find an answer in the strange hard
face before him.

"Ah don't know 'bout nothing right round heah.
Ah'se got uh brother whut works at uh saw mill
down in Florida, but dat's hard work an' uh long
way from heah," he ventured after a moment's
thought.

"I don't care how hard it is, or how far. It's the
only thing that'll make a real man of me, Daddy."

"Well Ah can't help sayin' Ah lak yo' spunk. Ah
allers thought it was in yuh, boy, an' ef'fen you sho'
you means whut youse sayin', Ah'll give yuh uh
letter to my brother an' if you ain't got nough
money, Ah'll stake yuh. De mill's fifteen miles
fuhm Jacksonville, jes' uh flag station but you kin
git dere awrite. It's called Johnson's. Ah ust'uh
go out dere to meet pay days an' dere's lots uh
money in circulation out dere awrite."

"Thanks Daddy, I'll get there all right and I'll
send you back your money as soon as I get started,"
William replied, a relieved look in his eyes.

"There's just one thing more I want to ask you,

don't tell any one and especially Ethel where I've gone," he added.

"Sho Ah kin keep uh secret—when you want to leave?"

"On the next train," William replied, rising.

"Dat'll be in 'bout uh hour. Ah'll write dat letter an' you kin be on yo' way." Daddy hurried away, and an hour later William was on his way to what he hoped would be a new life. He hated to leave Macon without telling his mother goodbye, but decided it would be best. She would ask questions, and no doubt would want to ask Owen Gordon to lend her the money he could earn to pay his way through college. All of his life she had made things too easy for him. During the trip he thought of how she and Jim had worked and sacrificed so that he might sit around and take things that he had no right to accept. Her constant worship had made him selfish and robbed him of the manhood he might have had. He could not find it in his heart to blame her for the many slips he had made because of these things, but he felt he must get away and find out for himself if there was any character in his twisted make-up worth fighting for.

After a night spent in the nearby city, he arrived late Tuesday afternoon at the mill.

The double row of one and two room shacks in which the mill hands lived surrounded with tall pines, looked desolate and mean in the waning light of the setting sun, but all around them was life, pulsing and vivid; little children ran shouting to and fro, and busy women sang as they hurried about their clean kitchens getting the evening meal for their men folk.

William had never been so far from home before, it was all strange and new. He wondered if he could muster sufficient courage to face the inquisitive eyes that watched his every move.

A group of men laughing and joking came towards him, one swinging along his overalls' jumper thrown across his arm, his dark brown face streaming with perspiration that stood out like glistening drops on shiny satin, looked at him inquiringly for a moment before he asked.

"Lookin' for somebody, stranger?"

William took in his short stocky form and friendly eyes. He felt at ease. There was something likeable about him that warmed his heart as he showed him the letter Daddy Jenks had given him and explained it had been given him by the man's brother to whom it was addressed.

"Yes, Ah knows Charlie Jenkins. We all does. He ust'uh work heah awrite but he done left heah six months now," the stranger informed him, handing the letter back.

"Well, all I wants is work. Maybe you can tell me if I can get a job here," William explained disappointed at not finding Daddy's brother working at the mill.

"My name's Ben Jackson, stranger, dat is, it wuz, but de boys heah calls me B.B.," the stocky stranger informed, extending his hand.

William knew he was going to like him as he took his hand and felt the hearty welcome he wanted to convey.

"My name's William Carter," he responded warmly.

"Well, it won't be long. Dey gives everybody

round heah a nickname.   Ah guess de boys'll jes'
bout call you yaller," B.B. laughed. "Dese other
boys heah," he indicated, taking in the group, "is
Spider, Full Breaches, Tin Pan, Long John an' dis
little fellow heah is Big Boy," he laughed pointing to
two hundred pounds of bronzed bulk.

"I'm glad to know you all," William acknowledged cordially, looking around the group.   There
was not the same open friendship in their eyes that
B.B.'s held and William sensed he would have no
easy time making these men like him.

"Now 'bout work," B.B. continued, walking
towards his shanty, William falling in step beside
him.   "Ah guess yuh kin git uh job round heah, as
we is short uh hands right now.   Most uh de boys
done gone down in South Florida to work at uh
new saw mill down dere in Nocotee caize de wages
is bettuh den dey is heah."

"Yeah," Full Breaches put in.   "De wages is
bettuh an' de crackers is bigger an' bad'er," the
men laughed and William joined in heartily.

"We'll see 'bout yuh gittin' on in de morning an'
yuh kin bunk wid me ef'fen yuh wants to, yaller boy.
Ah ain't married so we all kin batch together,"
B.B. offered.

"Thanks, I'll be glad to," William replied.

Later that evening he met Aunt Silby who cooked
for B.B. and the rest of the unmarried men.

"Ah see Ah got'uh take care uh dat cough you
got," she commented, as she bustled around getting
the supper of collard green fat pork and corn pone
on the table.

William felt at home with B.B. and the kindly old
woman, and spent his first night at the mill hap-

pily dreaming of the good he could do among these
people, who while they were not educated nor
learned in the ways of the outside world, were
honest and happy to do their job well. He wondered whether he could find the same contentment
they had found, and tried to feel that he was one
of them. It would be hard to curb the old feeling
of superiority he had always had but he was determined to try.

Wednesday morning B.B. took him to see the
"Big Boss" as Lemuel Johnson was called by his
negro mill hands. He was a big man standing almost six feet tall, his ruddy face topped by a mass
of red bushy hair and loud voice made him a force-
ful figure, but he was known throughout the state
for his fair treatment of employees. His keen blue
eyes seemed to look right through William, as he
remarked:

"Well, you don't look like you'll make much of a
millhand Carter, but I'm short so I'll give you a
try."

It was settled and he was put to work piling lumber. It was hard work under blazing sun that
burned through his rough work shirt into his tender
skin, often there followed drenching rains that soon
passed leaving him wet and sticky. But William
sang with the other men and tried to forget his
misery.

> "Ah got'uh gal, huh man,
> Ah loves my gal, huh man,
> Ah piles dis rail, huh man
> Throws it high, huh man
> Cause Ah loves my gal, huh man
> Till de day Ah die, huh man."

And on and on they worked and laughed and sang
fitting their song to their daily task. At the end of
the first week William's hands were raw and bleeding, but Monday he was at his post with thick bandages covering his wounds. At night Aunt Silby
treated them, bathing them in strong salt and water
and spreading goose grease on his bandages. Most
of his fellow workers disliked him. He was different, they felt it. He was too fair and too well
educated and was therefore compelled to think he
was better. He sensed their feeling towards him,
and tried to be friendly, but he realized they would
not let him be a part of them. Only B.B. was different. A friendship grew between them that was
sincere and lasting, but even B.B. knew nothing of
his past. He told no one where he was from nor
who his family was. B.B. did not ask and William
volunteered no information. He spent most of
his time reading an old worn bible he had found in
their shanty.

During the long hot nights he prayed for strength
to resist the many temptations that surrounded him
in the rough and tumble mill life, where every night
card and dice games were played in one of the
shanties.

On pay days the games lasted until early Monday
morning. On these days women flocked to the mill
to reap a reward of the dollars offered by the men
for their charms.

William held himself aloof from these women
but it was no easy job. He was good looking and
his very indifference made him more desirable.

One of the most persistent reproached him one
Saturday about his apparent coolness.

"Say yaller boy, how come you allers tries to get away to yo'seff when Ah comes round? Ah could sure go for you," she coaxed.

"Don't mind me. I'm just not interested," William replied.

"Well, it ain't no sense uh you workin' yo'seff to death in de mill. You jes' don't fit round heah. Ah could be mighty nice to yuh ef'fen yuh'd come to Jacksonville an' let me," she offered.

William smilingly refused, but a few nights later he kept a rendezvous with her in the depths of the dark pine woods. He emerged feeling ashamed and disgusted. Later that night when B.B. came to the shanty from a game he found William standing knee deep in a big wooden tub of hot water scrubbing himself as if he wanted to tear the skin from his body.

"Gee, Yaller, you sho is hankerin' for bein' clean, washin' dis time uh night," he laughed.

William said nothing. He was sick at heart. After all his promises he had found himself weak and still a prey to the lust that had come near ruining his life before.

* * *

June passed, and July with its hot long days dragged slowly but came to an end eventually. During the Spring and Summer he had written his mother regularly. He had received no letter from Ruth, but his mother had taken pains to mention her in every letter he received. She was still working for the Carmicheils in Valdosta. Of Jim his mother said little but she was careful to tell him how glad Owen Gordon was that he was trying to earn his money for his schooling. He often wondered why his mother had always been so desirous of his knowing Owen Gordon's interest in his welfare and related to him every opinion he offered.

As August came in, William felt the long hot days harder to endure. He had saved most of his money each week and had long since sent Daddy Jenks the money he had lent him. He was glad the men around the mill seemed to have learned to like him better and had stopped teasing him as he sat reading while they played cards or dice nearby.

The woman who had lured him into the woods had not returned to the mill the following pay day, and when he heard that she had gotten into trouble and was working out a sentence on the prison farm, he could not help feeling relieved, and thanked God fervently he had been saved from another affair such as he had had with Ethel.

He became more reticent than ever and spent more time reading the bible.

"Say whut yuh say fellows we make Yaller heah de preacher uh dis outfit?" Full Breaches suggested one night, as they played cards.

"Dat's uh good idea, den when de old Reverend Coleman don't show up, we kin have church anyhow," B.B. agreed good-naturedly.

From then on everybody around the mill called William, "Preacher" and on the Sundays the old minister did not show up, he carried on the Sunday school for the children and read and discussed the scripture later for the mothers and fathers. He would not let them call it preaching, but they considered it better sermons than the Reverend Cole-

man had ever preached, and William was happy—
his only worry was the dry hacking cough that had
held on through the Spring and Summer.

September with its long rainy days had almost
gone when Lemuel Johnson called William, who
was piling lumber in long even stacks under the shed
at the back of the mill.

"Say you yaller nig . . ." he started when William interrupted with: "I heard you the first time,
boss," turning his head to hide the angry flush that
mounted to his forehead.

"Well, I was gonna say I wants you to run this
wench machine here. Mister Casper who's been
running it, won't be round any more. I've been
noticing you, you ain't any too strong and maybe
you can handle this machine better'n you can them
logs. Nothing to do but sit and pull handles. B.B.
will show you how, course it's a white man's job,
but I guess you'll do for a spell," he finished, walking away. He had seen the flush of anger on William's face but somehow he liked him, and what he
had heard of his sober habits, made him like him
better.

The new job was easier and paid fifty cents more
a day and William was pleased. He had been working at the mill four months and except for one occasion when he had gone to the city to buy new clothes,
he had kept his promise to give up gambling. On
that trip he had yielded to the temptation of trying
his luck in a skin game in one of the places he and
B.B. had visited, and after an hour's play, had
found himself relieved of almost a month's pay. It
had taught him a lesson he thought he had learned
back in Macon and strengthened his determination

to prove himself strong enough to resist his old weaknesses. And had done no more back-sliding.

He felt as he started on his new job, he was being rewarded for his fight against the passions that had ruled his life. Sitting all day on the wench gave him plenty of time to think and plan his future.

October ushered in more damp rainy days. His cough worried him more than usual. Even Aunt Silby's strong portions of red onion juice boiled down in syrup and lemon juice did not relieve him. He was weary when his day's work was over, and night after night he threw himself upon his bunk with a promise to write his mother the next day only to awake mornings after a restless night filled with dreams of home and Ruth, more exhausted than ever.

October was almost gone and he had not written the promised letters nor had his cough improved. He felt miserable and were he not so determined to save a certain sum of money, he would have given up his job and gone home.

It was Saturday and the last day of the month. All night William had lain awake listening to the rain that pelted down upon the shingled roof of the shanty.

The mill hands arose at four o'clock and at five-thirty the machinery started moving for the day's work.

William walked slowly towards the mill. The rain-soaked ground felt damp and cold beneath his feet in spite of the heavy shoes he wore. Clouds hung low and grey obscuring the rosy pink of the new day. Large rain drops clung to the surrounding bushes on either side of the narrow twisting

path that lead to the mill. He had just seated
himself on the wench and reached for the switch to
start the great drum moving to and fro when Full
Breaches rushed towards him, his eyes bulging with
fright, his breath coming in quick little gasps.

"Wait uh minute, Preacher," he paused to catch
his breath and continued, "don't yuh start dat thing
dis morning caise dere is gointer be hell to pay
ef'fen yuh does."

"What you talkin' 'bout, Breaches?" William
asked.

"Jes' dis, dat white man, Casper Bennett, whut
ust'uh run dis wench done comed back heah an' he's
running mad caize Mister Johnson won't give 'im
his job back an' Ah done hearn him tell de boss
ef'fen he don't run dis wench, dere ain't no damn
nigguh gonna run it, an' he's headed dis'uh way."

"Dat sounds serious tuh me, Preacher," B.B.
added, his eyes filled with apprehension.

"I see Mister Johnson's car headed this way.
Maybe he'll catch up with him 'fore he gets here,"
William exclaimed, pointing to the car in the distance and trying to assume a composure he did not
possess.

"Boy yuh better git, Ah'm thinkin'," B.B. warned,
trying to pull William to his feet.

Hot rebellion rose in William's heart. He had
done nothing to have to run away for. The job
had been given him openly and he had performed
it well. He would allow no one but the owner of
the mill to dismiss him. His old stubborn determination rose within him. He would show Casper
the mere mention of a white man's name could not
frighten him. With a quick jerk he freed his arm

from B.B.'s grasp, and started his machine. The long arm of the wench started moving and almost instantaneous with the first throb of the machinery two shots rang out in quick succession. A sharp burning sting ran through William's left side as a bullet struck him somewhere below his shoulder blade. His body slumped to the floor of the machine and lay still, the bullet had pierced his left lung and rendered him unconscious.

Lemuel Johnson sprang quickly from his automobile. He had drove up in time to see the whole affair but not in time to avoid what had happened. Running up the steps he was at William's side and calling to the men, who had run for cover when the shots were fired, to help him lift the wounded man and carry him to his car.

"You get in the back of the car and hold him, B.B.," he ordered as they carried William's limp body to his car. B.B. got in first and the men helped to place William so that his body rested across his knees with his feet and legs on the folded small seats in front of them.

"You men get back to work," Johnson ordered to the negro workers who stood around undecided what to do.

"And Richards," he called to the white timekeeper standing near. "If there's any more trouble, you get in touch with the sheriff, have him send a posse. Better call him up anyway and tell him what's happened."

"Does you think it's safe for these men to go back to work?" Richards inquired doubtfully.

"Sure, that skunk won't start no more trouble.

I got to get this boy to the hospital.   It ain't but fifteen miles and I can get him there before a doctor could get out here," he replied as the car shot down the road towards Jacksonville gathering speed at every turn of the wheel in its race with death.

CHAPTER XXV

While in Byron, Sara Lou, a little more bent and
feeling many years older, stumbled along the dusty
clay road daily to the village post office to inquire
for mail. Every day the answer from the kindly
postmaster was the same:

"Nothing yet, Aunt Sara. Soon as something
comes in, I'll send it out to you."

"Thank yuh, Mr. Carmicheil," she'd smile feebly
and trudged back home again slowly, her heart almost breaking with disappointment.

And long past midnight Jim would hear her praying softly:

> My Lawd an' strong God.
> Ah done bowed heah humbly at yo' feet.
> Make me yo' footstool Ah pray Thee,
> Look down in pity on my humble plea,
> Kaise Ah ain't got no other name to call
>   on but yuh, an' yuh alone.
> Ah bows heah to humbly ask yuh to send
>   my boy back to my arms
> And to de cradle uh his birth.
> If it is Thy holy will.
> Snatch him as a bran from eternal burnin'
> And keep him from all danger,
> Seen an' unseen.
> And send him back to me 'fore my heart is
>   stilled by de hands uh death,
> And my voice is hushed to pray no more.

On and on her soft pleading voice would break the stillness of the night. Pain would clutch Jim's heart and he would join in silently with his mother's prayer for William's return.

During the Spring William's letters had come regularly and Sara Lou had been happy and proud of his independence in wanting to earn the money for his college course.

Planting and helping Jim get the place running smoothly had taken much of her time. Ruth spent the entire summer working in Valdosta and she had all of the housework to do as well as work in the field and over at the Gordon house. There had not been even time for her usual care of the neighboring sick or the church aid but they had been happy months.

Jim had fallen into his usual steady plodding from before sunrise to late at night. Owen Gordon's orchard and the garden that he insisted on planting, had taken a great deal of his time but he had gotten them all in shape and kept them going nicely.

July had passed. The cotton had claimed much of his attention, but he had kept busy trying to forget the terrible experience through which he had passed during his eighteen months in the chain gang, awaking some mornings afraid that he would find himself chained to his bunk. He had become more reticent than ever—thinking much and speaking only when he was compelled to.

August with it's hot blistering days and swarms of flies and mosquitoes brought a new interest to the Settlement. The much-talked-of Swamp Angel was to hold the big mid-summer revival meeting at their own Calvary. Saint and sinner from far and

near would attend, and sing and pray to their
heart's content.

The meeting, the first to be held in Byron in several years, opened on the second Sunday in August.
The church grounds were strewn with long tables
covered with snowy white cloths. Everything eat-
able from home-cooked corn bread to roast hog
meat could be bought. Women in their clean ging-
ham aprons with snowy head rags tied over their
neatly wrapped hair on which sometimes perched a
straw hat, sat stiff and attentive; men dressed in their
Sunday best beside them. Preaching and praying
was carried on continuously. The best moaners of
the community grouped themselves to give concerted
help to the preacher.

Outside around the tables the women committees
from the different churches called their ware and
tried to outdo each other in their sales.

"Rite dis'uh way for yo' hot fried fish," or
"Roast polk meat over heah!" and "Git yo' hot
peanuts an' roast tatters over heah!" could be heard
even above the din of praying, shouting people in
the church.

A little distance away in the surrounding woods
boys and young men hid among the tall saplings to
shoot dice or to play cards, cooling their throats
occasionally with the moonshine smuggled there to
cheer the sin-sick souls.

The Swamp Angel, resorting to his aisle walking
with the worn old bible on his shoulder, brought
many sinners to the mourners' bench but through it
all Jim sat erect, tears streaming down his cheeks
until candidates for baptism were asked to come to
the altar. Then he arose and walked slowly down

the aisle. Sara Lou ran forward and caught him
in her arms but he gently disentangled himself and
started telling the congregation how his soul had
been saved while in prison. On and on he talked between the tears, walking up and down the aisle in
his fervor. Men and women on all sides amened
and shouted, as for almost an hour, the usual silent
Jim swayed the congregation.

Sara Lou's cup of happiness was filled. She
shouted all the way home and neighbors rejoiced
with her until the little village became fired with
their religious zeal.

The following Sunday she walked beside him as
he was going to the River to be baptized. Somehow her thoughts kept going back to the Sunday
when William had walked thus to the river. He
had looked so tall and handsome and different from
the others. Her heart ached for the sight of him,
the touch of his hand, but she consoled herself with
the thought of him some day walking at the head
of his own converts, maybe a larger crowd than this.

Through the months that followed William's letters became shorter and less regular but they continued to cheer and encourage her. Then came
October when they ceased entirely. She lived on
each day with the hope that the next day would bring
the letter she longed for. But day after day brought
disappointment. Her shoulders began to sag, grief
and despair showed in her eyes.

Owen Gordon stopping by to leave some orders
with Jim, one day, saw the many lines that furrowed
her face, the purple shadows around her eyes and
with pity guessed the cause.

"When you hear from William, find out how

much that school you're so set on him attending is going to cost, Sara. I guess I can let you have the money," he said kindly, as he was leaving.

"Dat'll be fine, Mr. Gordon. Ah sho thanks yuh an' Ah'll be rite glad to tell him," she replied gratefully.

But no letter came from William. Laggingly she helped with the cotton and trudged to the post office without results.

Ruth, who now worked for and lived with Mrs. Carmicheil, who had come back to her home in Byron, visited her often but could not get up sufficient courage to talk to her about William, her heart was broken because Jim continued to avoid her. She longed to talk it over with him, and beg him to forgive her for seeming to accept William's love.

One day, as she walked out to the hickory nut tree under which the strands of their hair were buried, she saw him hurrying away. She called him and when he did not answer, ran and overtook him.

"Listen Jim," she began anxiously, "Ah been tryin' to git uh chance to talk to you but you jes' keeps out 'uh my way. Why do you do dat?"

"Jes' kaise yuh done promised to marry William," he answered, walking on.

"Ah ain't never goin'ter marry William. Ah loves you Jim 'fo' God Ah does," she pleaded.

"Yeah, maybe yuh thinks dat now dat William ain't heah but Ah ain't so sho," he quickened his steps.

"Ah ain't never loved William, Jim," Ruth almost sobbed.

"How come yuh promised to marry him den?"
Jim asked.

"Ah ain't never promised to marry him. He jes'
talked me into sayin' Ah guess Ah would. Please,
Jim, don't think Ah ever loved William kaise Ah
ain't. Dere was times Ah b'lieved Ah hated him
but he jes' kept pesterin' me and you had wrote me
we wasn't engaged no more."

Jim walked a few paces ahead in silence as Ruth,
trying to keep up with him, pleaded.

"Less us make up Jim an' marry."

"Not till William comes back and tells me wid his
own mouth you an' him is broke up," Jim answered
firmly.

And Ruth realized it would do no good to argue
with him further. Jim had always been stubborn
and set in his ways.

With the cotton all picked and ready to be ginned
and sold, Jim had more time to himself and spent
most of it in a manner Sara Lou had never known
him to before. Several times she walked up on him
hidden behind the barn, his bible across his knee,
studying it laboriously.

"Whut's yuh doin' readin' de bible so much uh
late, son?" she smiled.

"Oh nothin' Ma. Ah jes' lookin' up de sermon
de Rev. preached lass Sunday," closing the book.

"You ain't thinkin' on bein' uh preacher, is yuh,
Jim?" she asked seriously.

"Maybe Ma. Rite now since dey done made me
uh deacon, Ah might be called on to say somethin'
some time an' Ah laks to be sho uh whut Ah says,"
he answered.

Sara Lou smiled happily. Jim's conversion had

for years been her daily prayer. If William was only home or if he would only write and say he was all right, she would be very happy. But as October drew to a close and November passed slowly, her sorrow became almost desperation. Ruth now seldom came to see them. Mrs. Carmicheil was kind and had given her a nice room but there was lots of work which kept her busy.

Sara Lou, her tall form becoming more bent each day, found a strange consolation in her daily visits to the post office, although she received no mail. Neighbors gossiped and tried to guess what had happened to William but Sara Lou always on the alert to shield him, would explain:

"Ah guess maybe my William done jes' gone to Atlanta and started in dat Atlanta Preaching school tryin' to 'sprise me wid de news when he's all straight an' everythin'."

Walking from her house they would discuss her excuse and shake their heads sadly over the deep silent sorrow that was eating at her vitals.

Long nights in December dragged on with just herself and Jim, who was always reading now. Sitting alone—waiting—always waiting to hear something from her beloved William.

The approaching holiday season held no joy for her but she prayed unceasingly that they would bring her boy home, and lived on her faith.

* * *

Monday morning, Christmas eve dawned bright and clear with a crispy chill in the air that sent one's blood coursing delightfully through his veins. A holiday spirit filled the otherwise dull village of Byron with excitement. Early shoppers idled around the general store discussing the topics that interested them most. In the tree lined streets children shouting with happiness ran beside their parents, who dragged large green Christmas trees from the surrounding woods.

At the little wooden railroad station the usual loafers lounged around, their jaws protruding with huge wads of tobacco. Long streams of brown spit spattered the tracks, as they diligently whittled slender wooden sticks and waited from force of habit, the incoming train. It's three short blasts were soon followed by a grinding stop. A single passenger alighted.

No one recognized in the pale, stooped emaciated man, as he walked slowly down the three wooden steps to the street, the straight handsome William Carter they had all known.

Early in December Daddy Jenks' brother had returned to the saw mill and been told about the stranger who had inquired for him, saying he had brought a letter from his brother. He had written at once to Daddy Jenks, telling him about William having been shot, and although he had recovered from the serious bullet wound, he was still in a Jacksonville hospital seriously ill with tuberculosis, and no one knew who his people were nor from where he had come.

Daddy Jenks had lost no time getting to Jacksonville, and William had awakened from an afternoon nap one day to find him and Ethel standing at his bedside. He had felt happy and relieved when Daddy explained Ethel's presence with: "Ethel's my wife now, Carter. Ah couldn't git rid uh de pest so Ah ups an' marries her."

Daddy had scolded him for not letting him know he was sick but William like most tubercular patients, had not considered his condition serious and expected to be able to go home any day soon.

It had taken several weeks for him to get sufficient strength to make the trip, but Daddy and Ethel waited and brought him to Macon with them. But he had insisted on making the journey to Byron alone and Daddy had reluctantly let him have his way.

During the seventeen miles' ride, he sat motionless staring unseeingly at the fast moving scenery from the window. The months he had spent at the mill, the weeks he had suffered in the hospital not wanting to let his mother know because of the anguish the knowledge of his illness and accident would cause, the long, restless nights filled with thoughts of Ruth whom he realized he could never possess—passed through his mind in retrospect.

Stumbling feebly through the short streets of the village, visions of his home with its green, cool, fertile fields stretched inviting arms to him. He would be well and strong here in no time, he told himself over and over.

An automobile came swiftly towards him. He raised his head as it came abreast. Owen Gordon at the steering wheel saw him and stopped the car beside him, saying quietly: "Get in, William, I'll take you to Sara."

Jim, mending a broken place in the front porch, lay down his hammer and came quickly to the side of the car when it stopped at the gate. Owen Gor-

don assisted him in getting William into the house,
leaving as soon as he finished getting a bed ready
for him in the parlor downstairs, with an abrupt:
"I'll send Doctor Clarke right out, Jim."

Alone again in his car, his hand hastily brushed
a moisture very much like a tear, from the corner of
his eyes.

Sara Lou, who had been hastily summoned to the
bedside of Aunt Salisbury whom old age was re-
moving from her world of roots and herbs, had
been mercifully spared the anguish of seeing William brought home dying with tuberculosis and took
it better than anyone imagined she would when she
came home and found him there.

Even Doctor Clarke, who told her in the kindest
possible way that William would hardly live to see
the New Year, was surprised that she did not break
down entirely.   But after her first uncontrollable
burst of grief, her real characteristic ability of self
control exerted itself as she, seated in her favorite
rocker in the dining-room, swayed back and forth,
moaning pitifully.

"Ah done ask God to send him home to me an'
he did. Ah ain't tell him how. Ah jes' sayd please
send him home. Ah al'lers loved him with all my
heart. Maybe too much kaise God is uh jealous
God an' ain't wanted me to worship no other God
but him. Maybe dat's why he takin' him from me
kaise Ah worshipped him. Oh Lawd, have mercy
on my pore boy. Save his soul if yuh kaint save his
body, Lawd?"

Prayers and tears mingled in a steady stream all
day while the minister and church aid members
grouped around trying to console the grief-stricken

woman. Sissy for the first time since she ran away
some years earlier, came from Macon to help and
comfort her in her great sorrow. Ruth forgot the
wall of misunderstanding that had grown between
herself and Jim, and came as soon as she heard of
William's illness, to help care for him. Neighbors
overflowed the house, anxious to do what they could
for the grief-stricken family to whom Christmas day
seemed a hollow mockery.

Day by day William grew weaker, sometimes
drifting into semi-consciousness, his eyes closed, his
sunken features rigidly still between spells of spas-
modic coughing that racked his frame. At other
times he lay, his large, black eyes roving restlessly
around the room.

Sara Lou stole noiselessly into the room from
time to time and seated on the side of his bed, ran
her fingers through his damp curly hair mumbling
words of endearment into his ears, as her hot tears
watered his face. William, aroused, would pat her
hand affectionately, a twisted smile flitting over his
waxen face.

Ruth and Jim would finally coax her away and
lead her back to the dining-room, where she again
took up her rocking back and forth, mumbling
prayers to herself.

Saturday morning Doctor Clarke came again and
told Jim what he had already seen since the first
faint rays of sunshine had penetrated the room.
William was dying. Gently he bathed his forehead
and wiped the moisture from his lips. Ruth seated
on the opposite side of the bed, watched him tenderly care for the brother, who had hated him and
so cruelly wronged him. In her heart a strange

calm pervaded. William had said little to anyone during the days he lay so near death. She wondered whether he had made his peace with God, and fervently prayed he had.

The day dragged slowly on. Midnight, dark and still, broken only by the howls of Jim's old dog Towser, enveloped them. William lay quiet and unseeing until a few hours before dawn when he opened his eyes and let them rest on his brother, Jim.

"I'm leaving you Jim for good," he whispered weakly.

"Yeah, William, is dere anythin' yuh want?" Jim asked, trying to hide the catch in his voice.

"I wants to tell Ma about me causing you to go to prison."

"Ah kaint let yuh, William. She don't know nothin' 'bout dat uh none uh de things youse done. De faith she's allers had in you is been her very life. Don't take it from her now when she ain't got nothin' to live for," Jim pleaded.

"All right, Jim. I guess you're right as you've always been," William acknowledged and after a moment's rest, said:

"Call Ruth over here. I want to ask her forgiveness and yours for the many things I've caused you to suffer."

Ruth, who was standing at the window, came to the side of the bed. William reached for her hand, lightly it rested in his. His voice a thin whisper, broke in places, as he spoke.

"I want to ask you and Jim to for-give me, Ruth, for all the trouble I've caused you. I lied to Jim and caused him to break you'alls engagement but I loved you, Ruth, I still loves you. It's been the only real thing in my life. But Jim loves you too and you love him. I know it now and I want him to know it too. You two must marry and be happy, after I'm gone. Promise me you will."

He closed his eyes, exhausted. A coughing spell racked his frame. Jim hastily raised him in his arms and placed a glass of water to his lips. Ruth looked at Jim timidly, as he rose to place the glass on the stand.

"Ah'll marry you, Jim if you still wants me," she whispered.

" 'Course Ah wants you, Ruth," he replied looking into her eyes, his heart beating suffocatingly.

William's eyes were again open. He smiled up at them. A single word fell from his lips.

"Brother."—His eyes closed again. He lay still. Jim looking down on him, wondered why he should love him so much after all the wrongs he had heaped upon him. His heart seemed ready to burst with sorrow because he knew his brother would soon leave them forever.

Their mother came softly into the room and kneeling beside the bed, buried her face in the covers at his side. Tenderly Jim knelt beside her and assured her that William had not left them but was just resting quietly.

Outside the early dawn cast fitful shadows through the leafy boughs of the trees that grew near the house. Jim placed his arm around Ruth's waist, and led her over to the window to watch the sunrise painting the skies a rosy pink beyond the

Eastern horizon. Faint shafts of light like long pink fingers reached far into the room.

From the dining-room came the voices of the church aid sisters singing softly.

"Ah'm gonna lay down my burden
Down by de ribber side,
Down by de ribber side."

Jim spoke to Ruth softly. "Ah feels lak de words uh dat song Ah'm layin' down my burden."

"To find happiness an' study war no more," Ruth added.

"Yes, you an' me honey and Ma," he held her close to him.

"Yes, Jim, we three."

Sara Lou kneeling beside William's bed, heard him whisper "Ma" and placed her ear to his lips to hear what he was saying.

"Take me in your arms," his words trailed off.

Protectingly she placed her arms around him and drew him to her breast.

"I-want-them-to-sing-in-here-for-me," came haltingly from his lips, as he smiled up into her face.

Ruth, turning from the window, pointed to the bed.

"Look Jim!" she whispered, "his eyes is open. He's smilin' and uh ray of sunlight is shining right aroun' his head. Ain't it purtty? Less go over dere wid An' Sara."

"William wants de church aid sisters to sing in heah for him," Sara Lou said, looking up at them.

Jim called them from the door. They entered the room singing softly through their tears.

"Ah'm gonna lay down my burden,
Down by de ribber side
Down by de ribber side
Down by de ribber side . . ."

William's eyes closed slowly. His hand rested
upon his mother's bowed head. She gathered him
closer into her arms. His smiling lips became still
and set, his body stiffened. Ruth and Jim kneeling
on the other side of the bed, hid their faces in the
covers.

Sara Lou leaned down and kissed his pallid lips
and straightened his body upon the narrow bed.
Then burying her face on his breast, sobbed wildly.

Bravely the women sang on to the end of their
song.

"Ah ain't gonna study war no more."